HALF
OF
MAN
IS
WOMAN

ZHANG XIANLIANG

HALF OF MAN IS WOMAN

Translated by Martha Avery

W.W. NORTON & COMPANY

New York   London

Printed in the United States of America.

Library of Congress Cataloging-in-Publication Data

Chang, Hsien-liang.
[Nan jen ti i pan shih nü jen. English]
Half of man is woman / Zhang Xianliang ; translated by Martha
Avery.—1st ed.
p.   cm.
Translation of: Nan jen ti i pan shih nü jen.
I. Title.
PL2837.H762N313   1988
895.1′35—dc19   88–10015

ISBN 0-393-02586-1

W. W. Norton & Company, Inc., 500 Fifth Avenue, New York, N. Y. 10110
W. W. Norton & Company, Ltd., 37 Great Russell Street, London WC1B 3NU

1 2 3 4 5 6 7 8 9 0

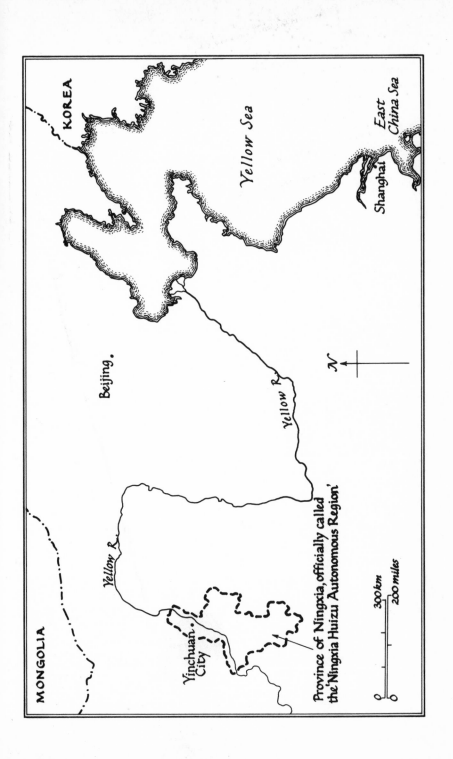

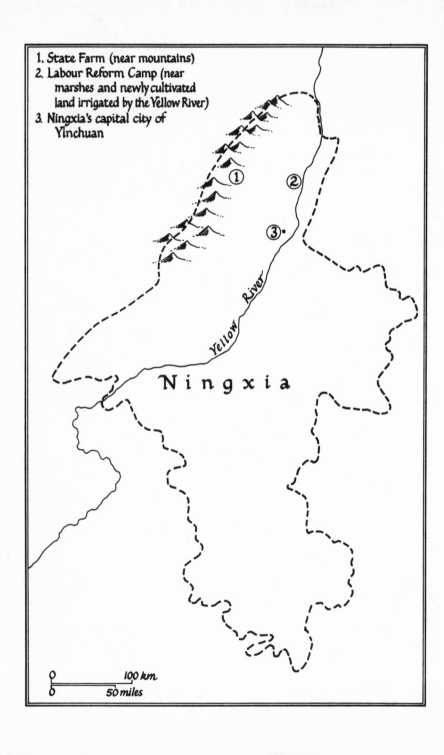

1. State Farm (near mountains)
2. Labour Reform Camp (near marshes and newly cultivated land irrigated by the Yellow River)
3. Ningxia's capital city of Yinchuan

Yellow River

N i n g x i a

100 km
50 miles

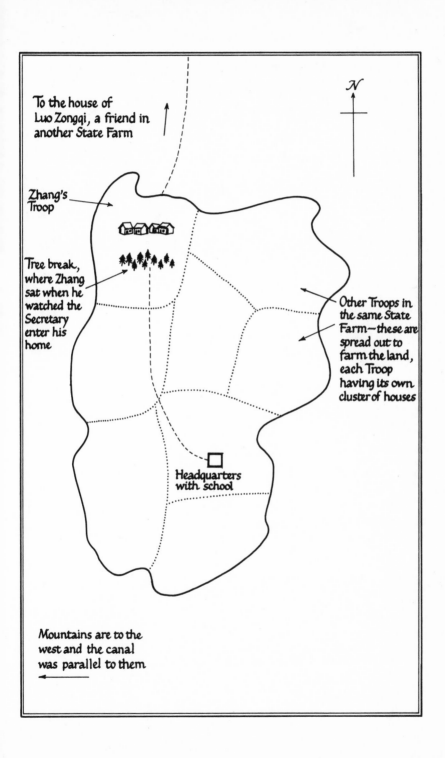

To the house of
Luo Zongqi, a friend in
another State Farm

Zhang's
Troop

Tree break,
where Zhang
sat when he
watched the
Secretary
enter his
home

Other Troops in
the same State
Farm—these are
spread out to
farm the land,
each Troop
having its own
cluster of houses

Headquarters
with school

Mountains are to the
west and the canal
was parallel to them

N

中國是一個神秘的國家。她不但
在外國人眼裡難以理解，在中國人心目
中也是一個謎。正因為她是一個謎，所以
她才可愛。這本書向讀者透露出了
一些謎語，請讀者去猜測她。

張賢亮
一九八六年十月十六日

AUTHOR'S FOREWORD

China is a mysterious country. Difficult to understand, it is an enigma to foreigners, and also a riddle to the Chinese themselves. Its very impenetrableness is what makes it so attractive. This book gives some hints to the answer to the riddle. I hope its readers will come to their own conclusions.

Zhang Xianliang
NOVEMBER 1986

TRANSLATOR'S INTRODUCTION

Half of Man Is Woman was published in China in late 1985. It immediately became the object of enormous controversy. About a political prisoner in a labour camp, it is also about lust and impotence. In China, these subjects are normally still taboo, but here the author uses details of his own life to expose the anatomy of a mass psychosis. By describing individual loss of control over private functions, from language to sex, he condemns the pervasive impact of totalitarianism.

Zhang Xianliang writes from his own experience. For two decades he was either in jail or in labour camps in north-west China's equivalent of Siberia—he is qualified to write of China's Gulag.

From 1966 to 1976, the period covered by this book, China experienced a triumph of absurdity, the attempt to politicize every detail of life. One quarter of humanity lived in a state of anarchic chaos. This book describes that chaos, on a personal level. It describes a language in which words mean their opposite, to the point where people refuse to speak at all, a society in which wives inform on their husbands to gain political points, a world from which civilization has been scraped away, revealing the most basic and primitive of animal reflexes.

Half of Man Is Woman is not about some future *1984.* In China, the Orwellian nightmare has already visited.

This is a book about survival in an insane world. Zhang describes a country that went mad. Along with all Chinese, he himself was part of that madness—short of dying, there was no way to avoid it. Zhang is, in the novel and in real life, a survivor. After 'crawling out of a pile of corpses' in a labour camp during the famine of 1960, he lived through another two decades of political hysteria. He writes about human resilience and the costs of survival, and he asks questions: under a totalitarian system, at what point does a person or a country decide to say no? At what point does a person lose the power to say no? What does a survivor hold back as his core of integrity, and what has a survivor, by surviving, lost?

This novel was published before the current crackdown on writers in China. As part of that crackdown, Zhang's latest writing has been banned. The reason given is that his work is too vulgar. It is less vulgar, however, than it is human and political. One of his main themes is that China's political system has desexed its population. It has not only instilled in its people profound distrust, which ranges from distrust of the Government to distrust of one's own relatives, it has castrated the will of people to stand up for themselves. They have been made both mentally and physically impotent. In *Half of Man Is Woman,* Zhang wonders if China's entire intellectual community has not been emasculated.

Zhang Xianliang was born in 1936 in Nanjing. The People's Republic of China was established in 1949, and Zhang went to high school in the early years of Communist rule. In 1955, as a young man of nineteen, he was assigned to teach in a cadre school in the north-west province of Ningxia. In 1956, Mao Zedong began the 'Hundred Flowers Movement' which is currently described in China as 'a trick to entice snakes [intellectuals] out of their holes'. In the brutal campaign following that movement, those who spoke out against Mao's policies were accused of being 'rightists' and were either killed, jailed or ostracized. Zhang was put in jail at the age of twenty-one, ostensibly for writing poetry.

For the next twenty years, he was sent back and forth between prison and hard labour in China's Gulag. Once a person has been labelled an outcast in China's polarized society, he becomes a natural target for the next movement that sweeps the country. Mao's policy of continuous revolution required a focus of attack for each successive 'struggle'. Like the others in the labour camps, Zhang repeatedly served as such a focus.

In early 1965 Mao Zedong lost control over most of the Communist Party apparatus in China's provinces and cities, particularly in Beijing, and in 1966 he launched the Cultural Revolution. Begun as a power struggle aimed at toppling the leadership of the Party apparatus, the Cultural Revolution developed its own momentum which brought China close to civil war. Zhang Xianliang spent the ten years of the Cultural Revolution in jail, in a Ningxia labour-reform camp, and working on a State Farm. The camp and the farm are described in this book. The novel begins in 1966 and ends in 1976, after Zhou Enlai's death in January but before Mao's death in September. Various factions were vying for power as Mao died: the 'Gang of Four' was arrested one month after Mao died and the Deng Xiaoping reform faction took over power in late 1978.

The country slowly began to recover from the self-destruction of the previous decades, and intellectuals and others expelled from society were 'rehabilitated'. Zhang was rehabilitated in 1979. In the peculiar language of this event, formal apologies were made for his having been 'wrongly dealt with' for roughly half of his life. He began to write again, still in Ningxia, describing what he had seen and experienced.

The interweaving of politics and poetry in this book may strike a non-Chinese reader as contrived, but to a contemporary audience in China it is only natural. Personal lives and decisions are unavoidably tied to politics. The warping of minds is a difficult subject to address when one has been through the warping process oneself. Chinese know this, and have found Zhang's work powerful. It has hit a very deep nerve in China today.

Zhang's audience in China includes a great many young people. To them he represents a person who not only experienced what he writes about, but who, unlike most of the older generation, was not broken by it. In *Half of Man Is Woman,* the protagonist feels that if one wants to influence the world, 'the least one must do is shout—never mind that it is a muffled shout from under a blanket of repression.' This book is such a shout. Zhang hopes that there are people listening.

No translation can do justice to the subtleties of expression and the slang that make this story so alive in the original. The author and the translator hope that even in this form the work will help non-Chinese readers understand contemporary China.

Martha Avery
MARCH 1987

PREFACE

Why haven't I written it all before? Maybe it was bitterness that held me back, maybe it was shame—the shame of wanting to hide something of the past. One is often one's own worst enemy.

The sun is slanting through the window now, covering the east wall with warm gold. From its perch on a picture a moth has flown to circle the room. Soon the sun will disappear, to take up tomorrow a path known from the beginning. And the moth? It may die before day returns.

Everything wants to live forever. Consciously or unconsciously, all aspire to the joke of eternity. Not I: I have had my eternity. So in fact has everything, even if only for a second. A second on earth is enough to know it all.

In the course of a lifetime, feelings sift out, indescribable feelings that lack any bones for analysis. They precipitate, congealing somewhere in a person's heart. There is no way to explain their insoluble kernel. People find it hard to recognize even themselves. But those indefinable feelings have an eternal meaning. Washed out from the waves of a lifetime, they are what will last.

The sun is sinking; evening is coming on. The dream is approaching again—is it the kernel's outer husk?

Water is flowing in a ditch by the road, jade green to the

bottom, like a mountain stream. Little fish, two or three inches long, collect under grasses washed along its banks. Black backs dart in and out, silver bellies flash like stars. The silent air is heavy with light. Ruts deep in the sandy road run ahead like railway tracks. I walk down the middle of the road, my footsteps slow, yet light. Floating dust rises, kicked up by my shoes, like early-morning mist, making the world hazy and indistinct. I feel I have a strangely different strength of sight, that I can peer through the thick dust and see what lies behind my consciousness.

I see a cat, grey with white stripes. He raises his back at me in fright, astride one of the tracks in the road. That is the cat 'we' lost.

The cat disappears in the silence of the dream-world.

I see four ducks swimming in the drainage ditch. I can tell that two are female from their upright necks and tails. They swim silently against the current of the ditch. They draw me into the remembrance of deep emotions.

Involuntarily, I follow. They wag their tails then, at a patch of reeds in a pool, turn in a circle. Riding a returning eddy of water, they thrust their way into a thick bank of reeds and disappear.

In my dream I continue to walk through a mist of dust. With some effort I pull up heavy legs, yet walk lightly, like a bird flying against an erratic wind. Past the pool, the ducks again burst out from among the reeds. These aren't four large ducks, however, but ducklings. Clothed in golden down, they seem to melt in the yellow light. They were there, those ducklings, swimming happily, puffing up their chests and looking straight at me. Their turned up beaks expressed a taunting amusement.

I realize those were 'our' ducks that I saw, the little ones are as they were as ducklings they used to be. Time is

xvi

flowing backwards: can I follow it? Back to that time, 'our' time, even in a dream?

Afterwards comes only confusion, a trancelike dream within a dream. As I wake, I know that the confusion is washing through the waves of my lifetime. The significance of a life, of eternity, waits in the midst of that trance.

The sun has come up again. The moth has disappeared, whether or not it still lives. I want to clarify the lines of the dream, to make them distinct, follow them back. I want to re-trace the path in writing, putting it down honestly. If there were nothing in our lives to be ashamed of, how would we judge them?

The moth has died. Whoever feels responsible for the brevity of its life has the right to censure the paths it took in its solitary flight.

The light is hitting me straight on, shining straight into the bottom of my heart. I float in its colour, leaving this noisy, dusty world. I seize the inspiration and take up pen and ink. In another moment I might change my mind.

PART 1

1

I may have seen her before and never noticed. I may never have seen her at all. This time, she made a lasting impression.

I was supervising hard labour in the rice fields after being transferred two months earlier from a place called Dazu. A prisoner myself, I had been in charge of a large gang of men, part of a larger Brigade* sentenced to 'reform through labour'.† When we were transferred to the rice fields, I was again put in charge of a small Detail.

The man who requested my transfer was Wang, Gang-Leader Wang: a local cadre,‡ a small old fellow from a farming family. He pulled on a cigarette he had rolled and began the conversation. 'Supervisor, are you? So the bosses trust you. Damn, those twelve are hard to manage. Nothing but problems. You whore, if you can handle those twelve, you can run a factory of eighteen hundred when you get out.'

---

*Throughout the Cultural Revolution, military terms were used for all organizations in China. According to the author, the practice was stopped in 1979.
†'Reform through labour', or 'laogai', camps are prison camps. The word is still used for the camps: the translator saw it on the gates of an Inner Mongolian prison camp in August 1986.
‡A cadre in modern China is either a public-official in a government organization or any leading member or administrator at any level, high or low.

He was squatting on the high bank of an irrigation canal. I had come up from the mouth of a ditch that watered a large field, and I stood with bare legs in front of him. He seemed to have more to say, but he didn't say it, just quietly smoked. His dry, thin little face, mapped with wrinkles, displayed deep thought. I didn't know what he was thinking, but I knew the pose: it was the inevitable prelude to giving a prisoner a special job. Deep thought displayed great seriousness, and emphasized the boundary between him and you. It showed that he had carefully thought through the coming assignment. It even hinted that he might have changed the verdict on you, a verdict imposed by a higher order of collective wisdom. It clearly indicated the importance of the new responsibility and also his trust in you. Cadres with no schooling, who felt uncomfortable talking, often used this silent technique to increase your respect. Wordlessly they made you realize that from this point on, from the simple fact of this trust, your burden was heavier.

Hard labour is not an ordinary kind of reform. It is reform of the most serious kind. A new job within it, or a new 'trust', could bring potential 'reward for meritorious service'. It could even increase the odds for an early release. An interview of this kind was therefore often the turning-point in a prisoner's life.

Wang's silent façade hid good intentions. He kneeled on the canal bank, smoking, as I stood below, switching from leg to leg, using the heel of one foot to rub the other bare instep.

When the rice was planted the mosquitoes surrounding me had not yet been born. Now they attacked in delegations, whining and biting, driving a man to distraction. Tiny enough to bore into the ears, eyelids or armpits, their bites raised blisters out of all proportion to the cause. Rubbing my feet and waving my arms, in a sort of shuffling dance before him, I awaited Wang's orders.

He didn't say a word. Well protected by his cigarette smoke and his cap, he was less eager than I to move. The Main Brigade had already receded in the distance, marching along the top of the canal. The evening sun was picking out their black prison uniforms as they approached some willow trees at a bend. From the back, with shovels over shoulders and arms swinging, they looked almost spirited.

This bend of the canal passed a small village, where some of the local prisoners had families. My own family-feeling was limited to being one among fellow prisoners—in the whole world, I belonged to nothing more than a particular labour brigade. As if to clinch my identity, a familiar tune came rippling across the newly planted rice,

Reform, reform, reform that reform. Hey!
Home in the evening, home to a ladle of chow. Hey!

Despite my position in front of Wang, it was hard to hold back a smile. This was our 'Song of the "Reform through Labour" Gang', which narrated the daily life of a prisoner. We sang it to the tune of a light-hearted Ningxia folk-song, and we had composed the words ourselves in the local dialect. In Mandarin, which was a foreign tongue in these parts, it came out 'Down with the kitchen, down with the kitchen, down with that kitchen!'

That 'Home in the evening, home to a ladle of chow' was strongly evocative for us. It was a ladle thick with rice noodles, sprinkled liberally with chopped green onions. Working with rhythmic precision, the cooks in the kitchen stirred steaming hot tubs, muscles moving in their rough

5

arms. As they stirred they dripped in great muddy drops of their pungent sweat, literally flavouring our dinner with the strong sauce of mankind.

I wanted to get back to that work gang, rejoin the mechanical trudge, and most of all, have my 'big ladle'. In that song one could almost hear the sound of hungary stomachs.

Gang-Leader Wang was silent, and as long as he felt like it, I had to be silent too. I had done hard labour twice before, and I was thoroughly versed in the laws of the camps. It was because of knowing these unwritten laws that in my third sentence I was honoured with the management of four Divisions: sixty-four men in the Main Brigade.

On the Outside, a person of dubious political leanings is shunned. He is an outcast who cannot be trusted. Those who have committed some moral offence, on the other hand, are considered merely unfortunate: they suffer only from 'internal contradictions'. On the Inside, things are different. The values, concepts, the very way of thinking held so tenaciously by a labour gang is at odds with the rest of China. It is because of this that the life of a prisoner offers certain insights, and also certain rewards. Within a labour gang it is the political prisoner who is trusted, although admittedly the trust comes in limited ways. 'Criminals'—or moral degenerates—receive very different treatment.

A labour camp is a kind of independent kingdom, set up with all the necessary occupations of life. As a result, the principle of using a man's skills to the utmost is practised like a religion: whatever a man can do, he will soon find he has been appointed to do. If a doctor enters who used to clean latrines on the Outside, he is soon Chief Internist, treating patients. With the Outside as it is, a gang labour camp is the more rational place.

Despite my ludicrous posture, with all four limbs swatting about, and despite my momentary lapse of discipline,

6

Gang-Leader Wang did not reprimand me. He continued to smoke. We both knew that my obedience in standing before him had another layer of significance. It was still possible that he might toss me a shred of news, leaked in from the Outside. This dry, thin cadre was a good man at heart. After a lifetime of contact with the yellow earth of the high plains, his nature was as straightforward as the dirt itself. Farming in the old ways for hundreds of years had imbued his people with traditional values. All this business of 'class struggle' was so much nonsense to them.

Wang wouldn't punish us when we cracked obscene jokes or sang our irreverent 'Labour Reform Song'. He would, on the contrary, take off his hat, rub his bare pate, and let out an expressive line of appreciation: 'Ha, you whores! Damn you, whores!' Hearing that the Vietnamese had downed so many American planes, it was 'Those whores!' again, to praise the Vietnamese generals. We even noticed on the day he brought his grandson down to the fields that he caressed the child and said, 'You whore!' As a result, we prisoners felt a kind of familial acceptance when he used the word on us.

Our gang was in the rice fields pulling weeds in the spring of 1966 when the Cultural Revolution was getting started. Gang-Leader Wang went into town to learn about it, together with a group from the local police force, and they were given a tour of the Province's 'Exhibition of the Triumphs of the Great Cultural Revolution'. Coming back, he bypassed home and his meal and made straight for our patch in the fields, slapping his pancake of a hat on his legs as he strode along, bounding over ditches to stand in front of me. 'Zhang, you damn whore! Those damn let-it-all-hang-out poems of yours! They're up there on the wall, in letters big as walnuts!' His weathered thumb and finger made a circle to show how big a walnut is. The forceful image gave my poetry a kind of physical strength. 'Those words were gigantic! Man, you can write!'

The general understanding in the countryside at the time was that the significance of words lay in the size of their writing. The authorities had already begun to select sentences at random from the *Little Red Book*, and write them out in large black characters. To Wang's mind, those poems I had written in 1957 had clearly assumed an equal importance.

My poetry was considered 'proof of guilt', and had been singled out for public criticism. Listening to Wang, though, the other prisoners shot me sidelong glances of respect.

Nine years had passed since I wrote those poems, yet they still brought them out to 'parade before the masses'. On the Outside, China still held together, and on the Inside, I was still a prisoner. Didn't those poems also indicate, however, that I had not been forgotten? In China if one was singled out in the midst of a 'Mass Movement', there was no escaping the ranks of history. The fate of someone singled out, though, is at the whim of the world. It has little or nothing to do with the will of the man.

I straightened my back, coiled a fistful of weeds and threw it on the bank. I looked out at the distant peaks, mute and incurious. Bending over again, I parted the rice shoots to find the weeds underneath, and from the surface of muddy water came sparks of clear light, dancing and shining. History, changeless and changeable, was in that poetry of mine, as it was in myself. To be a human being, one had to meet unceasing change with a quiet centre, and at the same time hope for unceasing change, to counter what had happened and what was happening now.

When I next straightened up to throw another bundle of weeds on the bank, I exploded with a feeling of tallness, as though I were the hero in a tragedy. All the prisoners bending over around me were like the robbers with Christ at Golgotha. I felt myself the 'Son of God', and first a feeling of superiority and then a sense of compassion welled up within me. Thank you, Wang, for bringing me this news! A prisoner, confined and humiliated, must survive by making himself feel bigger.

By autumn, the rice was already cut, but history Outside was turning faster than the seasons. We prisoners were on transport detail. We would take a large bundle of rice stalks, wrap it in straw and carry it to the side of the field. There we would pile bundles into stacks and tie them securely together with the 'back rope'. Squatting down in front of a stack, two arms would be thrust into the cross of the rope, and with an arching of the back and a hoist, a great pile of rice would be firmly on the back of a standing man.

I was the supervisor of this effort, so naturally I carried more. In a labour camp there is no other mark of recognition, no family pedigree, no higher education, no 'clean record' or 'unclean record': there is only the status accorded to work. 'Reform through labour' was our assigned occupation, and that is what we did. If you did it better, you got special treatment. You got the distinction of being allowed to manage others, being allowed to shit on others rather than be shat on. You got 'trust', and the title of 'free prisoner'. And when the day was done and you marched back in the ranks to the 'big ladle', you didn't get one, you got two.

Work creates man, bringing out an instinct long ago submerged in advanced culture. It takes man back to that primitive state when he gloried in the process of creation: the feeling that he was emerging and changing, that his essence was being enriched. Go to a labour camp and try it for yourself! Step back in time, to a process of modernization. Feel again the satisfaction of being so far back you are moving forward.

Five years had passed since I first felt that primal urge, since Hai Xixi and I competed in hard physical labour, while Ma Yinghua* gave me strength. I had felt the strange happiness countless times. When a shovel met my hand, the damp of a hemp bag soaked my shoulder or rice weighed down my back, I entered a mindless oblivion, as if I had put on magic shoes and could jump out into the abyss, could even jump into death.

When I hoisted rice no amount was enough—a greediness came over me, a need to see how much I could take. There is nothing like a heavy load to prove that the world is materialistic. One stack of rice can be as thick as a cow's middle. The average prisoner can lift two or three; I would not stop at five; six was not enough, I had to lift seven. As I staggered past Gang-Leader Wang, he would let out his own kind of praise: 'Hey, you whore, you can pack it better than a mule!'

> *Hell! What's a mule compared to me.*
> *I am what I am.*
> *Away with self-pity,*
> *Away with self-love,*
> *Put out more spirit,*
> *Fight fate to the death.*

Because I shouldered more, Wang sometimes helped me. When I had piled up the stacks and was preparing to hoist the load, he would run to give the final push. Having that

*These are characters in a previous work by Zhang, set in 1961. The author was released from prison camp in a condition of near-starvation, and was nursed back to health in a village.

10

extra arm made all the difference. Like a weightlifter heaving a heavy dumb-bell, if you can get your two legs under you and stand up straight, you can keep any amount of weight on your back.

'Don't kill yourself,' he would say. 'You push too hard, you spit blood and that's it for life.'

History Outside was outpacing this daily routine. As I secured the ropes and prepared to lift my load one day, Wang came across to help me. Instead of giving a push, however, he sat on the rice. 'Man, you whore, you. Much better off in a labour camp.' I heard him behind me, an odd tone in his voice. 'Showing off, are you? Well, let me tell you—day before yesterday I went to town. Who was there being paraded down the middle of the street but the Party Secretary of this whole province. Party Chairman too. Wearing these big paper hats. Beating on broken washbasins [in place of gongs] and shouting, "I am a capitalist roader, I am a capitalist roader." Man, you're a lucky one. You go ahead and show off. Remember that exhibit I went to see—the "Achievements of the Great Cultural Revolution"? What the hell, now the Red Guards say it was all a front. A trick put up by the "capitalist roaders" to cover their own crimes. They say our province has never had an honest-to-god Cultural Revolution. Time to begin. Secretary and Chairman, can you believe? And behind them, a long line of others, "rich landlords, bad elements, rightists" they call them: people just like you. All wearing those damn paper hats. Some even had their faces painted. Man, you whore. The one who put you into this labour camp must have been your own Creator. Otherwise you'd be out there too with those bastards, letting people "rectify" you to death.'

The spikes of the stalks scratched my face. The smoke from his cigarette found my nose. It's funny that when you

11

most need to smoke, just a whiff of the smell can satisfy the craving. I felt my body relax. With events changing so fast, could the turningpoint in the fate of a country, of a man, be far away?

Then I really piled it on—seven stacks weren't enough, I wanted eight. Startled, Wang yelled out, 'You whore! Trying to kill yourself? Don't forget you've got another two years to go here! It's up to you whether you live through it or not.'

Who could have known—who would have dreamed— that a prison gang in a labour camp would in China be considered a haven of peace?

That was then. This time, however, tormented by mosquitoes, I waited in vain for any news. Nothing came out of that wizened face but the curling stream of silent smoke. Nearby, a mechanical cultivator, brand no. 24, had been pulled in by the tractor and parked on the road. After baking in the sun all day a foul smell of engine oil seeped out, assaulting the natural smells of the muddy earth. It was as if the land were rejecting these modern contraptions, repudiating their very odour.

The nauseating mixture was getting hard to take. 'Gang-Leader Wang, anything more?' He looked around, as if he had just noticed I was there. 'Nothing more.' Rummaging through his pockets, he pulled out a half-smoked, hand-rolled cigarette. 'Go back.'

'Go back,' that meant to the labour camp. I took the cigarette he had given me and pinched off the end still wet from his mouth. The whole thing fell apart. Hell, he wasn't even as good at it as I was. That didn't matter, since I had my own cigarette. The gang was issued monthly pocket-money now, and also cigarettes: it was already a different world from 1960. I pulled out the aluminium needle-box which I had scrounged from a rubbish heap next to the

Troop's health unit. I carefully put his tobacco in, and then drew out a whole cigarette of my own. I lit it up. 'Go back.'

His long silence was infinitely eloquent. The chaos Outside was becoming more than even he could understand. His silence confirmed its existence like a final stamp. This was something I could comprehend. In the labour camps, each one of us was a Hegelian: from 'nothing' we could pull out 'something'. There is fundamentally no empty spot in the world, nowhere devoid of time or place. Those seemingly blank spaces are filled with the liveliest of hope: the hope of prisoners.

His transferring me to the rice fields made it possible for me to see her.

2

Since prisons were invented, there has never been a cleverer idea than using prisoners to guard other prisoners. The twelve that I was to supervise, sent from various Troops to work in the fields, were not as hard to manage as Gang-Leader Wang supposed. He spoke from the perspective of a cadre, a separate class from the prisoners themselves. In saying what he did, he was putting me, too, in a different category from them.

In fact, though, a feeling of camaraderie soon developed in our group. We were separated from the Main Brigade, which was based several miles away across an expanse of rice paddies. Our small Detail occupied an old house made of earthen bricks on the top of a hill. From it we could look over at the production brigade of a commune across a canal.

There was no watch-tower, no electrified wire. No jailer carried a gun beside us. The sound of dogs barking and birds singing gave a sense of being home. When flowers on our side of the canal were in bloom, the bees of the commune came buzzing across, as if they had erased the lines of fortification between men. The 'free prisoners' who constituted our group were either serving a short sentence or just finishing a long one, making an escape attempt unlikely.

14

Who would want to escape from such a garden anyway, during the times that China was going through?

At the time the rice was coming up, the oleaster trees began to shed along the banks of the canal. Small golden flowers would drop into the water, some drifting down with the flow, some stopped by willow branches in an eddy. These in turn caught more, together with willow catkins, and at places the surface of the water rippled with the mixture of yellow and silver. After a day of work in the fields, we would squat by this canal to eat dinner.

On the other side, standing under the willows, would be row after row of village children. They stared silently at us, this band of black-clothed men, stared as if our every movement was extremely strange. Our clothing had an aura of the mysterious, like the black gowns of teachers. What had these men done? What fate caused them to be gathered here? A terror of what might have been, of the outside world, of the future, was born in their young minds.

If the Main Brigade happened to be marching to work in the fields, especially under the escort of security guards, then the assembled audience would be larger. Peasants coming from distant villages to visit relatives would even make 'watching the prisoners' a festive occasion.

'Hey, look at that one! Still wearing glasses.'

'Say, that one, yes him, that guy's handsome.'

'So what? You want him for a son-in-law?'

'Drop dead, will you. I'm not that old.'

This would quickly erupt into an argument, as the women bantered back and forth. Our little stretch of canal was an open-air theatre. After a while, a lonely tiredness would settle over us, even if the work of the day had not been hard. To cheer ourselves up, although Wang had not ordered it (singing also was under orders), we would voluntarily sing a song. Among all the 'Revolutionary Songs' we most liked two.

The sun goes down behind western hills,
as red clouds drift,
Soldiers return to camp after shooting practice,
return to camp.

And:
We . . . men of the Communist Party
Are just like . . . seeds!

When they reached the word 'seeds', the younger prisoners would stand on the banks of the canal and make eyes at the young women.

Wang didn't care what we sang. He would simply let out a hearty 'whore' if we sang vigorously and all together. This continued until security guards happened to pass by one day. They objected to the authorities, the 'labour reform authorities' as they were known, who then issued a regulation: 'In this "extremely revolutionary period" prisoners are to sing only those songs which attack "reactionary elements".' We were to sing songs like 'If one doesn't thoroughly smash all things that are reactionary, then they won't be defeated.'

By 1967, however, these authorities were superseded. All those in the Public Security Bureau, the Investigation Bureau, the Legal Bureau, had themselves been 'smashed and pounded'. These noble men had considered themselves superior to the lowly labour reform cadres from the villages, and had carried out their own form of martial law.

According to Mao's *Little Red Book,* it was the lowly who were most intelligent, while the 'noble' needed guidance. Consequently, suspicion of the Book appeared among the

16

'noble'. No matter what your class or faction, you could draw what you liked from it. The *Little Red Book* could be made to justify any ends.

That term 'reactionary elements', for example—what were they? How could you be sure that other people meant the same thing you did? Of particular concern to the 'noble' was the crew of prisoners—among that unfathomable group of derelicts, how could you know exactly who they were calling 'reactionary elements'?

An order was eventually issued forbidding *Little Red Book* songs altogether. Yet at the time, no other songs were permissible. As a result, we began to sing our own—our anthem became a song that we had written:

> *Reform, reform, reform that reform. Hey!*
> *Home in the evening, home to a ladle of chow. Hey!*

A man was appointed every day to bring back the 'ladle of chow' from the Main Brigade to our field detachment. We were allowed two iron pots, and our man always brought them back full, whatever the food was.

The theory of 'to each according to his labour' had been repudiated on the Outside, but in the labour camps it was ironclad law. When the cucumbers and tomatoes were ripening, for example, we would help ourselves. Those in charge of the vegetable patches were 'free prisoners' like us, so we formed a pact, and we also lived by the dictum, 'to each according to his needs'. We prisoners ate fresh vegetables earlier than anyone, before the gang leaders, and before any of the cadres or their families. We had discovered that freedom is relative. If, in the worst of situations, you were able to obtain a small measure of it, then your reward would be disproportionately greater.

With a belly full of two ladles—for me it wasn't one

17

ladle—as well as a mound of tomatoes and cucumbers, we would be stuffed to the point of immobility. We would lie back on the slope of the canal, heads cradled in our arms, and feel the approach of tranquility. As the sun went down behind distant mountains, a cool quiet came over the wide irrigated fields. Slowly, experimentally, frogs and toads would call back and forth, first rising, then falling, in a long lazy sound. Abruptly, a whole field would then awaken, raucous with happy and angry croaks. The creatures seemed intent on pulling the world back from the grasp of humans, and their voices promised victory.

A breeze brushed up a spray of golden lights on the water. I closed my eyes and entered a peaceful oblivion. This was the sweetest state of mind for a prisoner, but was only obtained with discipline. Until there was a turning-point in history on the Outside, we ourselves had no control over what would happen. It was best to sink into mindless-ness.

What could we have thought about anyway? The world Outside had grown beyond the bounds of the groping laws of Marxism; the books had been thrown away. It was said that this stage of development was exactly what Marx had foreseen. None the less, even Wang had no explanation for what was happening, while I was shut off in a different world. The blankness of Wang's silence could be filled with groundless hope, but it held no clue to what was going on in the world. However, as Spengler said, 'Ignorance is not grounds for a defense.'

I told myself to quit thinking and just be a prisoner. Although I was still ashamed to admit it to myself, that is what I had become to the marrow of my bones—more than half my life had already been spent in that singular occupation.

After lying on the bank for long enough, the prisoners would begin to stretch and liven up.

'Say, wouldn't it be something if a spirit came to visit us tonight!'

'Sure, just so long as she's not a witch. Best to have one that's made up—rouge, lipstick, all that.'

'Screw that, the hanged ones have their tongues stuck out. Long, like that, and red—they give your face a lick and you're done for.'

'One wouldn't be enough—we'd need a batch of them. Thirteen, one for each of us to hold . . .'

'Our leader doesn't want one, he's a bookworm.'

'Bookworm? Even bookworms get hard-ons.'

I couldn't help laughing along with the others. With my eyes closed, I could feel their attention on me—they looked on me as someone elevated and apart. Despite that, I felt an identity with them. After the 'communization' of China in 1958, the onus of additional 'regulations' had been added to the existing laws of the country. These new regulations seeped in an unprecedented way into every crack of village life. Every farmer felt the truth of the ancient Greek fable: somewhere the sword of Damocles was hanging over them in those regulations, and they lived in fear of the day that it would fall on their heads.

Hearing them tell one another the details of their cases was like listening to wind sighing through a forest.

'Tough, eh. You don't steal, how can you live? Nothing in your stomach . . .'

A flat-nosed man had stolen chemical fertilizer used by his production team and resold it. They sentenced him to five years, but you would think he felt lucky: 'Worth it. I was able to buy medicine for my old mother. They gave me five years, but they didn't take the money back.'

19

'Yeah, I'm lucky, too.' The misfortune of another prisoner had been that the commune's cow died on him: they said he had overfed it. 'The court asked me, would you rather do hard labour or pay for the cow? I thought it over—in the labour camps you still get something to eat. So I came on in. It's not so bad, just that there aren't any women. Hell, last it out a little longer, eh?'

At times they would ask me, 'Captain Zhang, what got you in here?'

'Me,' I would say, 'I got in for nothing.'

Their mouths would widen in an understanding laugh. 'In for nothing' had become a daily occurrence in the camps—as when you eat to capacity, you burp, when you get too chilly, you catch a cold. No one asked for details. Nobody said, 'Why would they send a man to do hard labour for nothing?' It was that uncomplaining nature, trusting life to Fate as though it were a leaf floating on a river, that 'let it blow where it will' attitude that expressed the meekness of our race. Among them, I too had my doubts. When all seemed controlled by Fate, what use was there in thinking?

I knew why they had thought of female ghosts, and specifically ones who had died of hanging.

The house we lived in had been built in the 1950s, when the labour reform camp was first set up on this wide plateau. It was called an 'independent household', from the Japanese terminology used in old strategic-warfare textbooks. Built of earthen bricks at some distance from the Main Brigade, it deteriorated through the years and was gradually abandoned.

According to the legend, a lovely girl had lived in the nearby village. Rather than submit to the marriage her parents had arranged for her, this sad young lady fled to the abandoned building that now served as our home. Our place was not a bad choice if you wanted to hang yourself, and there in our house she took her life. It must have been easy to swing a rope over an old exposed beam. Who was going to visit such a desolate place, the house with its notice, 'strictly forbidden to enter'? Who was going to wander in and stop a young woman from ending her days? Older prisoners who had been Inside ten years still found it enormously interesting.

'Damn, she was pretty! Still wearing red shoes, two thick plaits hanging down, all glistening, all shiny. A white, white face, long eyelashes. When we lifted her down, her body was, oh, so soft . . .'

Some of the men said her pants were wet with urine, said her tongue was hanging out. Most of the older ones considered that talk blasphemous. Among the hard core she was firmly held to be a spirit.

We late-comers, not having seen it all at first hand, naturally lacked any feeling of reverence. We only wished that we could bring her back to life, have by our sides a living, breathing body. 'Hang on a little longer!' In the midst of our aching and yearning, she was an object of comfort to us. Virtuous, unnamed maiden, forgive our thoughts!

Every so often, the Main Brigade would show a movie in the evening, and Wang would order us to go: the movies were considered a form of 'education'. One person stayed behind to keep night-watch, and I always volunteered. Even as a prisoner, being leader required a certain propriety: one accepted a degree of sacrifice in order to win the respect of one's men.

One night was magical. A light wind rippled over the rice fields, crying, talking, scolding. Frogs croaked as the water moved gently under its touch. Outside our muddy window it was lacquer-black. The flame of an oil lamp, no bigger than a bean, kept me company.

21

When everything was quiet, and all I could see was the shadow of my own body on a wall of mottled mud, I began to think, 'Thirteen. Thirteen!' That most unlucky of numbers could summon her.

From a beam above, she came floating down. First a hazy cloud of colored mist, she materialized into a beautiful girl. As the old prisoners had said, she had two gleaming thick plaits, long eyelashes over bright, moist eyes, and in the dim light of the oil lamp her skin showed pinkish under translucent white. She was still wearing a winter robe and on her feet were red shoes. Our crude little home was transformed.

Lightly brushing off her clothes, she drew near timidly. With a voice as human as my own, she said, 'Tragic, oh so tragic . . .'

'Come,' I said to her, stretching out my hand. 'Your life was tragic, mine is too. Let us two be together . . .'

'But you're the one I'm talking about.' She put her hand on my shoulder as her soft body pressed close to mine. Looking at the book spread out before me, she said, 'You're the one who is miserable. After a person is dead, all the grief is gone. Every evening I watch you wait for the others to go to sleep—then you get up to read. Why? You're ruining your health.'

Her voice had a mildly scolding tone. Holding that slim waist more tightly, I told her, 'You're not so lucky yourself! Why did you go and kill yourself when you were so young? Living is always better than being dead, isn't it? Oh, if only you were alive!'

'I couldn't go on living.' She swayed slightly, making me feel I was entering a dream. 'They were making me marry someone I couldn't—you think I could carry on?' Continuing in a low voice, 'If you had been there, things would have been different.'

I drew her to my chest and sat her on my knee. I caressed

her hair. 'It's all society's fault,' I began. 'We still haven't achieved a real equality of the sexes, still haven't arrived at a stage of marriage through free choice. That's why I read. To find out how to have equality between one person and another.'

Impatient with my lesson, she squirmed on my lap. 'When will that ever be! It will take generations—I don't even dare to think. Our county Secretary talked like that. The loudspeaker even talked like that. What a load of rubbish. Being dead is fine, anyway. But if you were to take me as a living person, I'd come alive for you.' She raised her head, and with sudden emotion said, 'You're my real man. Don't take it from the loudspeakers. Let me sing you a song—I've been wanting to sing it so badly. Let me sing how good life could be, sing for a man I could love.'

Softly, she began to sing. The tone was pipe-like and delicate. A bed of golden lilies spread out before my eyes, willing a man to step on them: a field of lilies I had never seen before.

Watery glass shows a face at the window,
Smiling, she looks out at her lover.
One door of two swinging doors quietly opens,
She calls her lover to come inside.
Eyebrow to eyebrow, eye to eye,
They speak their hearts with the dancing of eyelashes.
Pairs of pigeons fly towards the south,
I'll throw my life in with yours and sleep with you.

Then the men began to return.

I could hear their voices in the distance. In a moment, a soft mist was all that was left of the song, the warm breath, of her body. As my comrades came through the door they piled a heap of tomatoes and cucumbers in her place.

'A thief doesn't work for nothing,' one of the prisoners

23

said. 'Eat up! You see this cucumber—hard to find any so crisp.' He gave it a few wipes with a fist much dirtier than the cucumber itself, then considering it clean passed it over to me. To call him a thief would have been fine with him. At a time when it was unnatural not to steal and every peasant did so, thieving was not shameful.

The men began to spread their cotton mattresses and covers over the brick kangs.* A stench of sweat immediately filled the room. When all were settled and in bed, they began to talk about the movie.

'That man in the movies, I'll give you ten to one he made it with the girl. Both in the same Division, I sure don't believe they didn't do it together.'

'Southerners all fool around like that, it's hot down there . . .'

'I've heard toilets in the south aren't split for men and women.'

'Well, you know in Japan men and women take baths together.'

'In Japan, what about China! The time I drifted into Shanghai, I still remember one hot day, I saw a group of men and women with my own eyes, all humping around together in a pool of water.'

'No clothes on?'

'Clothes on! What do you mean, clothes on? How could they hump around in the water like that with clothes on? All damn bare bottoms!'

'Ahh, well then . . .'

But I, embracing my maiden, entered the realm of sleep. I made a little cave in the bedding close to my body, and here her soft but completely empty body slept.

---

*A kang is a brick platform heated underneath by a flue from the stove. It is used to sleep on at night and to sit on during the day.

Once the labour gang somehow got hold of the movie *Lenin in October*. After watching it, they were most taken by the scene where Vassily kisses his wife goodbye: 'What about that! So they 'eat the old tigers' in these shadows on film!'

'Ha, so you hold onto the face like that and chew!'

'You've chewed your wife before—haha! Have you chewed her? Tell us, tell us! "Come out with it and we'll be lenient, resist and it'll be tough.' "

The prisoners clearly remembered the terminology of interrogation, which came quickly back to their lips.

'What, chew that filthy face? When I said goodbye I threw a leg over my horse, and was off to the west of the river . . .'

They would not kiss a 'filthy face', yet the other parts of the body, touched so thoroughly, were not considered filthy? Love is an expression of culture. In a place without culture, in a person lacking it, all the gentle refinement of love is gone. All that remains is primitive physical lust.

> Come through the door and blow out the light,
> Come grab hold of my jade stalk . . .

The flame of the lamp was blown out, and the room where a girl had hanged herself was dark. The men who snored began snoring, those who ground their teeth began grinding, as one by one the prisoners went to sleep. The man who had fed his cow to death sang a few bars of a song, ended with a few smacks of his lips, and sweetly entered the land of dreams. In this room all those dreams, of all those men, were of women. Like sparks of static electricity, they glimmered in the minds of lonely men.

What of myself? I could not have said what was immoral and obscene and what was not. I knew that in my body, in the flesh of a strong man of thirty, the demon of desire was powerful. The Buddhist sutras ask the question, 'What is it that is called the devil?' The answer, 'That which takes away intelligence and perception, that which harms the proper way, virtue and goodness.' The she-devil could destroy a man's mind, take away his instincts for good, his morality, education, intelligence. She could wipe them away, leaving nothing but degradation.

What the hell, though, here I was doing hard labour! They had branded me a 'class enemy' ten years ago, and I was now in the labour camps for the third time. They're the ones with a death-hold on me, not some she-devil. Buddhism talks about the 'eternal successions of life and death'. I didn't seem to have even one chance. Morality seemed of little use to me.

We prisoners slept without clothes on. One reason was to save our clothes—except for one black uniform, everything else was either sent to you by your family or purchased. Another reason was lice. Inside the covers, my rough hand scratched a muscular chest. The scratching was like stroking a wild animal that at any time might leap out snarling. 'Love' had been extinguished in me long ago—both what I had felt and those I had known had disappeared.

It was because I loved her that I couldn't make her go through life together with me. It was because I loved her that I couldn't come too close. Wanting her was hypocrisy, that could only lay a debt upon her life. Letting her go was giving her freedom. I knew also that if the heart once softened it became impossible to meet grim reality with the necessary steel. I had seen too much. I had seen men ground up and destroyed by reality. They were the ones

26

who had been soft. They had fretted about what was 'right', and they had loved.

Pure love, the fear and trembling of first love, the fragrance, the illusions of romance, where were they now? Eradicated by prison clothes. Eradicated by lining up, yelling out a number, being counted, marching to work. Snuffed out by bitter struggle.

The physical needs of an animal were what remained. What frightened me was not that around us there were no women to love, but that if put to the test I could not have found love left in me. My emotions had grown as coarse as my skin. There was as much gentleness in my eyes as in an eagle's stare. Sex is, after all, a native talent: with the loss of love we return to the physical.

As I stroked my chest, I felt a sharpness from inside, a pain against my ribs and in my brain. I heard the insidious breathing of the animal, felt it as a scorching undercurrent, felt it coursing through all the veins and arteries of my body. This was not my own self, it was another being inside me, and it was frighteningly possible that it might burst out. Tearing me to shreds and licking its bloody lips, it would pounce on the first woman it saw.

I finally slept. In my dreams were women, yet not women, Woman: shadowy and ungraspable. I envied the farmers sleeping around me in the hut, since early marriage was the custom in this region. This year I would be thirty-one, yet in my whole life I had never truly known a woman. The others had had the full experience. In their dreams they could review the entire process of knowing the opposite sex. Throwing off the chains of their imprisonment, they could reach extreme pleasure in the escape of dreams. But I knew only abstractions. I saw the formless line of a soft

27

body, undulating, I saw the colours of Picasso in his later period, moving uncertainly in a cloud of smoke. This, I tried to persuade myself, this was Woman!

At times she took a more familiar form. She melted into other things that gave me pleasure. She was the gentleness and gracefulness, the beautiful curves of my cigarette-smoke. She was the flavour and resilience of my steamed bread. She was the rustling, skin-white paper of my book. She was the well-used smoothness of my shovel handle. With all these things in mind as she came to me, I entered the abyss. In the darkness I, too, found a physical pleasure.

3

The most grueling work in the rice fields came between the time the seedlings were planted and the time they began to stand out above the water. These forty days had a name, the 'Period of Preserving the Seedlings'.

After this period, we thirteen men were allowed to lie back and relax. Five hundred acres of rice, around forty for each of us, had come up smooth and even, like a sheet of green jade. We could then have been called back to work with the Main Brigade. Familiar with the rhythm of farm work, however, Gang-Leader Wang respected this time of release as compensation for forty days and nights of intensive labour.

An additional reason for his leniency was that at this time the labour camps were continuously being supplied with fresh recruits. The Great Cultural Revolution was creating a world-record-breaking number of 'criminals'. The authorities were fully occupied making arrangements for wave after wave of new inmates. Why should they hurry to bring us old ones back?

Coming in from getting our food, the flat-nosed man had run into a new prisoner in the vegetable patch, brought in under security guard. According to him, the news from the Outside was that walls out there were completely covered with court decisions. It was a blessing we had come in early—otherwise we too would be arrested and paraded right now. Come in early, leave early, we were thinking: the thirteen of us were pleased, taking our current status as prisoners to be a favour that fortune had bestowed on us.

Once the seedlings were up, the entire plateau was covered in tender green. Everywhere was green: green mountains, green water, green fields. Even the air seemed heavy with a kind of verdant fragrance, the juices of nature. Wild storks spread their silver-grey wings over the green, paying no attention to the wire fences or the 'strictly forbidden to enter' signs below them. Landing, they stalked the fields on long legs, looking in their silent seriousness like Gang-Leader Wang. Wild ducks began to build nests in new reeds by the sides of irrigation canals. Painstakingly they built their little homes, as the sun glanced off their coloured tails and their calls shimmered over the wide rice fields. A wild wind rolled across the tops of the seedlings as they quietly absorbed the nutrients of the earth. Nature was rich and substantial, sufficient unto itself. Only man was found wanting, and aching for something more.

Gang-Leader Wang often came down to the fields, a man apart, pacing, with hands behind his back. Up and down the dikes he walked, investigating our work. Army-green jacket slung over one shoulder, he would squeeze the buoyant heads of rice as if he were playing with a toy on a spring. Once the seedlings were up and safe, we no longer followed anxiously behind his rump. We looked after ourselves, each to his own devices, catching fish, snaring wild ducks or spreading out our prison uniforms and lying in the shade of the willows.

This interlude lasted until one day Wang surveyed a field, then came up to me and barked, 'Look sharp. Tell all those whores to get things cleaned up. Sweep out the mouths of

30

the ditches, and look at the dikes—where they're thin make them wider. Big Gang's coming to pull weeds. Be here in a day or two.' At that we set to work.

As we finished breakfast on the morning of the third day, a man who had been sent out to open the water-sluices ran in, shouting, 'The Main Brigade's come!'

Everyone was excited, and I was no exception. I had no relatives in the Main Brigade, and no friends, but the black-clothed group still held a strong attraction. Before this assignment, my days and nights had been spent with them. Camp rules had molded us together. We were raised with common daily habits, common daily laws. The system had come to define us, to the point that we alone understood its language. Moved by their arrival, I put down my work and ran outside with the others.

Been a while, old fellows!

An early-morning mist had still not lifted. Only the tops of the willows and poplars were touched by sun; darkness lingered below. We stood on the high ground of our hill looking out over the canal to the north, and as we watched, the spectre of a grey and shadowy line moved towards us. The grey colour turned black and faces became distinct as the men approached. Countenances one after another, grim, sombre, handsome, malevolent, open, defeated. They passed by on top of the dike, following the sound of marching.

What black magic had brought these disparate faces together? What force had swept them up into this group? Appallingly, it had branded each with a new identity. The lines of the labour camps were stamped on every face. You could not say they looked ill, for at the busy season the food was not bad. Still, each one was marked with desolation. From nose to mouth were 'snake wrinkles', named for the so-called flying snakes entering their holes. These bitter lines could not be seen on ordinary citizens, but on a prisoner they revealed his current status and established a lifetime claim to a crippled mind.

Without amusement or superiority, we watched from the hill. Sadly, silently, we watched the men file past. Only from outside that line did we recognize the oppression. Only from an outside vantage point can we see the tragedy of our lives. The villagers watched also, but their emotions were different: what they saw, as they stood to one side, was another world. What we saw that morning was ourselves.

As we watched, we realized the peculiar function of this black-clad delegation passing in front of us. Once you had been swallowed up by its ranks, 'you' were gone.

If you want to see your own face clearly, you have to move the mirror away a certain distance.

'Order! March!'

One of our group threw a glowing cigarette down. The guards glared but didn't interfere. A prisoner walking along the dike quickly scooped it up, greedily dragged twice, and passed it like a baton to the next man. All prisoners were given a tiny allowance, but we 'free prisoners' found it easier to buy cigarettes.

Following that success, we tried a cucumber and then a tomato, anything we hadn't eaten yet. Suddenly, like an American football team, throwers and receivers were in high spirits. Across the disappearing morning mist came a wave of laughter.

It would be wrong to think a labour gang spends the whole time moping. We could never have survived the tedious passage of our sentences. We always found something to be glad about. The line broke step, which made the guards yell louder, 'Move up there! Faster!' They took no stiffer action—hard to use guns to prod and beat laughing men. Perhaps they were not convinced that these men had committed crimes.

As they passed by I thought, 'Just like old army comrades.' But who were the enemies of this pitiful Division? I doubt if any of us could have answered, although we had all been judged to be 'class enemies' long ago.

The line of men passed on. Dust slowly settled on the dike. Far off, the ones ahead were already beginning to pull off their shoes and preparing to work in the rice fields under Wang's supervision. Our cucumber-throwing men still had mischievous smiles on their faces. What should have been crying had turned to laughter—lord, was this our weakness or our fortitude? Suddenly, someone pointed to the north again and yelled happily back to us, 'There's more!'

The man who had overfed the cow stretched out his neck and gave a long, hard look—then laughing slyly, said, 'They're women!'

Yes, they were women.

From that distance, it was hard to tell. The man had probably based it on a sense of smell. Their prison uniform was also black, their hair was short. When I was sent to camp for the first time, one could still differentiate. At that time they still permitted female prisoners to wear their hair in plaits. After 1966, the winds of the 'Smash the Four Olds Movement' suddenly blew in, and within one night every head in our camp was completely shaved.

I remember there was one old 'free prisoner', a woman of about sixty, a devoutly religious woman who worked in the vegetable patch. That night they cut off her few thin strands of a bun. Sentenced to seven years of labour, she hadn't complained, indeed she even thanked the government for the favour. 'When I get out, I'm going to burn incense for old Buddha Mao Zedong,' she used to say. But when this old lady's hair was cut off, she screamed. 'A sin! A sin! The revolution has come down on my head!' She began a strange religious chant which nobody around could understand. A month later she was dead.

Four of us were selected to put her in the coffin. Following the sober figure of Gang-Leader Wang, we entered the 'Small Brigade'. Before a group of trembling female prisoners, we lifted up this spiritual old lady, but as we lifted we didn't quite get her straight. The piece of paper that had been on her face fell onto the mud, and two shrivelled eyes appeared, staring straight up. I tried to stroke them down with my fingers, but in that dry old body her eyelids still had spring. Like the soft body of a snail that shrinks into its shell, the eyes moved back—then opened wider, as if to rebuke my impulse to touch. Standing next to a dead body like that, particularly one who had died so unhappily, it was difficult to concentrate on the women about me. My curiosity was checked by an overpowering sense of death. This was a sightseeing chance in a million, but I didn't even glance sideways. I remember clearly, though, that when those eyes opened wide I heard the cries and whimpers of the crowd and a tiny metallic sound that could have been a bowl overturned in fright.

We put her in a 'crispy skin', our local name for the white-poplar-wood caskets of that time. Still this old lady could be considered fortunate. In 1960 when a person died, there weren't any 'crispy skins' for a proper burial—only the reed matting off a kang to be rolled up in. I came close to being rolled up in one myself.

Male prisoners were completely separated from female. We were separate to the point that we could almost forget the women's existence. Still, the farm was one farm, the road was one stretch of road. The women were in fact right by our sides. Some of the younger men among us, relying on a guard-dog's sense of smell, could sniff out where they had worked that day, which road they had crossed, even what work they had done. A rubber band dropped on the road could excite these boys' imaginations. The rubber

34

bands, used as bracelets, became small treasures, and they came to symbolize the femininity of the women.

How we watched for the tiny footprints of the 'Small Brigade', those narrow imprints like a child's pressed into the mud. We even enjoyed the bean skins that they left behind. All these became small paths in the grounds of an elegant garden, trails leading to the meeting of two sexes. Needless to say, the meeting was only in the mind. Unless both parties were 'free prisoners', a meeting would never become reality.

After evening roll-call, backs warming by the stove in our little home, the older fellows would regale newcomers with stories: stories of romantic goings-on under the black prison clothes. These old prisoners were the pack-horses of the Troop. Like a burden to be carried, the history of the farm depended on them for its transmission.

To hear them tell it, the women had a tougher life than the men. Their tender spirits were more lonely, and they found prison harder to take. They were always seeking comfort, support and protection. Some would even flirt with the guards through iron bars. 'Captain, is your little mouse thirsty? Want to suck sweet water?' Give these women a chance (though they would note that chances must be made, everyone knows they don't fall from heaven)— and nothing could hold them back. Give them a chance and they would positively leap into a man's arms.

Such women were passing by at this very moment.

The morning mist had gone. The sun's orange rays were hitting the dike, where myriad footsteps had made intricate patterns in the dust. This was a capricious path, strewn with bitterness. A day that had started out misty was a day without wind. The willows hung down limply. Jutting up to meet them were the reeds of the canal, stiff and arrogant as if disdaining even to notice the women. Lightly, the women

35

walked by, their provocative movements seeming to invite our examination. Yes, you could still say these prisoners' steps were light, even that some of them were coy: all women sent down to work in the big fields were young.

If we were to ignore that walk, however, and see them standing stiff as the haughty reeds, would we believe that they were women? I remember in Tolstoy's 'Resurrection', when Maslowa sets out on the Vladimir Road for Siberia: I don't know if it was white or grey, but what she wore was definitely a skirt. On her head was tied a kerchief. But here in China women prisoners wore the clothes of men. A baggy top like a cloth sack and a pair of pants stubbornly covered all that was specifically female. Sexless, these women had descended to a state even lower than ours. The term 'woman' was used only by habit. They had no waists, no chests, no buttocks, as one after another their dark red faces passed by. Although they lacked the 'snake wrinkles' of the men, they had the boorishness of female animals. Many of them chewed unripe sunflower seeds. Some shot sidelong glances at us, with the eyes of cold fish. They seemed almost smug, as if this were a form of flirting. Sunflower seeds stuck to their mouths, like a circle of white spittle.

My stomach suddenly turned and a stream of acid came up my throat. I looked away, I couldn't go on looking. They would destroy my hope for life itself. To think that the femininity I had enjoyed before, women I had loved before, had come to this. To imagine that they had been arrested and brought to this end—what was there left Outside that was still worth longing for?

I turned my back on the canal, and began to cough.

My god! Oh, my mother!

It suddenly came to me that the first primitive animal to use a leaf or the skin of an animal to cover itself must have been a female.

36

A hot summer steamed over the expanse of rice fields, as the scorching Ningxia sun burned every cloud out of the sky. It was a good day, a rich day, and within it all the millet, the reeds, the grass reached up to touch the azure sky. From where we worked to the mountains was a carpet of green, a verdant sweep of emerald that hurt your eyes.

Beneath that triumphant green hid our young rice plants, soft and gentle like a layer of down. With your aching back and tired eyes, just try to find them! The land was home to wild geese and ducks. It also bred every conceivable insect together with the tangle of plants. Prisoners had worked here from the 1950s, year by year filling in the swamp. Despite their efforts, the water wouldn't drain properly, and no food-crops except millet and rice would grow in the alkaline soil. Prisoners had hacked at the weeds for years, but short of being pulled out by the roots they only flourished with the extra blessing of fertilizer. The more we put on for the rice, the more the weeds grew. It was up to our hands to pull some out, hopeless to pull them all.

Nevertheless, it was hands that had to try. If there was anything the camps had, it was men's hands.

Move, you there, pull! Set those seedlings free! Having started with a mess of grasses and weeds, we sometimes faced a bare patch of mud when we finished pulling: no rice.

37

Dig out those long grass stalks! Pull up those reeds by the roots! Straw hat covering his head, Wang walked back and forth on the bank. How could we pull up the roots of the reeds? They lay coiled and interlaced underground, as if born of a giant python. How could we dig out the long grass stalks? They were buried deep in muck. The daily quota for each prisoner was five squares of land: rear up and head down, getting just one square finished was hard.

The men would secretly trample chopped-off weeds into the mud—throwing rootless bundles on the bank would bring on the wrath of the Supervisors. At the same time, if you didn't dig out the roots of reeds, when the field was irrigated their hollow stems would begin to pop. These popping sounds were like informants betraying the men.

'What do you mean I didn't pull out the roots? That was only me letting off a fart,' one of them slyly laughed.

'What a sonorous rear-end! But strange it didn't smell. Anyway, rather have a butt letting out grass-wind than what normally comes out of that mule.' The prisoners around poked fun at him, and across the field came the sound of laughter.

Yes, we found things to be glad about—how were we to survive those days otherwise? Somebody started to sing in a thin voice:

Older brother* has gone to do labour reform in the camps,
Leaving little sister* alone in an empty home,
Little sister, little sister, don't you worry,
In the labour reform camps there are rations to eat.

At noon the sun's rays intensified, pressing a deep green down onto the face of the earth. Wild ducks, frogs and toads

*lover

called lazily. The very air seemed to congeal to a rubbery mass. Occasionally, a hot breath of wind came wafting down out of the valleys of the mountains, bringing with it the scorched air of the desert on the far side. It set the reeds rubbing against each other with a metallic sound, and heated the muddy water until it burnt one's feet. The prisoners lacked the energy to talk. Silently, they hacked at the weeds.

Struggle to finish that daily quota. Don't you see that slogan stretched out by the field? 'Turn bad to good, the future is glorious.' I shouldered my shovel and walked back and forth in the field I was supervising. Ahead of me was a field of heads scorched deep brown by the sun, glistening with drops of muddy sweat, smelling richer than humus. Behind me were rows of rear-ends, lined up in the water. Their seats were covered with patches, and on the patches was plastered thick brown mud.

Above, a deep blue sky. Below, the dark green land. Transparent, profound, beautiful. But squashed in between these two were black lines of human beings.

Suddenly, a call sounded from across the fields. Our rations appeared on the high wall of the canal dike. Four horses hauled baskets of food in front; a donkey pulled a keg of water behind. Drowsily, the animals dallied in the shade of the willows. Damn you, you've already eaten your fill! Our buns had better be bigger today—difficult to survive on the small ones. At least at every mealtime there's something to eat.

Gang-Leader Wang blew the whistle and as if starting an insurrection the men made for the cart. Run fast, hungry men! The ones in front get the bigger buns, those behind get the ones at the bottom. If they're not crumbs already, they're pressed flat.

To a prisoner, eating is akin to praying. As with a Be-

39

liever, it takes total concentration. He who bothers a man when he's eating sees a criminal with bloodstained eyes, faces the snarl of a wolf, the bared teeth and warning growl of an animal hunkered over his meal. No matter how urgent the work, Wang knew not to hurry lunch. 'Even lightning doesn't strike an eating man,' he would say.

If the morning work had gone well, Wang allowed a rest at noon. Progress had been good today. After months of either being locked up or working in dry fields, the water had been a welcome change. Gang-Leader Wang was pleased, and allowed the men to sprawl out on the bank. Burnt by the sun, they looked like rows of fried dough-twists.

Sitting apart under a tree, Wang picked at his teeth with a stalk of grass. Like a shepherd surveying the flocks he had just fed, he squinted contentedly at the prisoners below him.

We field supervisors had other work to do. If we weren't careful the men would quietly sabotage the work, digging open the irrigation channels, trampling down the dikes. They put little value on their work, and they valued that of others even less. We therefore took advantage of the break to check the fields.

The criminals of the Main Brigade blamed the weeds on the supervisors. Not able to fill their quotas, they focused their frustration on us. Paddies we had painstakingly filled would suddenly be drained. Water that was flowing smoothly would suddenly flood, breaking down restraining walls. The only thing to do then was slowly mend the damage. The one thing in the world we had was time.

That noontime, therefore, I went out to do an inspection. The forty acres that I supervised were divided into four fields, each lined with ditches. A central irrigation ditch joined the four fields, with smaller run-offs intersecting it at

40

right angles. At the far end of the fields was the main drainage canal.

The main canal ran fill year-round fed by water coming down out of the mountains. In winter it froze to a layer of ice, and in spring it still had a bone-numbing chill. Between canal and fields was a tall, straight wall of reeds. The evil legacy of the old swamp, these reeds proliferated in the spring. By now, they formed a dense wall of green, straight as arrows and much taller than a man.

As I made my rounds at the far side of the field, I heard the hubbub of women coming from the other side of this wall. The Small Brigade was pulling weeds next to us—a 'free prisoner' in his fifties supervised their work. Gang-Leader Wang knew how to organize things. The man's eight years of hard labour would be up this year—he was unlikely to risk fooling around.

Standing there, I heard one of the women begin to sing. The coarse voice was scratchy and uneven, as if a cloud of grey fog were rolling uneasily over the reed wall. When it stopped abruptly, the sounds of the group moved off into the distance. In the silence, I could hear a new sound, light and clear from the reeds before me: a sound of splashing, like a bird fanning wings on the water.

It must be a wild duck, a flat-nosed, coloured-tail duck: just what we supervisors liked for making ourselves a fine meal. The camp rations were enough to live on, but meat was scarce. Catching fish and ducks had become a sideline with us. On the Outside, ducks are either shot or netted. In the camps, we learned to bag them alive with only our two hands: when a man entered the camps, he developed a range of skills that he never knew he had.

These foolish birds made their nests in tall, thick reeds. Unable to take off and land like helicopters, they naturally formed small trails coming and going from their homes.

41

First they would land in a field then, following the trail, they would waddle home. They left home by the same clear route: we often saw them by the side of a ditch, sticking out their heads to look at the sky. It was like the ritual of a person going out to take a look at the weather.

We kept an eye out for those trails—a meandering seam where the grass had been parted would lead us straight to their nests. Supervisors were allocated flashlights. Using these at night, we followed the ones we had noted by day. At the end we were certain to find a nest, and in it would generally be two large ducks, often with eggs or nestlings. The ducks would freeze in the glare of the light—sticking out their necks in mute appeal, they would dumbly stare at it, unmoving. Their shiny black eyes, dark as black jade, revealed a stupid innocence long since lost to mankind. What light was that? Had the sun already come up? Taking advantage of their dazed state, we would reach out and grab a neck. Some evenings we bagged as many as ten.

Quietly, I moved towards the sound of splashing. My feet were bare, and I used the shovel to part the reeds carefully. Fortunately, the wind that had come up at noon was blowing. The reeds were rustling like a forest of trees. The breeze split the light on the water into a thousand reflections. My feet were already under water, and soon the steep slope would drop off. The sound of splashing was clearer. After a splash came the long slow drip and trickle of flowing water, as if the droplets and the wild grasses were quietly whispering to each other. This didn't sound like a wild duck.

Curious, I pulled aside the stalks of the reeds, and looked over at the other side of the ditch. I froze in amazement. What I saw was a person!

A woman!

A completely naked woman!

42

5

She was bathing. Not daring to go into the middle of the water, she stood on a clump of grass on the bank of the far side. With cupped hands, she teased the water up over her body, splashing her neck, her shoulders, her waist, her hips, her stomach. Her body was lithe and firm. From between the two walls of green, the sun shone straight on her, making her wet skin shine like stretched silk. That skin called for a man's touch—especially her breasts, shining with a wet luster, moving as her body moved. Two delectable shadows curved under those breasts.

Her whole body rose and fell as she splashed, sporting like a dolphin. Curving in an arc in the air, it would unfold in a beautiful motion. The skin was milky ivory, and glowed with a natural beauty. She vigorously rubbed wherever the water fell on her, until her whole body exuded life.

At each shock of the cold water, her face would flash with pleasure. It was a face that invited, a face of happy vitality. Her short wet hair was smoothed back on her head, giving the look of a boy soldier to what were feminine features. Her eyebrows gave a grace to the boyishness, narrow and long over deep eyes. They were indescribably lively, shooting up as the cold water hit.

She seemed to have forgotten everything—that this was

a labour reform camp, that someone might run up to 'criticize'. Forgotten her past and her present, forgotten the set of clothes beside her, the black badge of her position in life. She bathed intently, completely. She bathed as if to wash her very soul and make it clean.

She forgot herself, and I also forgot myself. At the start, I couldn't help looking, indeed my eyes kept returning to that most secret of female places. Then from it, and from the entire picture, began to emanate a feeling, the aura of a powerful force. Here was something magical, that escaped all that man abhorred. Here, almost, was a myth, an archetype that transcended the world itself. Because of her, the world now had colour. Because of her, I now knew grace.

Gradually, a desire to speak to her came over me, but I was afraid she would panic. Unwilling to break this vision, this dreamlike picture, I stood quietly watching.

When she had finished, she carefully dried herself with a piece of old cloth. A breeze continued to blow, and long wisps of cloud appeared in the sky. She began to feel chilly, and turning, bent to pick up the underwear that she had placed on top of her prison clothes. Turning round again she lifted her head and caught sight of me.

She didn't let out a sound, nor did she move to cover herself. She stared. In her eyes were anger, challenge and also doubt. She had to decide what she was going to do.

Miraculously, she smiled, then cocked her head to listen. The only sounds were the winds and reeds whispering like lovers. In no hurry to put on clothes, she dropped the underwear still in her hand. As if afraid of getting cold, she crossed one arm over the other. With a hand on each of her shoulders, she stood there facing me.

In the wind, the sun's rays turned a soft yellow colour. In that soft yellow light, her body shone.

She didn't make the slightest seductive move, let alone

say anything provocative. Her face bore no shadow of her smile. But her eyes, the tiny tremors moving the skin on every part of her body, her attitude of compliance were all being used to call to me.

An impulse to act reverberated within my body, urging me to spring forward, or at least to run away. Outside came a separate pressure, suppressing any action within. I tried repeatedly to swallow, conscious of terror, hope and cowardice. A feeling of impending catastrophe clashed with one of certain joy, and I began to tremble involuntarily. Was this a trap in front of me? Was it real or an illusion? Would it be right to spring forward, or the depths of degeneracy? A black-clothed fox stood there with me, fur raised on its neck, tongue hanging out. Salivating, crouched in the reeds, it stared at suspicious prey . . .

The reeds, marsh, sky, seemed to have darkened. The two of us stood in a stalemate.

Then, strong enough to knock me out, an instinctive self-preservation took hold. At the same time, in her eyes, on her rippling skin, I saw a frightening pain. I saw the tragedy covering both of us. Her thirst and her hunger were my own—she was a mirror to me. Into the desire to possess her came the equally male desire to protect her. My physical need disappeared, in its place was a mental ache.

The sharp sound of a whistle pierced the air from far away. It lashed my body like a whip, and I turned and ran.

After staggering out of the reeds I noticed the bleeding scratches that the sharp blades had made on my face, hands and calves. The soles of my feet were lacerated.

I spent the afternoon wandering aimlessly along the paths between the fields. Shouldering my shovel, I walked with head down, as though I were looking for something I had lost.

The old prisoner who supervised the neighbouring team

45

came over to ask for a light. 'Zhang,' he said, 'you don't look so good—you sick?' I felt my forehead—both hands and face were cold. Dully, I answered that I wasn't feeling well. Using that as an excuse, I approached Gang-Leader Wang and asked if I could return to the hut to rest. He grunted, which I took to be permission. Dragging myself home, I threw myself down on the kang.

It was here, in this lonely dirt-floored room, precisely on this mouldy bed that reeked of men's sweat, that I had spun out hours of thoughts and dreams of women. Every image I could conceive that related to lovemaking had passed through my mind here. Now, back on that bed, I felt the extreme vexation of having lost my chance. At the same time, I felt the self-conceit of having successfully come through a severe trial—yet what exactly that trial had been I could not say. What was the invisible demon barrier that had held me back? What had kept me from plunging ahead? The same desire, mental and physical, tormented us both. The same mark of suffering branded both our bodies. Why couldn't we take a moment of joy in the midst of hardship?

I began to despise the education I had received. Civilization was a cord that bound a man, restraining his actions, making him 'responsible'. The natural simple needs of a man's most basic nature became complex, became ultimately desirable and unattainable at the same time. Had I been one of the common farmers undergoing labour reform I would not have cared. But I also rejoiced in my education. It was education that distinguished me from an animal, that gave me self-control and the power, in a critical moment, to be 'human'. It was the force of education that gave me free-will and the power to choose, the power to exhibit the kind of superior behaviour that only humans could show. It was also education that made me realize I was responsible for my own behaviour.

46

Nevertheless, if I had taken her the world would not have been any the worse for it. The fact that I had turned and run did not make the world any better. I was a labour reform prisoner, a black ant—what right had I to comfort myself with the labels of morality and virtue? If I considered myself virtuous, then it was clear I had to call her immoral, which was hypocrisy. Hadn't that scene been played countless times before in my own imagination?

I was willing to be responsible for my actions—no one had ever taken responsibility for me anyway. It seemed that the collective responsibility of society was only organized to oppress and hurt me.

None the less, if we had made love, my fate from that moment on would not have been the same. They say that a person's fate is an unending chain of cause and effect—that if a butterfly flutters its wings in Beijing the weather in New York is affected. I would definitely be a different person, but how could I know if my changed fate would be better or worse? Perhaps the cords binding me would be cut away, and I could return to a primitive state, using the ways of a wild and savage era to meet life in this crazy world . . .

This sort of thought circulated in my head, making it whirl until it was ready to split with pain. At last, exhaustion obliterated everything else, and an empty whiteness came before my eyes. Morality and politics ceased to exist, along with 'prisoners' regulations' and 'labour reform ordinances'. I didn't exist. All that remained was her image, standing with crossed arms in the midst of that sheet of whiteness: her beautiful, enticing, fertile, glistening body.

All that was left in the world was her.

I didn't sleep that night.

Halfway through, some drops of rain began falling tentatively. Soon they were coming thick and heavy, and the fields and rafters began to beat out their sound. The eaves of our hut were like a pounding waterfall, shaking up the stillness of the night. A darkness spread, until it covered everything, as if a majestic god-creature were lowering its wings, about to land on this earth. Lying back in fear I felt an impending calamity as I prepared yet again to receive some punishment. Gradually my chaotic thoughts disappeared, I stopped thinking . . . about her. The rain stopped shortly before the light of dawn, leaving as abruptly as it had come. A solitary cock crowed plaintively from the far side of the dike: drops of water from the eaves made a lonely accompaniment.

As the disquiet of lust subsided, I began to look, in the smugness of morality, for the satisfaction I had not found in the physical. The curtains of 'woman' were being lifted in front of me, until layer by layer they approached the final one. With that final sheet would go the mystery of 'Woman'. Knowing that what lacked the colour of mystery turned flat and flavourless, I comforted myself with the thought that my knowledge of women had therefore

48

reached an optimum point: my imagination was still free to roam in this obscure state, weaving a tantalizing and romantic tale.

At the same time I realized that I was not good for much more than dreams. I could deal with the daily trials of life, but beyond that I was sunk in my own imagination. I lacked the quality of being able to forge ahead.

I also discovered the peculiar function of being 'civilized'. It lies not in directing but in explaining a man's behaviour. Not having acted, I could rightly applaud myself. Had I acted, however, I could have forgiven myself just as easily, and indeed considered it the action of a strong man.

The sky lightened. The grey light of morning came through the dirty glass of the window. The prisoners still slept soundly around me. Those who could think depended on thinking to live, while those who could not had their instincts and native talent. Reflection weakened a man— without it, one could still be whole and strong.

When you came down to it, at this particular time in China, thinking and not thinking came almost to the same thing. I was about to turn over and get up, when I fell asleep.

The next day the Main Brigade went to work as usual. The night of heavy rain had not left much trace on the sandy earth of the high plains, except for rivulets that had spilled over in places on the slopes of the dikes. But the water of the rice fields and marshes had spread out in vast sheets. On their surface were white flowers of froth, whipped up by the storm that had lashed the green plants in the water. The air was abnormally humid and the breezes still carried the feel of rain. The trunks of willows and oleaster had deepened to blackness, while the white poplars seemed to have been cast in gleaming silver. Toads squatted on the sides of fields and in the road, frogs hid among the grasses. They looked like farmers after a flood, like helpless refugees. The road itself was dry, though, and the dikes firm and walkable. The Main Brigade would pass by on this day as every day, to do their work in the fields.

As soon as the day was properly light, we field supervisors gathered up our shovels, and headed out to look over the damage. Had the water-sluices been collapsed by the rain? Were all the dikes intact? Groggy and confused, I could hardly tell. My mouth was bitter and sour, and I had no appetite for food. Passing the spot where I had entered the reeds the day before, I noticed they were split into two sides, like a breach in a high wall. The sight of this hole brought on a sharp pleasure, as well as the intolerable ache of indecision.

After a cursory look around, I turned to go back, running into the Main Brigade halfway along, as they made their way out to the day's work of pulling weeds.

'Rains all night and clears up in the day—makes a prisoner angry enough to pickle his guts!' A sharp-nosed criminal passed by me, letting off steam. If the rain had kept up they could have stayed in bed, burying their heads in sleep for the day.

Although the day was dark, the rain held off. Many unusual things happened inside the labour camps, but very seldom were they fortunate things. As a prisoner it was best not to harbour the slightest expectation—I had done so, and suffered as a result.

Out here, love did not exist. What did exist, I had learned, was physical lust.

The Main Brigade went by. In the distance, far behind, came the women. Now I realized what I had been waiting for. Suddenly I felt an excitement I had not experienced for years.

Although the air was grey and heavy, and even the drops of water on the grass by the road were dull and lifeless, to me the world took on lustre. Soon I would see her.

The women walking in front stared at me with curiosity, looking forward again only after they had passed by. She came at the very end, carrying a scythe for cutting grasses. In the dense grass that grew beside the fields, the practice was simply to cut away—no rice was growing there that needed protecting. Behind her walked a 'Captain' carrying a gun.

A kind of taunting amusement danced in her eyes, but also the light of familiarity, a kind of intimacy with me. We used our eyes to greet each other: 'Good morning!' 'How are you?' 'Did you eat well this morning?' 'Enough to make do . . .'

Her face glowed with health, and didn't show the slightest shame. Mine, on the contrary, had blushed with the memory. She wore exactly the same black prison uniform as the others, without collar or pockets, like the straight tube of a flour sack. Thick rough sleeves swung back and forth over thin arms. To me, she still looked beautiful, and to me, she was still naked.

She passed close by my side. When she was almost touching me, she suddenly lifted up the scythe and shook it in my face. In a voice that only I could hear, she said savagely, 'If I could, I would butcher you.'

She walked on before I had time to react. Her head did not turn around, like the others. The 'Captain' followed behind grumbling something, as the end of the Troop went past.

The barrel of his rifle gleamed a metallic blue.

I had waited, and what I got was that sentence. The soundless exchange of our eyes had been my own invention.

51

Following breakfast, I sat blankly on the dike. The wind tore at the lead-grey clouds and an orange sun began to appear at the end of the sky. Sounds of activity came from the village across the way, voices urging their livestock out of corrals. A thin and bony chestnut horse appeared, then stopped suddenly, lifting its head to sniff something in the wind. The water of the dike had soaked my lower legs, and its trickling sound carried a melody of mourning.

Feeling wronged, I quietly began to cry. I felt wounded, and felt that she also was wounded. Yet I couldn't say where we had been hurt.

After that incident, I did not see her again in the labour camp gangs. For two days, over one thousand people pulled weeds in five hundred acres of rice fields. On the third day the Main Brigade was transferred north. By the time the rice was yellow and ripe and we field supervisors had returned to its ranks, the Small Brigade had already been moved to another station. Later, I asked her name.

It was Huang Xiangjiu.

PART 2

1

Eight years had passed by the time we next saw each other again.

Again, it was a windy day. Rather than the damp winds of the labour camp, however, these were hot, dry winds, blowing over scorched gravel. Few plants could survive this wind and the barren stones. In place of the greenness was the bleakness of a north-western State Farm.* The scene had changed from rice paddies to a sheep pen, and the smell of fermenting sheep shit filled the spring air. Time had passed, and the stage was different: it seemed that only our positions in life remained the same.

I was spreading hay over the manure with a pitchfork. The wind caught the stray stalks, turning and twisting them

*State Farms were, and still are, administratively different from communes or villages, and were first set up on a large scale in China in the 1950s. They range from being straight prison camps/farms, through using convict labour on farms, to being regular agricultural farms. In western China, they were made up of people sent from eastern China to open up new agricultural lands in the west, as well as of local people classified as 'criminals' and sent from neighbouring areas. Many 'units' in China had their corresponding State Farm in the countryside: for example, the Chinese Academy of Sciences had a State Farm in Hubei Province, where scientists were sent to do physical labour. The army has State Farms throughout China. The most notorious State Farms have been in Heilongjiang, Qinghai and Gansu provinces. A State Farm consists of a number of 'Troops' spread out over a large area to farm the land. See map of this particular State Farm on page vi.

in the sun, making them dance like the locusts that plagued our lives out here. In the distance, a mist spread halfway up ridges of mountains, taking away their creases and their solidity, framing them like a picture. A narrow path snaked its way down from the foot of the mountains, coming to the sheep pen before leading on to the village below. Just before the village, it joined another path leading to the State Farm headquarters.

She came walking up this second path.

I had herded the sheep back from the mountains two days earlier, and had found the pen collapsing with disuse. A sheep pen without sheep in it is like a house without people-it soon begins to decline. All the posts were askew, and the corners were filled with spiders' webs. The mangers had been spirited away by somebody, not surprisingly. A manger is made of wood: dragged home at night it can be made into a cupboard. In a farming village nothing is without its use, and anything that can be used in daily life disappears when one isn't looking. When winter is coming on even flat building stones are stolen for covering the jars of pickled vegetables.

The manger was gone. Quite a few of the beams were also missing. Small wonder that an entire side of the pen had collapsed. Putting in a formal request, I asked the Party Secretary of our 'production brigade' to send someone to help me fix it. 'The sheep don't dare crawl into this hole. When one gets crushed to death, remember that it won't be me who is to blame.' Sheep were more important than humans. If you were to say that your home was falling down, and to ask for help in repairing it, forget it. But sheep—sheep were a different matter. Although it was the busiest time of the year at the farm, the Secretary promised to send a woman up to help.

'She just moved over to our troop, actually, from the

White Sands Commune. She didn't want to stay there any longer, so I arranged for her to come over here.' The Secretary gave a toothy smile. 'She did hard labour before too. In fact, she was at the same camp as you.'

My heart gave a jump. 'What's her name?'

'Huang Xiangjiu.'

There must have been more than a hundred women working at the camp when I was there, and over a thousand had been locked up in it at one time or another. Yet I had immediately thought of her. I have always felt I had the gift of prophecy. Very little that I have foretold in the past has not come true. My gift has been limited to premonitions, however, and everything that has come true has been for the worse.

Let this be an exception: let it be a miracle.

I watched for a while as she slowly climbed up the slope to the pens. She had two thin sticks over her shoulder, and a shovel. The wind tugged at her light green headscarf and pressed her army-green clothes to her body. Army-green was in fashion at that time. She threw down the sticks and shovel and leaned against the railing.

'Hey, this where I'm supposed to work?'

A far-away voice reverberated in my ears, 'If I could, I would butcher you!' The voice was suddenly near, the same headstrong, spoilt tone inflecting the words. I smiled to myself as I went forward to meet her.

'This is it. You found it, but what do you think you're going to do with these?' I kicked at the sticks in front of her, and said, 'How are these matchsticks supposed to make a pen?'

'Screw it! Thin ones are easier to carry.' She puckered up her mouth and squinted as she looked up at me. I waited, agitated. A moment later she drew in a sharp breath.

'It's you?'

'It's me.' I was glad that she could still recognize me.

'How can you be here too? And where've you been these last few days since I came?' Climbing up the railings, she came on over into the pen. I put my hands on her waist to help her down. In the vast dryness of the place, the only spots of moisture were under her arms.

'How could I not be here? Where else can branded sheep like us go, except to a State Farm? Who else would take us?' I could barely restrain my gladness and excitement, I felt talkative. 'The camps started the policy of going back to where you came from, didn't they? Well, this is the place I left when I went into that camp, so this is where I returned. I've been up in the mountains herding the sheep all winter. I came back day before yesterday. And you, how do you come to be here?'

'So, you can tend sheep can you? That's not easy.' She stopped moving about the pen and stood still, smoothing out her clothes. Then one by one she began to pick out the little bits of hay that clung to them. This careful action was so deeply feminine that I must have stared in wonder. I tried to answer in an offhand way.

'And what can't I do? It's been eighteen years since I first went in, in 1959. If I had gone to university I would have graduated five times by now. Here on the farm the only thing I can't do is drive the tractor—I'm not allowed to handle that. If I was, I expect I could learn that fast enough.'

She measured me up and down and then, laughing, said, 'How strange, that we should meet up here.'

'Strange? I don't find it so at all. Sooner or later the likes of us all get pulled together. The world is a very large place, but for those who have been in the camps it's very small. These past years I've run into a number of people who were also in labour reform. For example, of the five men lately tending sheep with me, four were sent out from the camps.

The only one who wasn't was a good-for-nothing who had been in the army. One of the four even spent time in jail with me. You find it strange? Come on, bring your shovel. Time to get to work.'

The months and years seemed to have left no mark on her. Perhaps I simply had not seen her clearly before. Over thirty now, she was slightly heavier than the woman in my memory, with a healthier complexion. Back then she couldn't avoid being like the rest, looking sallow and unfortunate. Tiny wrinkles had now appeared around her eyes and at the corners of her mouth, but her face was more expressive. The richer play of expression made her look even younger.

'It's been eight years since that time,' she said, helping me manoeuver the poles we were going to use as uprights for the sheep pen. 'What have you been up to these eight years? All on this farm?'

'No, not at all.' Using the shovel, I pitched in dirt. 'First I was "mass-dictated" for a year, and after that I spent another two years in jail. I went to jail shortly after being released from the camp, got rolled in by the Great Cultural Revolution. Then in 1970 I was sent in again, during the "One Hit Three Counters Movement". And you? How did you get through these eight years?'

'Me? Don't even ask,' she laughed. Then she stamped down the earth that I had shovelled in. 'Eight years: I married twice and divorced twice. That was about it. Luckily there weren't any children.'

I kept on working, not at all surprised. I had seen too much, and heard too much. In the end, there was very little that I could not imagine. If she didn't get along that way, how was she to live? Good fortune was a kind of miracle, misfortune was the norm. She, in turn, felt no surprise at my own experience. In that respect we both totally understood

59

each other. Her lack of any commiseration was fine —through the years, I had come to dislike the simpering sympathy of other people.

'You've been in jail twice over these years, well, don't laugh, I've been married twice. Comes to the same thing. At times, I think jail must be easier to take than marriage. The first time, I didn't tell him I'd been in the camps, and I lived in fear that he would find out. When he eventually did, he asked for a divorce. The second time, at the White Sands Commune, I told him all about my past from the very start. After that, he was always bringing it up again, holding it against me. In the end I couldn't take it, and I asked him for a divorce. First time, he didn't want me; second time, I didn't want him. One to one, even! So that's life. I'm not getting married again.'

'That's easy enough. If you don't want to marry, you don't have to. But me, if I don't want to go to jail it isn't my decision.' I teased her, 'Marriage is up to you, jail's not up to me. You've been a lot better off than I have.'

From the start we spoke to each other like old friends. There are all kinds of patterns in friendship. With some, you find it natural to be close from the beginning, with others it takes some time before the wheels engage. If the gears don't mesh, the thing does not go at all. We both ignored the hardships of the other, because we had encountered enough in our own lives. At the same time, we understood each other, because although the form of suffering we each had endured was different, the essence of what we had felt was the same.

Stalks of dry hay blew in the wind, floating and settling, making the sheep's pen flicker with light. Branches rustled in the wind. A hanging water pail swung back and forth against the well. I drew out water to mix with dirt for mud, and together we slowly built the pen.

60

Actually, I could easily have repaired the sheep pen by myself. Years of experience had taught me, however, that before you agree to take on a job you should always make some noise. If they send someone to help you, it saves you that much work. There is no contradiction between saving yourself work on the job, and the trance you can find in hard labour. A job is for someone else. Labour is your own. Only hired hands really know the difference. Right now, with two of us doing the job of one, we worked easily, with a tacit understanding. As we worked, I suddenly realized the solid pleasure in the life of a farmer: that of man and wife working together. As in the ancient poems of China, a certain beauty came from the fundamental concept of 'men tilling and women weaving'.

As we worked, we talked of people we had known. Of those acquaintances, that is, with whom we had done hard labour. Acquaintances further back were long gone, lost in a lifetime that seemed an illusion. It was in the camps that our lives and others' had some connection. Some had been pushed back into the camps, some were on the Outside, divorced by their husbands or their wives. Some had committed suicide, others had been killed . . . Talking it over, back and forth, we discovered that we had been the lucky ones: fate had seemed to smile particularly on the two of us. Although we had secretly felt sorry for ourselves, as we worked we began to cheer each other up.

'Why aren't you staying on at the White Sands Commune? Is life over there so bad that you want to come here?'

'All State Farms are the same. Life, hell, it's what you make of it.' She brushed back a lock of hair that had slipped out of her cheap nylon scarf and rolled her eyes up to look at it a moment. If there had been a mirror nearby she would have walked over to look in it. A mischievous expression passed over her face at that moment, and I noticed that her

61

hair was very shiny and very black. 'Since I was already divorced, what good was there in staying on at that place? Better to get as far away as possible. Your Party Secretary and ours are good friends, and yours is often over at our Commune. He's the one who fixed it for me.'

After a pause, she said, 'He's no good, that one.'

'Oh? How do you know? He seems all right to me.'

'Ha!' She gave a cold laugh through her nose. 'Men, I've seen enough to know. One glance in their eyes is enough for me.'

I thought that over. This Secretary's eyes had always seemed normal enough—perhaps I had never really looked. I immediately thought of my own eyes. Was she perhaps seeing something in them, too? I remembered what I had seen eight years ago, the scene as clear to me as if it had happened yesterday. It was impossible to know what my eyes might have looked like at that time. Nevertheless, in front of someone with such confidence in her ability to see through men, I had better be a little more careful. I quickly focused on something else, and taking up the sticks she had brought, ruminated over them for a while, as if considering exactly where they might be of use.

Just then the Secretary came climbing up the slope. Fortunately, we had stopped talking—she was standing there not giving a damn, and I was pretending to work.

'Not bad, not bad. You've really gone at it!' The Secretary's mood seemed uncommonly good: we had not, in fact, done that much. He glanced at me as he walked by, and I took the opportunity to look into his eyes. There was nothing unusual in them that I could see. He laughed, and as he did the fishtails shot out from their corners. This was a very clever man. When no one else was around, he was perfectly normal towards me. Our Troop had originally been known as the 'Gate of Hell'. Of all the Troops in this State Farm,

62

it had been the most severely controlled. Towards the end of the Great Cultural Revolution, it was turned into an Armed Brigade* and given responsibility for watching over the construction of the jail by the Agricultural Construction Division. After the 'Nine One Three' Lin Biao incident,† it was this same Secretary who had released the prisoners from that jail. The releasing of those prisoners was like dissolving a pinch of salt in a kettle of water, however. Their bitterness began permeating the others, and the entire population began to be flavoured by their suffering.

I have heard it said that this Secretary would often warn people, the 'masses' who enjoyed hitting other people with clubs or their fists; 'Don't push dogs into a corner,' he would say. Although he was comparing us to dogs, in those days of 'thrashing drowning dogs' even those words held a measure of kindness.

Since his coming here, the administration of the 'Gate of Hell' had loosened considerably. It had even reached a point where you could leave your house on a day off without first asking for permission. The 'Gate of Hell' hardly seemed itself any more.

The Secretary moved his laughing eyes over to Xiangjiu. Walking up to her he took her shovel and weighed it with his hand. 'Just got this?' he asked. 'The edge hasn't even been sharpened.'

Setting the edge on a large rock which had once propped up the manger, he gripped the handle and began to grind. His wide sleeves were like waves washing back and forth

*A Brigade in which workers are armed with guns and sub-machine guns as they worked in the fields. This was prevalent in the border regions of China.
†13 September 1971 is the date that Lin Biao allegedly died in a plane crash over Mongolia as he fled from China to the Soviet Union. According to Chinese sources Lin Biao was plotting to take power at the time, but his plot was discovered, he fled in a small plane with seven other men and one woman and was shot down outside the Chinese border.

from the motion, while his flexed body gave a feeling of strength and virility. After working at it for some time, he stood up and tested the edge with his thumb. 'See what that's like,' he said, handing it to her. 'That should be better.'

She shovelled some manure from the spot he pointed to, and laughingly agreed that it was indeed much better.

How quickly the Secretary had reversed her previous opinion of him! He had his ways, while all I had done was to grind my mouth away talking.

I turned my back on them, and began to lash the boards together, using a length of wire I had brought for the purpose. Taking my place, the Secretary began to plant the posts with her. The wind carried their conversation over to me.

'Secretary Cao, where were you before you came here?'

'I was out on the plains—you know the Xilingol Steppe? I was in the cavalry out there.'

'That's a beautiful place.'

'You've been there?'

'No, but I've seen it in the movies. Those miles of plains are really something.'

'That's true, the plains are a real treasure, especially in the summer-time. But when you're hundreds of miles from anywhere, not a house in sight, not to mention a woman . . . We soldiers were all young fellows, you know, and sometimes it got pretty lonely . . .'

He too had felt lonely?

'Then why didn't you take your wife?'

'I didn't have a wife then. What's more, as a Platoon Leader I didn't have the rank. To take a family along, you had to be a Battalion Commander.'

'Your wife is so pretty—isn't she the one teaching at the school?'

64

'Pretty or not, she's the one. They say that "after three years in the army, even a sow looks like a woman"! Well, I spent eight years in the army. I married as soon as I got out, and who cared if she was pretty or not!'

There was more than a tinge of regret in his words. It was not hard to tell that his choice would have been different today. The main features of his wife were her large mouth full of yellow teeth, two red cheeks verging on purple, and skin that was rough as leather. They said in the village that the water in her hometown had been to blame. Huang Xiangjiu's words had been sheer flattery, but who else was there in the village to compare her to? This woman was the wife of the Troop Party Secretary, and although she had never finished primary school and it was doubtful if she could write her own name properly, she was still the teacher in the village school.

Working together, the two of them found things to talk about. Secretary Cao seldom put on many airs, but today he was unusually frank. He told her this village was nothing compared to his old home, too much sand, too much wind, no decent transportation to get around. But here he could work as cadre of a government enterprise, which was better than being cadre of a commune back home. Moreover, back there his wife did not get along with her in-laws. He had decided to come over here, but if the opportunity arose to return to a 'national unit' back home, he would jump at it.

She expressed regret that the Secretary did not want to stay on. 'The State Farm needs a good leader,' I heard her say. 'The speed of a train depends on its engine.' Then, sighing, she added, 'Being a cadre is definitely better. You can get transferred wherever you like. If not a farm then you can go to a factory, if not a factory you can go to the government. Even if we farm-workers get transferred, it's just from one State Farm to another.'

65

Secretary Cao advised her to try and move back to her old home. All she needed was a unit to accept her there, and he would make sure the necessary documents went through. From the corner of my eye, I saw his hand make a motion—the flourish of a signature, and off she would go.

'Thanks a lot,' she said, 'but I've been through some trouble, you know. I don't really want to go back home, I don't have much of a reputation back there.'

'Oh that,' he said, 'that doesn't count for much. We call that merely a private "internal contradiction". Just a shame it happened before the Great Cultural Revolution. If it had been during, you never would have been sentenced to three years' hard labour. You should have seen the big-character posters pasted up at that time, exposing a lot of senior cadres who did the same thing!'

I had always wondered what crime she had committed. The Secretary not only had a handle on politics, he also had access to people's files, and naturally he would know. From what he said, it was clear she had been charged for so-called 'male-female relationships'. That was one crime that didn't differentiate between the high and the low. Unlike being a 'capitalist roader', for which she simply had no qualifications, anybody could do it.

As the two of them kept chatting, I became increasingly disconsolate. The sun was beginning to hang down in the western sky. The floating clouds drawn in by ridges of mountains were now curling around their bald tops. The wind had died down and now wandered tiredly over last year's dry weeds. To the south, on the yellow line of the horizon I could see a small puff of white dust. Dumbo was bringing the sheep back in. A shepherd headed out to work later than the Main Troop and got home earlier, but once the sheep were back they still had to be watered and fed— there was plenty of work to do.

66

With a rude bang, I pulled open the gate of the pen. It was like a fan that has lost several of its ribs, and wobbled and shook from the insult. 'Better get going,' I told them. 'The sheep will be here soon.'

The Secretary turned around to look at me. 'So, that's it for today,' he said, passing the shovel back to her.

Walking up, he offered me a cigarette. 'Here, have a smoke. The "Daily Supplement" says that for every cigarette you smoke you lose five minutes of your life. I don't believe it. How can you know which five minutes are being knocked off, anyway?'

'If you smoke, you smoke,' I said. 'Anyway, five minutes more or less is all the same to me.'

I took the cigarette and lit it, then offered him a light. After a long puff, he said, significantly, 'Doesn't matter to anyone. Right now, who's afraid of dying?'

That was true enough. Chinese were not afraid of dying. Especially now, when there was little point in living. But talking to the Secretary one had to be careful not to go too far. I changed the subject. 'I've just come back from herding those sheep in the mountains. Do you want me to stay up here with them, or come back and live in the Troop?'

'It's up to you,' he said generously. 'Herding sheep or not's also up to you. You've stuck it out in the mountains for a whole winter. If you want a rest, then come on back to the Troop. If you want to be by yourself with the sheep, then keep at it. Oh, one more thing—since you've just come back, take three days of vacation. How's that?'

'Fine. In that case, I'll come back to work in the Troop.'

On a State Farm, the easiest life is that in the Troop: you work regular hours, get holidays, and no matter how lazy you are the salary is not one penny less. Unlike a labour camp, solitary work did not offer freedom here. On the contrary, it could mean that you were chained to your post. If no one was willing to take over for you, there was no getting away from it. Sheep herding was, moreover, a dangerous risk for people like us to take. If the birthing rate of the lambs was high, we got no credit, and if the death rate was high, we were to blame.

The Secretary rubbed the dirt off his hands, shook out the legs of his trousers, and followed the snaking path heading off down the hill. Holding the shovel, she strolled over to me. 'Strange,' I said, 'he seems particularly humane today. Gave me three days of vacation, and I saw you two had a lively talk.'

'These people are real devils,' she said. 'He's not the same as before.'

'How not the same?' With some alarm, I realized that, up on the mountain for an entire winter, I had not seen a single newspaper, nor heard a single word out of a loudspeaker. Had there been some change in the world during my absence?

'I couldn't say for sure. I just felt something was different.' She looked out over at the cloud of white dust, gradually getting bigger on the horizon. 'If you're not busy tonight, come on over to our place to sit awhile. It's plenty quiet there, just two of us, and one of them an old woman . . .'

2

Dumbo brought the sheep in. Herd them in, count them up, water them, split them into pens. In a moment the cold, empty sheep pen was filled with exuberant life. Sheep pushing sheep, sheep butting sheep, baby sheep looking for mother sheep. Only the old ones stayed quiet, looking over their kind with a cold resignation.

Right: 275 altogether, not any less, and naturally there wouldn't be any more. For all their liveliness, though, they were still only sheep. For months, I had been missing people.

When the sheep were in the pen, they were no longer Dumbo's business. It wasn't that they ought not be his business, but he was incapable of doing anything other than herding them. He couldn't even count them: Dumbo served the function of a sheep-dog. At the moment, he was squatting silently by the wall. With his head hanging down, he was staring fixedly at the two pieces of car tyre that were the soles of his mountain shoes. I called out to him between yelling at the sheep,

'Hey, you go on home!'

'Go on home?'

'I say, go home and eat your dinner!'

'Eat your dinner?'

No matter what you said, it came back to you as an echo. Forget it, a man had enough to do worrying about his own life.

After a while, his old lady came by. She was a big-footed Mongolian woman, with a flat face that had been burnt by the sun to a deep yellow. While all the others were wearing army green now, only this woman still dressed in the old-fashioned style. She started to abuse him from down on the path, before even getting to the sheep pen.

'I declare, why don't you just die! Aargh! Why don't you just go off and die. You worthless piece of trash. You wouldn't even know the way home, if I didn't come to get you. You really should kick off, save your old woman a lot of trouble . . .'

'Don't scold him, big sister,' I told her. 'He brings you thirty-three yuan a month by living, doesn't he? Leaving aside the fact that he can't find his own way home, when he's herding sheep he's better than a dog . . .'

'That's right, and I cherish those thirty-three yuan!' The big feet plodded into the sheep pen. 'But this idiot doesn't know any better. He had money, and then went and gave it away. Who told him to give back that bag? That's over with, but having done it, he should have just left it at that. But the man has to up and fall sick. I can't stop thinking about it. Lao Zhang,* I just can't make it out—what are people all about, anyway? Eh? You tell me, you're the one with the education. Can you understand a man?'

She put the emphasis on the word 'man', indicating clearly that she wasn't talking about her own husband. She was asking me about the nature of man, the quality of man, the significance of man. At a time when all that mattered was man's 'class', this big-footed woman living in a remote

---

*Put before the surname, 'Lao' is a term of affection and respect for a person, usually someone older than oneself.

desert was thinking more deeply. While the critics and the policy-makers screamed 'class', she was actually trying to penetrate man's nature.

Using her husband's whip to prod him a few times, this unlucky philosopher persuaded Dumbo to get moving. As she led the way, he silently followed behind, going down the narrow path towards home.

The sheep bleated; smoke began to rise from houses in the distance. Most families burned a particular kind of wood which produced a thick, heavy smoke. Like genii rising from their chimneys, the plumes spread over the town.

Dumbo was not really a mute. A few years back everybody was caught up in reciting the 'Three Articles'. Although he could scarcely read a word, in the phrase of the villagers, Dumbo could 'recite up a bubbling brook'. His family background—his class—was 'poor farmer'. You could go back five generations and not find a blemish in that sterling record. He had come back to his home town after getting out of the army. Unlike the farm's Secretary, he had little education, and the highest position he could dredge up was Team Leader. Moreover, it was Team Leader of something nobody else wanted: he became master of herding sheep.

Dumbo had always been a happy man, with no real grudge against anyone. He had carried a gun for five years in the army, but never lost the good nature of his peasant blood. None the less, when it came to fighting he would positively leap into battle, using his fists, biting and kicking. His devotion to his leaders was complete. His hatred for 'class enemies' was a result of his total belief in revolution. If the leaders said the 'cow ghosts and snake demons'* were bad men, then surely they were evil. Because of his sunny

---

*Literally 'cow ghosts and snake demons', this is usually translated as 'class enemies of all kinds', or 'forces of evil'.

nature, people liked him. Because of his devotion, bosses favoured him. Every year he was commended for actively studying the works of Mao.

Three years ago, the sheep were herded up into the mountains in the autumn as usual, to graze on the rocky slopes. Dumbo took four other herders with him, assembled from various Troops. They headed out to a stone sheep pen on a mountain pass almost in Inner Mongolia. It was from this place that I had just returned. The ground up there is strewn with large flat stones; a natural flood outlet coming out of the hills is also full of these grey-green stones. The grass growing between them flourishes—it has to be vigorous to survive. The local lore has it that sheep fed on this grass will absorb its sturdy spirit, so every year they are herded to this place to graze.

One day, the man we had not yet started to call Dumbo was driving over two hundred sheep along, when he suddenly made a totally unexpected find. It was a bulging canvas bag, lying on top of a rock. He opened it, looked inside, and found wad after wad of money. In such a barren wilderness, such a stretch of moonlike terrain, the only possible explanation was that the bag had fallen out of the sky. Dumbo stayed alone on the slope the entire day, never quite getting the money counted, trying to figure out what to do. Returning to the sheep pen at night, he secretly buried the bag away in the manure, and from that moment Dumbo fell ill. Talking to himself continuously, his lips would tremble without making a sound. It was as if he were counting out a string of astronomical figures in his mind. Of course, from then on he was incapable of tending the sheep, but he was officially Team Leader, and another man was found to substitute for him.

Not long after, a group of men from the Provincial Public Security Bureau came through. It seems the money had been lost by some Mongolians. They had driven a herd of horses up the Yellow River to sell, had made around ten thousand dollars and were on their way back home. No bank existed on the high plateau to take the deposit, so they had strapped the bag to a saddle and headed out across the pass. Along the way, however, they had a bit to drink. Without their noticing, the bag came loose and fell off onto the ground.

The Public Security men followed the path that they had taken home, making their investigation step by step along its trail. They figured that the men living in the sheep pens of this thirty-mile barren expanse were most suspect. Eventually, they found their way to Dumbo's pen.

The solitary sheep pen had never seen so many people. One by one, the herders were taken over to a jeep, where uniformed men were interrogating everyone. Dumbo was a Team Leader, and a good and proper 'poor farmer'. Also, he suffered from this strange illness. Nobody even thought of doubting him. At the first sight of those gun-carrying men, though, he came apart. He changed colour and his entire body began to shake. Without their asking, he voluntarily told them everything. The Mongolian canvas bag was dug out from the middle of a pile of sheep shit, and when it was counted not a penny was missing.

Overnight, Dumbo became famous. On top of being an exemplary 'Activist at Studying the Works of Mao', he became a 'Model Soldier' in the 'Agriculture and Reclamation System' of the province. He was made an 'Exceptional Party Member', and was pointed out to people as a guide to follow.

When a propaganda official was helping him set it all down in a Report, however, he chuckled and twittered, saying, 'The money was just too much! If it had been only a few hundred dollars, I would have kept it for myself.'

73

Naturally, this could not go into an offical Report. The propaganda man simply adopted the ready-made phrases of the newspaper articles to write his account.

Dumbo did not have the money, neither did he suffer from the illness any more. He had simply let out a true statement. This was not officially noted, however, and soon after Dumbo was called on to make a speech in Beijing.

He attended the 'Congress of New People' called by the 'National Agricultural System'. He even met the Big Bosses of the Central Committee.

Coming back from Beijing, however, he began to tell people that he had been stupid. Before going, he had not known what money was really for. After he had been to Beijing and seen all the goods on sale at the Wangfujing Department Store, then he realized you needed money to have a good life. Word of this got around to the delegation leaders. They called him in and proceeded to give him a lesson. If he went on babbling like that, they would have to classify him a 'class enemy'.

Crushed, Dumbo returned from the State Farm Headquarters a different man. From that day on, Dumbo was silent.

At the beginning, the nickname people gave him was 'stupid'. Unfortunately, at that particular time the adjective 'stupid' had taken on a complimentary character, and was used as a term of commendation. For example, the person who came daily to clean the Headquarter's toilets—this person was encouraged and praised as being 'stupid'. He had previously been a hydraulic engineer, and had with some difficulty overcome the appellation 'intellectual'. Now after much work he had obtained the glorious status of 'stupid', and been allowed to enter the Party.

People felt, therefore, that it was not quite fitting to call the shepherd 'stupid'. Later, as a result of the peculiar nature of his illness, we took to calling him Dumbo.

Dumbo was stubbornly silent, but who knew what was going on inside his head? When people looked at him, they felt a dark shadow passing through their own minds. Most personal tragedies were being caused by politics, by the 'Mass Movements' that were washing over people's lives. Dumbo's tragedy had been brought on by himself. When we thought about his case, we all had to recognize that the most common of desires still lurked in the bottom of our own hearts. Under the layers of political slogans, in the heart and mind of a very normal man, of a man who led a model life, was a naked feeling of simply wanting to live a good life. It was a frighteningly raw and honest, selfish desire. It was a feeling that refused to submit to politics. If it existed in Dumbo, how much more did it exist in us? No matter what political movements scoured us, it was impossible to flush that feeling away. On the contrary, it would sometimes crawl out of its own volition, and in a moment dissolve all the influence that 'politics' had on a person.

Looking at Dumbo, we knew that in our hearts too, beside the fighting spirit of 'unceasing revolution', lived that other, unnameable spirit. Dumbo's case had brought it into the open, while in the rest of us it still lay submerged. These insidious thoughts, like the trickling of water under layers of ice, were little by little gnawing away at the frozen world above.

Perhaps this had something to do with what the Big-footed Philosopher meant?

Dumbo simply hung his head, and followed the woman with the whip down the hill. Slowly they disappeared into the light blue evening mist. The smoke let out by the genii had capped the entire village. The sheep had settled down.

75

One baleful, tired-out old ram lay down in a back corner, breathing heavily. With his long beard hanging down, he looked as though he understood heaven's irony and man's sorrow.

I finished the work I had to do and sat down on the stone that Secretary Cao had used for sharpening the shovel. As I lit a cigarette, a habitual feeling of sadness settled in. This emotion came as punctually as the hour on the clock. When the sun went down and evening was approaching, when the sheep were quiet and soft clouds curled across the sky, as the wind sank across sculpted sand hills and silent plains and all the solitary, erect blades of grass became indistinct, then into my mind came this solitude, this loneliness.

Every day and night of my life, I had only sheep or the likes of Dumbo to keep me company. I was living in a society that was almost inhuman, that seemed a little swirl of mud flung out from the careening revolutions of human-kind. In all the vast space above me and the unchanging emptiness of nature around me, I couldn't find one particle of evidence to corroborate what I had read in books. Our world had lost its link with human society.

This state of immobile suspension sometimes made me want to take action, to move. At other times, it made me hopeless and depressed. Even more, it made me afraid. Both time and my mind were being silently eroded by the wind. In the end, I would be useless, as I slowly became like Dumbo.

Could you say that there was nothing in Dumbo's mind at all? On this Dumbo was mute. The world is cast of iron, without feelings or consciousness. If you want to influence it, push it, mould it, the least you must do is shout—never mind that it is a muffled shout from under a blanket of repression.

Today, however, as I watched the sun sink behind deep

green mountains from my sheep-pen perch, between the loneliness and the solitude came the thread of another emotion. It entered as soft as down, tickling and provoking my thoughts. Today, I have finally seen you again! Wasn't this the will of heaven? In all these years, the various women I had known had been forgotten. Han Yueping, Ma Ying-hua—I knew I would not see them again, and so wasted no time in thinking about them.

I did, however, remember Her, and every time I did I would doubt if it had really happened. Did I in fact have such a magical moment in my life? My heart had hardened, yet that sight of her had left an indelible mark. To this day, I was moved by that image, the beautiful lines of a naked body. It had excited me countless times, aroused a lust in me, made me realize that despite my outer husk of prison black, or blue, or now, labouring green, I was still a man inside.

Although we were living in a society that strangled individuality, at least I maintained the distinction of sex. That powerful gesture of hers, that brave and soundless call, had had the effect of raping me. I had not had the courage to meet it, but its effect was to stay with and in me: although at the age of thirty-nine I was still a virgin, I had lost my virginity at that moment.

All the warm embraces of the past were shattered by the memory of her trembling body; blood red rays of sun had pierced through peach-coloured clouds of morning. From that time on, I knew if I were to think of a woman, I would think of her. My innocence was lost in her body. I couldn't believe that she would enter my life for only that one moment. Without any basis for believing it, I knew I would see her again. Now, here she was before me. Things that happen twice in life carry with them a certain significance: it has to be fate.

I knew, however, that unused to warm emotions I had long ago been taken over by raw desire. The way one lives changes one's way of loving, one's purpose in loving, one's concept of love. Just like Dumbo, I was caught in an irreconcilable dilemma. On the one side was the voice of reason, held down and controlled by the force of culture; on the other side a primal, non-rational urge, aching to screw another living, breathing body. It didn't matter who she was, as long as she excited the male sex in me.

The floating evening clouds split into shreds . . .

As I finished my cigarette, the loudspeaker from down below erupted. This iron-grey instrument, opening its black yawning mouth, was the sole contact we farmers had with the outside world. It repeated the same tune every single day, proving yet again that the world had stopped in its tracks. The only thing that seemed to flow on was time—so the loudspeaker's main function was to announce the time: time to go to the mess to eat dinner. I stood up and rolled and shouldered my bedding. Without waiting for the man who was to take my place, I secured the gate to the sheep pen and set off down the slope.

What the hell—when I'd eaten, I'd go and look for her!

3

Squatting at the doorway to the mess, I finished eating. I clamped my rice bowl under one arm and shouldered my bedding with the other, and headed back to the dormitory where I used to stay. Entering, I tossed the bedding over the boards of an empty bed.

'What's happened to those two?' Looking at two empty bunks, I spoke to Zhou Ruicheng, who was sitting cross-legged on a bed nearby.

'Married and gone—we're the only two bare cudgels [bachelors] left here.'

He gave a fawning and submissive smile, as his delicate face looked up from the er-hu* he was playing. Only a small, sharp mouth could smile like that. I returned the compliment, saying, 'At least I haven't got an old lady like you. You're in worse shape than I am—you've got someone you can't go back to.'

Without replying he took up the instrument again, playing the plaintive Song of the Liuyang River. His playing was quite good, the lonely notes full of emotion. But Liuyang River was the only song he ever played.

Zhou Ruicheng was what they called 'surplus material'

*A two-stringed Chinese instrument played with a bow.

from the prison. He had been working in town as head of the supply group for the 'Agricultural Construction Division' until the year they needed more 'cow demons and snake spirits' to fill the jail. That year they pulled in people from all over—I was locked up with him there myself. Afterwards, when the prison was emptied, all the 'cow demons and snake spirits' went back home, some to their units, others to official positions. Only Zhou was not set free. His status was still unclear, and he had been living with us bachelors in the dormitory for several years now.

The sound of his instrument reverberated and spread inside the four mud walls of our room. I put out my bedding and lay down on my back, watching his pointed mouth and his little pointed beard. Slowly the evening darkened, and his frail figure shrank until in the end he was only a black shadow. All that remained was the Liuyang River, trickling and dripping from his unseen fingers, trying to escape through the cracks of the lonely room.

The room was lonely, the music was lonely, the air itself was lonely. I suddenly recognized what he was playing. Words praising our Great Leader had been set to the music, but originally it had been a simple Hunan folk-song. With a range of notes that was not too broad and intervals that did not jump too far, it gave solid expression to the aching of melancholy and of grief.

I sat up on the bed, and asked him apologetically, 'Thinking about home?'

In the darkness, all I could see now were his two eyes, staring ahead at the wall, or at the music, or perhaps towards some person or some other thing. After a moment, he carefully put down the er-hu, and said, 'Who's thinking about home? I'm just tired of living.'

Only in a 'Revolutionary Song' like this one did he dare to insert a little of his own emotion—like a 'free prisoner' using a public vehicle to transport a few of his own belongings on the side. If he could have managed to spit out what he was thinking to me, the two of us might have got along. He was well-educated, the graduate of a KMT military academy, versed in classical studies. I had never heard him speak his mind, though, and in fact one seldom heard him speak at all.

Once, I made the mistake of calling our collective dormitory the 'Bachelors' Committee', and this almost scared Zhou to death. Taking me aside, he whispered, 'What are you thinking about, Zhang, "Bachelors' Committee"! If the leaders hear about this, there'll be hell to pay. The one thing they are most sensitive to is any new organization.'

He had not, however, been incapacitated by his paranoia. Whatever psychosis he suffered, he was still capable of writing his Appeal.* He would often sit facing the wall, and with a beautiful, graceful hand, write the square upright characters of a formal letter.

'What about it? No answer?' The lonely music had made me sympathetic towards him. 'I came back from a winter on that mountain, expecting you'd have left for home long ago. All this writing, it doesn't seem to have been much use.'

'That's not so,' he said, earnestly. 'It would be useful, if the people on top could see it. You see, someone in the middle has been blocking the way. You should understand that I am someone who has "done meritorious deeds".'

'You've "done meritorious deeds"?' I asked him curiously. 'What meritorious deeds have you done? You mean, after the uprising you went over to fight in the Liberation Army?'

*A 'letter of appeal' to be 'rehabilitated', i.e. to have one's 'mishandled case' reversed.

81

'No, you don't understand.' He lay back, dejected, pursuing old recollections. 'When the Great Cultural Revolution had just begun, I was in the Division Headquarters, putting together information and studying it with the others. Lots of material on soldiers who had been in that uprising together with me was material that I provided . . .'

Then I understood. One of the rebel KMT officers on whom he had 'provided information' had been rehabilitated. He had returned to a position of authority and was now blocking Zhou's Appeal.

The 'meritorious deed' he had performed had had reverse consequences. Without seeing clearly, he had been fooled by the turn of events.

'I see. Go ahead and write anyway. Write a lot—there's bound to come a day when those above will get a look at it. There's sure to be a time when you can go home.' I comforted him, while I thought, 'Ha ha! You keep on waiting!'

I jumped down from the bed and walked outside. I had met a number of people who liked to inform—the 'Head of Administration' of this Troop was one, and here was another. Yet Zhou seemed to have put aside informing for the time being: he devoted himself entirely to writing his Appeal. First he had framed other people, and now he had to defend himself. This too was a kind of 'Man's Fate'!

The dark night exuded the baked stink of an overflowing cesspool. Was the weather about to change?

Mixed with it, however, was the clear smell of oleaster flowers, a fragrance that seemed to go straight into a person's innards. Spring was definitely on its way.

Their room was lit by one large light bulb that clearly exceeded regulation size. I screwed up my eyes in the unac-

82

customed brightness as I walked in. 'Eh? What are you two up to in here? Playing Chinese chess?'*

She raised her head in greeting and chuckled, 'Who's playing chess? I'm just helping Old Lady Ma write her "letter of appeal".'

The two were sitting facing each other, heads bowed over a table made from a wooden carton. On top of the carton lay a sheet of white paper, and I noticed that she was holding a pen.

'Lao Zhang, now that you've come, I figure it's better that you should write it,' Old Lady Ma said. 'You've got the education.'

'Excuse me, I've never written an Appeal for anyone,' I said. 'If you wanted to get married, now, I could write that for you. And I guarantee the application would pass.'

'You devil, you,' she scolded, 'me get married? Who would I marry? You think I've gone mad?'

Laughing at her, I answered, 'With Zhou Ruicheng. His woman ran off with someone else and I'm afraid he doesn't know it yet. You two would be just right together—he's writing a "letter of appeal" too.'

Old Lady Ma grinned. 'You rogue, you've never been quite normal. My young friend, that mouth of yours has been your trouble all this time.'

'You're wrong there.' Very casually, I sat down on Old Lady Ma's bed. This bed was exactly opposite where she was sitting. 'This man has always been normal and proper. It's just that people take serious things as a joke now, and crazy talk for real. Anyway, the charges they have used to indict me with the last five times have not been for something that I said, but something that I wrote. And you're still

*A forbidden pleasure.

asking me to write your "letter of appeal"? I'm afraid the more I wrote the worse things would get—in the end they might even send you in again!'

At the age of eight, Old Lady Ma had been sold into a Shandong household as a child bride. She had been working there for eight years when Liberation came. Her husband was ten years older than she, and in the chaos he disappeared and no one ever saw him again. The Chairman of the 'Poor Farmer Committee' noticed her, but this sixteen-year-old young bride foolishly rejected her good fortune. Loss of face at her refusal made him vindictive. He waited until 1958, before finding his chance for revenge during the Great Leap Forward. He 'hatted'* her with the title 'Landlord Element'. She fled the province, running in the end to this backward country State Farm to work as a labourer. Even as she ran, a 'Wanted Circular' pursued her. During the 'Socialist Education Movement' of 1963 it finally caught up with her. The Farm then branded her a 'Refugee Landlord', and sentenced her to three years of punishment. Although she had finished the sentence long ago and was now released, she was still considered a 'Landlord Element'. Her only reason for writing an Appeal was to have this inappropriate 'hat' taken off her head. However, in the past she had told me that the 'Poor Farmer Committee' Chairman was now the Party Secretary of her old commune. Re-examination of cases in her old home town had necessarily to go through the local government:

*Derived from the practice of placing tall paper dunce-caps on 'criminals' and forcing them to parade through the streets chanting their crimes, the term 'hatted' meant losing civilian rights and becoming an outcast in society. A 'hatted' person was given the lowest menial job available and the lowest salary ranking, his or her family was ostracized and their children were often not allowed to go to school; the wife or husband of a 'hatted' person was often forced to get a divorce.

she might as well throw the Appeal into the wastebasket.

As long as they're living, people must have hope. I didn't have the heart to extinguish that hope, so the only thing to do was joke with them.

'Lao Zhang, you should write an Appeal too. Just look at you, you're almost forty years old. If you were rehabilitated, you could teach in a school.' Old Lady Ma looked at me, speaking earnestly.

People always think that the things they most love to eat are what everybody else should eat too, and they try to make everybody sample some.

Pulling cigarettes from my pocket, I glanced at Old Lady Ma's face. She was only four years older than I, but it looked as though every day she had lived had been etched in wrinkles on her face. It was no wonder that even seventy-year-old men called her Old Lady Ma.

Go back home! I thought, just go back to your home town! That face of yours is your best 'letter of appeal'! Let that Committee Chairman, now the Commune Secretary, get a good long look. 'Do you still recognize the pretty girl you once desired?' If he still has any conscience left at all, he'll rehabilitate you.

It is doubtful, however, if that kind of person has an ounce of mercy in him.

In the end, she kept on hoping. Not only was she hoping for herself, but she spread this hope around for others to enjoy as well. The beneficence hidden underneath those wrinkles made her face shine out at times with the light of that sixteen-year-old girl.

'My case isn't the same as yours,' I said, lighting a cigarette. 'I was first a "rightist", and then later a "counter-revolutionary". I don't know which it would be better to try to get repealed. But you, if you can get your "landlord

85

hat" taken off, then everything should go well. Write, write, there's bound to be a day when someone will clear it up for you.' I sincerely wished her well.

'Ah,' she drew a long breath. 'It would be good if it could be cleared up. These days of wearing a "hat" are difficult.' Turning to Xiangjiu, she asked, 'Where did we get to in that letter—1963? . . .'

'Wait a moment,' Xiangjiu said, putting down the pen and leaning back against the wall. 'We have a guest, let's leave it for a while.'

'Oh yes, yes,' Old Lady Ma hurriedly apologized. 'You see, I was just thinking of myself. You two sit awhile, I'll go out and look for some ink.' And Old Lady Ma significantly withdrew.

She had a keen eye, that one. She had not, however, known how to appreciate the favours of the 'Poor Farmer Committee' Chairman. As a result . . .

The scent of oleaster deepened, like just before a thundershower, wafting in from the window and the crack in the door. In the dormitory, everything inside wanted to get out, but in this room everything wanted to get in.

I asked her, 'Why don't you write your own Appeal?'

'It would be pointless,' she responded. 'Who can clear up things that relate to feelings? If it wasn't me that was wrong, it was him. Since I've already done hard labour, what use is there in bringing it up? Anyway, even if they rehabilitated me, they couldn't bring back those three years.'

There was nothing I could say to that. She understood the situation better than I did.

She was wearing a white shirt. The buttons at the neck were open, exposing a triangle of skin above her breasts. Her skin was still ivory. One didn't need to touch it to know that it was warm and smooth . . . I gave a little smile.

'You're really the one who should write an Appeal,'

86

she said. 'Start from the "rightist" problem—everything started from there. If you were rehabilitated, just as Old Lady Ma said, you would have no problem at all going out to teach . . .'

'No, it's precisely because I would have to go back to that "rightist" problem that I don't even try.'

'How long are you going to wait?'

I moved my eyes off that triangle, and tried to think of how to answer her.

'Maybe you don't know,' she said, 'Deng Xiaoping's already been rehabilitated.'

'Ah?' This was indeed surprising and happy news. No wonder everyone had suddenly begun to write his 'letter of appeal'. 'Is that really true?'

'Naturally. He's already out and working again.'

This was probably what she had wanted to tell me during the day! It was something that should have been announced to everyone. They should have read it in the newspapers, heard it from the loudspeakers, learned about it through radio announcements. In addition to those must certainly have been tens or hundreds of red-headlined documents from the Central Government. This was a remote town, however, a village of outcasts clumped together in an uncaring landscape. News of major affairs that managed to reach this place through the press were like a string of hieroglyphics, a chain of bizarre notations: it was what it appeared to be, and yet it wasn't that at all. You had to reach the real news through those tortuous markings, through the Maze of Minos that they laid out. People fated to remain outside Authority could not hope to comprehend them.

With utmost effort, the highest levels of government attempted to pass news down to us, like passing a baton through innumerable hands, one by one. By the time it reached this village, it was like the sun's reflected light that

87

had been to the moon and back before touching our lives. Even then, our senses could only detect the vaguest of its reflections.

In this village, major matters, such as whether or not the grain ration had been increased, down to smaller events such as the Secretary's asking me to smoke one of his cigarettes today, had to be sifted carefully for their significance. Rational comprehension was out of the question. Ultimately one had to depend on instincts. As a result, everything took on an air of the supernatural: meteorites, earthquakes, strange foetuses, hairy children, and every manner of abnormal natural phenomena were on an equal footing with the end of the Vietnam War, the visit to China of Sihanouk, the big-character article on Yao Wenyuan, the order of protocol of names attending national banquets, as well as all the little scraps of rumours that issued from every alley. All played an equally significant part in affecting our lives. The indiscriminate doctrine of the 'unity of man and nature' had run rampant: we had returned to the Dark Ages.

I had tried to comprehend the order of things from works of philosophy, of politics and economics, and what was written in the books was clear. It had supported me in life, and become the guide to my spirit. But as soon as I came up against reality, all turned into chaos. News reports suddenly seemed non-linear, and took on an undeniable arbitrariness. They seemed to have escaped from all convention, and even fled the bounds of intuition. They were like the interference that a plane puts out to confuse the radar signals of its trackers.

This last news was out of the ordinary. My intuition had also told me that things were changing fast Outside. Like smoke passing through a cigarette, a stream of heat passed through my veins and arteries. A boat had been overturned—it didn't matter if the bow or the stern had gone over first. What mattered was that someone had clambered back on top of that great boat, and had taken on the responsibility of being captain. The first thing he would do would be to order a rescue operation. Where the boat would go on the vast open seas once it had been righted again was a question for the future: it would have to wait until those who were in the water had been hauled back up on board.

Her eyes questioned mine as she watched me, wondering. A pair of woman's eyes are not sheep eyes, but they have the same meekness, doubt, alarm and vacillation. What could I say to her? An obscure intimation could not yet be considered understanding, and even if I was correct, the maze was too difficult to enter. I was not the sort who wanted to send the ship to the bottom, although there were those already in the water who wanted everyone to drown along with them. My only concern was that the ship should have me on it! I just wanted to get back on board, dry off my clothes, clean my wounds, stretch my four limbs in the heat of the sun. And I wanted one thing more; I harboured a secret hope. I wanted to participate in determining the course of the ship. The experience of the last eighteen years had clarified one thing for me: one person might be able to hold onto the rudder of the ship, but one person was not enough to steer it where he wanted it to go.

But could I say these things to her? The light bulb was uncomfortably bright. For the past few months the only light I had had in the sheep pens came from the kerosene lanterns of the last century. I liked their warmth in the midst of darkness. In the darkness I could imagine the murmuring of soft talk, soothing my lonely nerves . . . and here in front of me actually sat a living woman. She herself sat in front of me! She was talking to me, in a gentle voice that was leisurely and cordial. That voice expressed more than words, however, with its timbre full of overtones and implications. I suddenly became aware of the meaning of the questioning light in her eyes: there were only the two of us in this room, one a man without a woman, and the other a woman without a man. Was there nothing to talk about except 'letters of appeal' and 'rehabilitation'?

Not only questioning and doubt were in her eyes—there also flickered hope and acquiescence. It was as though she had already taken a position, and was waiting for me to make the first move. As though she had prepared in advance to crumble under my oncoming attack.

I sat on the bed on one side of the room, she sat on the bed across from me. Between us was a strip of brown earth less than two metres wide. This strip was like the challenging line on a life-sized chessboard. If you considered the other side to be invincible, then it was. If you didn't then its power would dissolve into nothingness, obliterated by something as small as the flick of a finger. Time trickled on in the silence. A tiny smile appeared on her face, strange and mysterious. That brave and soundless call, that call from the midst of loneliness, was repeatedly echoing between us again. Although she was fully dressed, the contour of her body was clear beneath the blouse. A naked body again appeared before my eyes.

The passion of politics flows from the same source as the impulse of lust, both secreted internally from the endocrine glands. Both incite a man to abandon himself, to plunge forward—decisively, bravely, foolishly, taking and possessing—receiving fulfilment and happiness in the act of self-sacrifice.

Today was a day of auspicious events—how was it they all seemed to crowd together? It was a day worth celebrating, and I already felt half-liberated. Over my face came a strange and mysterious smile. I knew she could understand:

just as she could read a man's eyes, she must know what I was thinking. That yellow-coloured glandular secretion surged violently; I felt drunk. A feeling of apprehension and unwilling good fortune came over me, a kind of delirious alarm. I again felt my mouth go dry, as I had back then in the middle of the reeds . . .

As I was preparing to say something, do something, Old Lady Ma pushed open the door.

'I've looked everywhere and there just isn't any to be found!' She shot a searching look at our faces. 'Life is hard, even getting ink to write a "letter of appeal" is so much trouble.'

'Try going to the office,' Xiangjiu urged her, 'the accountants are sure to have some there.'

'Yes, that would be something!' Old Lady Ma feigned a look of simple fear. 'Secretary Cao would immediately say, "You, writing? You've got no relatives to write to, let alone any friends, and you say you want to write a letter? I'm afraid you must be writing a complaint against your leader!"'

We all laughed, which broke the ice, as her face again revealed the naïveté of a sixteen-year-old.

'You two have got it right after all,' she said. 'If you don't care about "rehabilitation", it doesn't get to you.' She again sat in front of the wooden crate, and picking up some sewing to work on it, came straight to the point. 'I'm not joking now, you two are a perfect couple.'

Xiangjiu didn't say anything, but she smiled a little. Old Lady Ma had good intentions, but she was definitely too eager and too impatient.

'I suppose you're referring to neither of us writing Appeals. But then you're writing an Appeal, and so is Zhou Ruicheng—aren't you two also a perfect couple?'

'Don't be silly.' With needle in hand, she made a circle

91

around her ear to show how crazy I was. 'I'm telling the truth. You two have both done labour reform, so neither of you could resent or suspect the other. Your age is about the same. Lao Zhang, you've been educated, and her education isn't so bad either—she's been to middle school at least. As soon as she moved in here, I got to thinking about it. I've just been waiting for you to come back from the mountains to tell you.'

'Now, now, now.' Xiangjiu was laughing. 'I'm not getting married again. I've been married enough for one lifetime.'

'How can you not be married? From the day that they're born, women are meant to be partners for men. Nobody wants me, it's true, but if anybody did, I would be married too!' Old Lady Ma was certainly full of determination.

'What do you mean nobody wants you?' I said. 'That Committee Chairman wanted you. Your troubles began because you wouldn't have him.'

'That wouldn't do!' she said righteously. 'He already had a wife and son. If he hadn't had a family, I would have gone with him. He wasn't a bad man at all—tall, handsome, he was the right material for an official. That "hat" he put on me was only meant to bring my pride down, nothing more.'

It looked almost as if she still loved him. He had routed her out of house and home, and put her through hard labour for three years! 'Why did you become a refugee at the very beginning?' I asked her.

'Basically because we didn't have enough to eat at home. I didn't leave on my own, either, there was a group of us that fled together. Except it was only me that came to such grief.'

'Think about it a little,' I said. 'That no-good Committee Chairman of yours still put out that "wanted circular".' I wanted to say: stop being so infatuated.

'That's true, but all he wanted to do was catch me and bring me back. He wanted me in front of him again. Who could have known then that we would run into all these Movements . . .'

There was no way to reason with the woman. As Huang Xiangjiu had said, who can see things clearly when it comes to feelings? I looked at her—she was facing Old Lady Ma and laughing. What was hidden in that laughter, sympathy, ridicule, or encouragement? Encouragement to bring up the subject of us again?

When I left their room, the night was full of stars. From out of the darkness came a young woman, an 'intellectual' sent down from Beijing as an 'educated youth, working in the countryside and mountain areas'. Her name was He Lifang. She was singing a Kazakh song, called 'Sending You a Rose':

> *My price isn't really too high,*
> *Just nylon stockings and two gunny-sacks.*
> *If you feel apologetic, then*
> *Add to that a watch with Roman numerals.*

'Brother,' she walked up next to me and softly said, 'come to my place and sit for a while—how about it? You must have saved up a lot of "Unity" on that mountain all winter . . .'

'What would I be doing coming over so late?' I said. 'I'll come over tomorrow.'

'Easier to do things when it's late. Our man's gone off to Beijing to visit relatives.'

'Aren't you afraid what Hei-tz will do to you when he gets back?'

'Ha ha! He's like this on the Outside too, depending on his two fingers to make some money.' Her eyes flashed like

93

a cat's in the inky dark. 'Here in this town, who cares what you do?'

'Go home and sleep,' I told her. Hei-tz was a friend of mine.

The trickle of water was slowly eating into the layers of ice above . . .

I raised my head to the sky and drew a long breath. Could I ever expect to understand people?

Luo Zongqi's two feet hung in mid-air as he straddled the centre beam. No thicker than a man's arm, it had to serve as the mainstay for a small kitchen he was building onto his house.

He set a nail in position and poised his hammer to drive it into place. 'You've been "rectified" by them for almost two decades, and you're still that naïve? I wouldn't be too hopeful if I were you.' He drove the nail home, and then continued, 'Look at me, will you—I've been "rehabilitated". I'm back to holding a regular job, small as it is, and with this home you could say I'm master of my own little square of earth. But I ask you, do I have any say over the course of events?'

Bang! Bang! Bang! He looked not only angry, but as though he wanted to wake me up. I had walked twelve miles that morning, from our Troop over to his. The sun had been brilliant, reminding me of the ocean. I had come to ask him for guidance, for the significance of the 'news'— those hieroglyphics, for help in making my way through the Minotaur's maze. He had not yet led me into the first corridor, however, when the brilliant sun had darkened.

I continued to drink his tea greedily. It was a good strong brew, and it had been a long time since I had had any. This kind of tea could wash away the grease of meat from one's body—I felt that just one cup could change me from being a carnivorous animal to being a man. Civilization is truly amazing. A rhythmic sound came from inside the bamboo curtain blocking the door. Stuffing for my dumplings was being minced by Zhu Shujun, Luo's wife. One would have thought that meat and noodles would already be sufficient—why must the meat be wrapped inside the noodles before it was considered good enough to eat? I was not used to any of this.

A small garden had been made by levelling the land around: the hollyhocks were already tall, though not yet blooming, sprouts of tomatoes, hot peppers and aubergines were pushing up, and between them the yellow earth had been raked fine until it looked as soft as a piece of carpet. Two white butterflies circled blindly in the light, and near the wall was a low apricot tree. This was a regular life. I had the feeling of having come home, although all around was unfamiliar. Lying back in a canvas-seated chair, I closed my eyes, with the need to talk growing strong inside me.

Luo Zongqi continued to harangue me. 'I'm Head of the Troop here, you know, but who do you think they've made Party Secretary to work with me? I'll tell you a story, so you'll get the idea: This old woman was originally Party Secretary at the Qinliang Farm. When the Cultural Revolution came along, naturally everybody was swept up into it and she was bundled into jail. Her daughter then sent a letter to her in the "cowshed". It said, "Ma, they won't let me get into the Red Guards. They say you're to blame, so I'd like to break off contact for a while. Let's pretend to do it, since I think a short time will be enough." What did this woman say in response to her daughter? She abjectly confessed that she was a "renegade three times over". She wrote that she wanted her daughter to break off relations in earnest—no kidding—with "no tender-heartedness she wanted to draw a clear line"! She wanted her daughter to "resolutely carry Revolution to the end"!

'As a result, the daughter, that seventeen-year-old child, became a brutal thug. I've heard she personally broke the bones of two old landlords. You think about it—a daughter told not even to recognize her mother! Who is a child like that going to listen to? Only an evil mother could raise such an evil child.

'That's the woman they've appointed as my Party Secretary. I'll tell you another story—you can see for yourself what she's like. There's plenty of empty land around here, so I said, let the farmhands plant a little on the side, give them a little more to eat. When the vegetables they planted were just getting out of the ground, she sent in a tractor and ploughed them all up. I was furious. I told her, China has 9.6 million square kilometres of land—to plant a few extra aubergines is surely only adding to the wealth of socialism! Why not let them grow? She said, the wealth of socialism is in its national collectives—anything produced by an individual belongs to stinking capitalism. Then she recited a whole string of Quotations—no way I could beat her in that game.

'Ever since then, when we meet we don't say a word. I go east, she goes west. Lao Zhang, think of it, a Troop Leader and his Party Secretary, and the two not on speaking terms—with things like that, you think we can get any work done? We don't even average our differences, we totally cancel each other out, which means we end up with nothing.

'I can just imagine how Xiaoping* would have handled it. At least that old woman has never "rectified" me. You

*Deng Xiaoping

know, Xiaoping actually went rowing round Zhongnanhai, friendly as could be, with someone who had "rectified" him! Lao Zhang, what they're trying to do is put a group of people who still haven't recovered from a severe shock together on the same boat with a bunch of starving wolves. What do you think the result can be? I'm afraid the tragedy is going to go on and on.'

He stopped hammering for a moment, looking down at me from on high. The look in his eyes made me think of the baleful pessimism of that tired-out old ram.

I stretched, returning his look with a disconsolate smile. 'Lao Luo, the tragedy has been playing for too long. It's been around for a good eighteen years now. I don't know if the audience has the same feeling, but this actor is just plain tired.'

'There is no audience in China,' he answered shortly. 'One side plays the "rectifiers", while the other side plays the victims. Then after a while they switch positions. You're just tired of being in the side that gets "rectified", that's all. What do you think? Would you like to play "rectifiers" for a while?"

With his tall, gaunt body and his rugged face, he could have passed for Sherlock Holmes if his flashing eyes had been a little deeper and the bridge of his nose a little higher. The two of us had spent two years in jail together, from 1970 to 1972. We shared my one blanket, one bed and one rice bowl. The Troop Secretary who had preceded Cao Xueyi was in control then, and even the chopsticks that Luo's wife sent him were confiscated.

Once, when we were trembling from the cold together in my wad of bedding, I remember telling him, 'You know, I don't believe Lin Biao died well.' What evidence did I have, he wanted to know. None, I said, but he was very like a labour prisoner I had known who was summarily executed.* His nickname was '400-Watt bulb'. He had also been bald, like Lin Biao, and his face looked just like Lin Biao's. He used to try to keep warm by laughing lightheartedly. Every time he went through the daily routine of 'qing zui' [admitting his errors and asking for pardon], instead of hanging his head down in the usual manner he would prop his head sideways, as if he were thinking about something. He wrote a very lengthy confession, and I heard he wrote that he had first been 'criticized' in 1942 in Yenan.† After that, he shielded 'rightists' in 1957. By 1959, he had become a 'right-leaning opportunist' himself, and in 1966 he was swept into jail together with those in the 'Liu-Deng Capitalist Headquarters'. He wrote that he had no idea where this Headquarters was, or what campaigns it commanded. This irritated the 'Revolutionary Committee'. We others in the jail knew that if he hadn't given so much historical background, which was just a millstone around his neck, he would have been 'rehabilitated' as a high-level cadre long ago.

Luo collected his materials and started climbing down from the beam, talking as he carefully picked his way. 'I've been through it all,' he said. 'Right now the only thing to do is protect your own little life—build yourself a little kitchen, make some furniture for your home . . . you know, I made that sofa over there myself from the tyres of a truck. It's great, just as good as one with springs—go on, try it.'

As he reached the ground I saw that his body was still lithe and limber, despite being over fifty. 'Not bad, eh?' he noticed my glance. 'Everybody should spend some time in jail. First, it keeps you trim. Second, you realize that your

*In conversation, the author told the translator that he believed that this labour prisoner was in fact Lin Biao, not merely a man who resembled him.
†This was the first Party purge and rectification campaign aimed against intellectuals.

real comrades are the ones you've done time with, not the people you work with in some office.'

We pushed aside the bamboo curtain and walked on into his house. Sitting on the sofa he had made himself, I began to talk. 'Lao Luo, this tragedy we're playing out isn't only due to individuals. It's clear to me that it's our system that's at fault.'

'Sure, but if you want to change a system, first you have to harmonize human relationships.' He poured himself some tea. 'For instance, putting me and that old woman together. The two of us couldn't even agree on building a public toilet. You can forget about our agreeing how to change a whole system.'

Cheering up a bit, I admonished him, 'Don't forget about theory, now. I get the feeling that what we're doing in China right now has nothing to do with Marxism but rather with Linism. You know the KMT had their Three Principles and called them Minisms, well, we have ours, and call them Linisms.'

'How do you see that?'

'It's obvious. We've got Bukharin, who basically invented the idea of the Cultural Revolution. Our Great Leaders think they did, but Bukharin applied for the patent long ago in the International Communist Movement. Then we've got Dulin, who talks about willpower, violence and force. And we've got Bald Lin—he's easiest of all. Bald Linism is simple: find a man to worship!'

'Better watch it,' he laughed. 'It's no wonder you're constantly under attack! You're "counter-revolutionary" all right.'

At that moment, Zhu Shujun came in carrying a plate of steaming dumplings. 'A "counter-revolutionary" and an old "right deviationist"—the two of you had better sit at the table and get something to eat!' Laughing heartily, she

100

shooed us to our seats. 'Lao Zhang, you haven't been to our home for over a year now, you'd better eat properly tonight.'

She stood by proudly as we took our seats, her sleeves rolled up, her chubby hands on her hips. Then back she went to the kitchen, her daughter holding the curtain aside for her as she emerged again with more steaming plates. The simple home took on the atmosphere of a banquet. It had been a long time since I had had an intelligent conversation with anyone, although I said exactly the same things to the sheep every single night.

'Going back to theory,' I continued. 'Right now we're simply messing everything up.' I took up a pair of chopsticks that were darkened with use, and speared a meat-filled dumpling. The relief of talking made me feel as though I were sitting at the head of a conference table, presiding over a very important meeting. 'Our real responsibility right now is to return to true Marxism. For example, when that old woman recited Mao's Quotation to you, you could have countered by using words from Lenin. You know, Lenin said that it isn't just stupid, it's also suicide to try to stop all private non-governmental exchange completely. He didn't even forbid small capitalist trade, and he would certainly have allowed a few aubergines.'

'Sure, that's what Lenin said a long time ago,' Luo Zongqi mumbled as he ate.

'Isn't that all we're doing right now, though, juggling around the words that people said in the past? You use the Leader's quotations to counter me. I use someone else's words to counter you. It's just like Marx said, "Dead men have a hold over the living." '

I chose another dumpling. 'Our minds have no time for new creations now, they're totally preoccupied with playing with words. Even if we want to develop in new directions,

101

in these suffocating times we first have to fight our way out with words. It's proof that our "theory" is nearing a final stage. The final curtain will be when it has led us all the way to the end of a cul-de-sac.'

Luo listened intently as he chewed. He cocked his head to one side, as some people did when making confessions. 'So what do you think we should do?' he demanded.

'Now? Right now, we can't even start talking about what to do. Lenin was right when he said that when a country is on the verge of bankruptcy, its workers come first.'

I thought of the farm-hands in our Troop, of Dumbo, Old Lady Ma, Hei-tz, He Lifang. 'We have to allow them to live the lives of real people. We can start changing the system afterwards, reforming the economy . . .' With that, I began to reel off my theories on how I thought the economy should be reformed.

'Hey! Enough, enough!' Luo Zongqi was laughing. 'Lao Zhang, have you ever thought of writing it all down?' He said seriously, 'You could put it into a dissertation. Right now it's no use to anybody, but in the future, it certainly might be . . .'

'Ha! You think it's safe for me to write? Do you remember Zhou Ruicheng? I live together with him now in the same dormitory. That bastard loves informing on other people. Just let one line of anything I've written fall into his hands, and I wouldn't be around to eat your dumplings any more.'

'Lao Zhang,' Zhu Shujun had stood by this whole time, encouraging me to have just one more dumpling, 'I think the only thing for you to do is have a family. Have your own life, your own little room—then if you write something, who's to know? The rules have relaxed now, I'm sure you'd get permission.'

'Get married in order to write a dissertation?' I laughed,

and the daughter joined in agreement from behind her mother.

'Even if there were no other reason at all, I still think you should get married. If you have any trouble with finances, we can help you out.'

'Money's not the problem. I just don't have the person!' In fact, I was thinking, I do already have her.

As I walked back layers of clouds were hanging low on the horizon, grabbing the line of the land and sweeping away with it before you noticed, moving out to cover the mountain ridges. Thousands of black swallows swooped back and forth, lacing the green barley and dark sky together, calling shrilly to each other as they worked. The air was full of the meaty smell of wet earth. The barley brushed restlessly against itself, waiting for the rain to fall.

The road coming to Luo's house had been bright and clear, the road returning was dark with quickly growing clouds. In the darkness, however, a hope was trembling, a tiny flicker of happiness was moving. Beneath the melody of gloom was a counterpoint of brightness.

I strode on across the open country. Two heavy drops of rain spattered against the yellow dust, raising small boils on the ground, as if some little animal were burrowing.

Then abruptly, the broad land was singing with rain. Cool water dashed against my face, which I realized was flushed with heat. In the midst of the thunderstorm, my body seemed to be its own warm stove. Luo's parting words made it burn the hotter. Marriage! The word itself could hardly be spoken out loud. I had thought of marriage many times in the past, but had never thought that I could marry in my unfree status. Nor had I ever thought of marrying someone in the same situation as myself.

Dreaming is such pleasure! I imagined a bride draped in filmy white, floating towards me under a comforting blue sky . . . and the bride was she! Never before had I thought of a wife in concrete terms. The filmy white raiment had entered my thoughts, but except for that, all had been indistinct. When my own standards of beauty changed as I went through life, my vision of 'wife' changed along with them, so that I was always supplied with the perfect companion to meet my pleasure.

Then, as black prison clothes replaced the filmy white of wedding dreams, the wife in my thoughts became a woman, nothing more. Put another way, any woman would do as a wife. With the loss of freedom, and any possibility of leading a normal life, what good were sublime hopes going to do me?

Without a particular hope, one was never going to be disappointed. And yet, with true cunning, I found a way to make hope out of no hope. I found rationalizations to consider myself fortunate. A light sentence or punishment could be made into the most fortunate of lucky flukes: it could have been so much worse! The series of punishments rolling through my life could therefore actually make me wild with joy. My vagrant and homeless life could be turned into one rich with experience; the hunger and cold could be seen as bracing tests for what was still to come. I could persuade myself that I was being tempered for a great responsibility that I was to be given. I made myself into a modern Don Quixote, who took demons to be windmills instead of the other way around. In this way, I made life tolerable.

In reality, to be married meant to marry her. To have a home, and for the time being it would have to be either the room Zhou Ruicheng and I shared or the one she and Old Lady Ma shared, to have a home was to have a home with her. Still, as the great drops of rain plunked solidly on my head, I realized that I would then be firmly tied. I would be lashed to the shattering life of reality. I was certain to lose my comforting dream-world, that ability to intoxicate myself with exalting thoughts. Like the raindrops around me, I would be separated violently from the clouds, and driven everlastingly into the dry earth, to be absorbed, to be turned into a mess of mud.

In the end, though, that naked, glistening body hypnotized me. Soft, quivering with excited flesh, it called to me. Radiant with heat, my entire body was giving off steam. As the cool drops of rain fell they sizzled, burned as on an iron.

Luo Zongqi was right! I needed a home, a nest, a few square feet to call my own. Even people in prehistoric times had caves to protect themselves. It is said that the old 'King of Nests' of China was supported by the people because he had invented places to keep the body safe and to keep life going. To me, a home meant a few square meters out of the 9.6 million square kilometres of China that I could make into my own independent kingdom. Master of that tiny plot, I could concentrate my thoughts there and plan, plan for the future of the rest of that vast land.

The tragedy would eventually play itself out.

Passing over a drainage ditch, one of my shoes got stuck; when I pulled, the shoe was left behind, mired in the mud. With carefree abandon, I left it behind. She'll make me a new pair, I thought. Limping along happily, one foot high and the other low, I returned to the dormitory.

'Oh my, why didn't you hide in the trees for a while!' Zhou Ruicheng greeted me with dismay, as he lifted his head from the sheet of white paper in front of him. He was still hard at work on his 'letter of appeal'. Write! I thought. You just go ahead and write. Yours is a real tragedy, and one that is continuing.

'Look at you, you're wet through.' He gave me his usual

defeated and fawning smile, and on this day I was particularly annoyed by the sight of it. How could I have tolerated living with this kind of man?

'Hell, what's a little shower like this? I saw a lot worse when I was out there herding sheep.'

He looked out of the window for a moment, and his face took on a sly gloating look at my misfortune. 'Look! The sun's coming out!' It was true. Outside the window weak yellow sunlight appeared, shining against the wall of the building next door.

'Heaven's against me too.' I climbed onto my bed, grumbling. 'Lao Zhou, this crazy life we're living—when do you think it will ever end?'

His thin, wizened face suddenly turned apprehensive. Was I going to say something 'counter-revolutionary' again? If so, should he report it, or not? Would it give him more trouble? And if he reported it, what if I denied it?

'You see, the only way to end it is to take a wife—I think that then you could call this craziness finished.' To ease his mind, I said out loud what I was thinking. Looking up at the darkening beams overhead, I thought, how could we fix up this room? . . .

5

'How about herding horses for awhile?' Cao Xueyi asked me casually.

Seeing that I was willing, he took his cigarettes out and handed me one. 'It's a pretty easy job, only twenty-odd animals. You don't have to go way out into the mountains, so you'll get back regularly in the evenings. The night-shift man handles the evening feeding, so you won't have to worry about that either.' He seemed to be doing his best to take care of me, trying to give me the easiest life possible. In fact, I knew there was no one else willing to do the job. Right now, it was hard to get people even to go out and work in the fields. Nobody was willing to put any effort at all into learning something new.

'Well then, who's going to herd them with me?' I asked as I lit the cigarette.

'Who do you think would do?'

'I think Dumbo would do just fine.'

He laughed. 'How is it you just happened to think of him? If I brought him down, who would herd the sheep?'

'Then ask someone else to come lend me a hand. Looks as though you'll have to ask someone from the Main Troop.' We both knew that in these times of shouting and recriminations, Dumbo was the ideal companion.

107

He thought awhile. 'I'll see what I can do.'

We were squatting on the slope at the edge of a field, watching the irrigation water come gurgling in, slowly washing around the shoots as it spread out on the ground. The thunderstorm of several days ago that had wet me to the bone had hardly been enough to water the crops. This spring the wheat was coming up well, though, and some of the shoots at the edges of the field were already leafing. In farming terms, they were enjoying what we called the 'better conditions at the fringes'. Growing away from the rest, they could absorb plenty of sun, air and water. Humans seemed to feel the opposite need and did their best to crowd together in a pile.

I would have done so myself, but I could never seem to get in. Every time I tried, I met the resistance of a 'Movement'.

Was it going to be possible after getting married? To live a normal life like others, raise a family, have a cosy little home? When I was undergoing interrogation in jail, the examiners would often shake their heads at me, and say, 'Zhang Yonglin, you're definitely not a simple man! You're already over thirty years old—what have you been waiting for? If the body's still around, don't tell me the heart has died! I bet you're just hanging on for a change of dynasties. You think everything will change with a change in power, and then you'll find a wife!' Even not being married aroused their suspicions and doubts, and in those days if they had doubts, you had obviously committed a crime.

The loudspeaker blared out again. Its metallic sound travelled a long distance in the humid air. They were broadcasting the noon news: '. . . . the spirit of the great coal-mining workers has undergone a profound change . . . Under the leadership of the "advanced collectives" and "advanced

108

persons", by studying Marxism, Leninism and the Thought of Mao Zedong, they have eradicated "hired hand mentality",* and have improved their attitude to responsibility. Carrying forward the spirit of Communism, unceasingly exhibiting the faces of "New Men and Women", they have smashed the concepts of "destiny" and "fate". They have cast off the chains and shackles of the "reactionary ruling class" prior to Liberation and have taken a great step forward in liberating their thinking. They have energetically pushed forward the development of production and technical improvement . . .'

Listening intently for a long time, the only thing I learned was that the workers in the coal mines also believed in 'fate'. Other than that one gleaned item of news, the broadcast had not told me anything.

I could have written 'news' like that, just squatting here on the edge of a field.

Remarkably, Cao Xueyi also snorted at the 'news', then with a 'Damn!' in the direction of the loudspeaker he stood up and twisted a branch of willow off a nearby tree. Like an actor riding a horse in a Peking opera, he went swaying off down the road, brandishing his whip.

After he had gone, Old Lady Ma suddenly burrowed out of the line of trees behind me and appeared at my side. One hand was gripping a shovel, the other was wrapped around a bundle of firewood. Single women were not required to eat in the mess—they could cook for themselves, and seemed to take a feminine pleasure in it.

'Lao Zhang, the loudspeaker's sounded, aren't you going back to town?' Clearly, the news for her was that it was time to knock off work.

---

*That is, doing no more than what you are paid to do.

109

'Not quite finished irrigating this field—I'll be here a bit longer. What's up?' I asked, as that innocent look came over her face. I had already guessed, however.

'She says you should go and talk to her yourself!' Old Lady Ma settled down beside me. 'No problem, I tell you!' She was certainly confident. 'Just don't believe it when she says she won't marry. She wants someone to come after her—women are always like that . . .'

'Well, what did you say to her?' I said, as I drew a little closer. 'And what exactly did she say? Did you tell her what I told you to tell her?'

'Yes, yes, I told her what you told me to tell her. And all she said was, "Let him come tell me himself." '

'You think she'll go for it? Don't go messing it up for me!'

'Didn't I just say, no problem? I said, no problem.'

The water of the Yellow River gurgled happily as it slowly spread into the wheat fields. I felt that my ego had been sufficiently bolstered by this news, and I didn't at that time think about the future. What was important was that I had taken a first step, and this first step had not been met with a blow. In my experience of the past eighteen years, not meeting with a setback was something new.

'Well, when should I go talk to her?'

'Dear me, what a child! You mean you think you'll wait for the Most Auspicious Day? Come tonight. As soon as you walk in, I'll walk out.'

'What do I say first?'

'You're asking me? Somebody as smart as you and you can't get started? I've already started it for you, anyway. If it works, it works, and if not, then it doesn't. But I tell you, it's guaranteed.'

'How do you know it's guaranteed?'

'Gracious sakes alive! You'll kill yourself asking ques-

110

tions. Haven't the two of us lived in the same room for the past two months? You think there's anything left I don't know about her? Look at her—she's been married twice already. What better could she expect? An official won't have her, no matter how pretty she is. A worker can't have her, since she can't get a regular residency permit. If she marries you, my only worry is she's so pretty that . . .'

This was not the sort of thing I wanted to hear. What I most desired right now was to be told how good she was, how difficult it was going to be to catch her . . .

When evening came, I walked over to their room. As I knocked on the door, I suddenly felt that this did not in fact require much courage, it was not as in novels a matter of great enterprise and spirit.

The room was quite like a real cave, except for the one light bulb which lit it. Other than the fact that it was considerably cleaner, the arrangement inside was exactly like Zhou Ruicheng's. All the rooms in the village looked rather like stalls for animals.

I felt like an animal entering it. The 'Great Criticizing' of the past ten years had virtually scraped away all advances made by human beings. The relationship of man to woman was back at the stage when apes were still in the process of becoming human. The physiological meaning of the relationship was all. Incest, snatching a mate by force, marrying by order of one's parents, betrothal gifts, lifelong marriage through free choice, all the way down to free love—these were all yet to come. In this primitive state, I still felt the barbarity of an animal on the prowl; merely sniffing around each other's bodies seemed to be enough.

As promised, Old Lady Ma laughingly said a few words to me, then gathered up her sewing and headed out the door. I had not understood a word of what she said.

'You've come! Sit down.' She put down the book she was

111

holding and patted the bed beside her. She seemed to know already that I was going to come—the bed had been made with a freshly cleaned coverlet.

'What book are you reading?'

I thought there might be something I could say about it. Picking it up, however, I found it was a *Practical Handbook of Electronics*—even I did not understand a word.

'What do you mean book? That is for Old Lady Ma's shoes. She uses the paper to line the soles.' She laughed. 'What would I be doing reading a book? The few characters I ever knew I've almost forgotten.'

'You could keep on studying.' Distracted, I put down the book, and noticed then that I'd put it where it would have been best to sit. All I could do was sit opposite, on Old Lady Ma's bed again.

She then picked up the *Practical Handbook of Electronics* and with her head down began to look through it for pictures. She seemed totally absorbed in it, despite the lack of any pictures.

I took out a cigarette and began to smoke. All this was too far removed from my expectations: this was definitely not the scene of a marriage proposal. It should have the scent of flowers wafting through it, under the moon, willows sighing softly overhead as we whispered sweet nothings to each other. It should be filled with laughter, with sweet mouths crossing forbidden boundaries as our emotions crystallized in a land of Paradise. But here, where was the Love? Was there Love? I cursed, and told myself Love had been replaced with Need.

For a moment, I wondered if my decision had been right. A feeling of alienation had come over me, as my whole being seemed to resist taking this one step. I began to scrutinize her carefully, and this time it was with the cold eyes of a buyer. She could not be considered beautiful,

112

although there was a seductive appeal to her face and her black, shiny hair. Unlike the weathered face of Old Lady Ma, hers had nothing in it to indicate the past. It was the mask of a young woman who is either lost in dreams or doesn't think at all. Its purity had a radiance that was beyond reality, that seemed to transcend the common and the vulgar. Looking closely, however, it could also have hidden stupidity. As I looked, it became an impenetrable mask. Was she really stupid, or was she merely innocent?

The upper part of her body was leaning against the wall with catlike indolence, as though she were idly waiting for something. The sight corresponded exactly to my mental image of her for the past eight years. Her upright breasts, her small curve of a stomach, just looking at her body you could feel its elasticity. There was no part of it that was unfeminine. The very air she breathed was feminine: to a man she was the ultimate in seduction. This awareness gave a sudden twist to my guts, as though they realized that they had been submerged in something dangerous.

The danger was urging me to plunge ahead, do anything, just to see what would happen.

'Did Old Lady Ma talk to you?' I finally began.

'Um.' She raised her head at last and looked at me. 'She did.'

'How about it?' It sounded as though I were asking her to go for a walk with me.

'Why did you ask her to do it—it's something we should talk about ourselves.' This was said as though she were asking me to loan her money.

'Yes, we should talk it over ourselves. It was because . . . because . . .' feeling very insecure, I began to mumble. 'Because I've never said these things before. That's why I asked her.'

'You really never asked anyone before?'

'Really,' I assured her firmly. In point of fact, I started my 'past' from 1957, since I did not feel that what had happened before then was part of my life.

'How can that be?' Although she spoke with a smile, she obviously had her doubts.

'Think about it. Starting from 1957, I became a pawn of the "Movements"—I became a "Movement Man". Between jail and hard labour, how was there any chance to find a wife, let alone talk about love?'

She expressed sympathy with a shake of her head. Then, laughing, she said, 'Would you like me to teach you?'

I took up her challenge. 'I'd be glad to be taught by you.' I already felt that life with her was going to be a great deal easier.

'Really, though,' she said, suddenly becoming serious, 'there's not much point in talking about love when you get to our age, especially with what we've been through. The main thing is to set up a home, start a family, live like everybody else.'

'That's exactly what I've been thinking,' I said. My mind was telling me, however, that we might not be thinking along exactly the same lines.

'And one thing, I'm not saying if it's about you or about me, but there's no need in the future to bring up anyone's past.' Her eyes hardened as she made this point, staring at me. I realized she was hiding her weaknesses by being tough. She was wrong if she thought she was speaking only of herself. Did she think that I had been so very chaste emotionally?

I nodded my head, 'Of course! That's the way it is, of course . . .'

There was an awkward silence for awhile, as we took stock of how far we had come. Until now, I had not quite been able to use the words 'man and wife', or even 'couple'.

114

First, there was the matter of the two metres of dirt floor between us, and second, it seemed as if we were simply talking business. Suddenly, I felt how ludicrous the whole scene was.

She also seemed to feel it, as she moved to take a green thermos jug of hot water from under the bed. She also brought out one earthenware cup. 'You want tea in it or not?' she asked. I answered that just water was fine. I took the opportunity to look her over as she poured, and only then noticed a look of warmth and gentleness on her face. The sound of poured water was like a whisper as it met the cup. Water too had no form, only taking that of the cup when it was required.

She put the mug of water between us on the wooden crate, and suddenly we had shortened the distance between each other. What should I do now? I felt like reaching out my hand and touching hers, but her next words made my nerves cringe.

'Well now, how much money do you have?'

Taken aback, I told her. 'I'd say about seventy or eighty dollars. But I can borrow some if it's necessary . . .' I was thinking about Luo's offer.

'No need. If you borrow you'd just have to pay it back, clear a debt, month by month. But how can you have saved so little? You've been living alone all these years!'

I felt my whole body go cold. I picked up the mug, and took a gulp of hot water.

'You know yourself—my wages are twenty-seven dollars a month and out of that I have to eat and clothe myself, and buy cigarettes. I could give up the cigarettes . . .' although as I said it, I knew I didn't have the determination for that. I had not given up smoking even in the worst times in the labour camps. The unfolding of the plot of this particular drama seemed to require that I say such a thing.

115

'You don't need to quit,' she said. 'In the future we'll save some money in other ways. I've saved a bit myself . . .'

She traced a line on the edge of the carton with her finger, pausing as though she were waiting for me to ask. When I didn't, she raised her head and said, pointedly, 'Much more than you!' I looked at her and simply laughed. She couldn't have saved all that much more. Prisoners released from the labour camps were on the bottom rung of the Farm's salary scale, twenty-seven yuan a month. It would have been surprising if she had prospered on that.

'I think it might be best if you took charge of household affairs.'

'Fine!' she said, seeming happy to have got the upper hand.

All this seemed remote and slightly bizarre to me. While she had been a figment of my imagination, she had done whatever I told her to do, been whatever I wanted. Now the dream seemed to have floated out from my brain, escaped my control and become an independent being. What it did had surprisingly little relation to what had been in my head. I had thought somehow that I knew her well, yet here I encountered a stranger.

Nevertheless, as a three-dimensional body in front of me, she was a great deal more alive. Her warm, slightly hurried breathing seemed to brush my face; her full breasts followed the rhythm of it, going up and down. Her body was as exquisite as in my dreams, so that my mental image and her reality were still inextricably rolled together.

Having settled that last subject, there seemed nothing more to talk about. We both sat silent, waiting and uneasy, her fingers drumming the edge of the crate, my seat on Old Lady Ma's bed becoming increasingly uncomfortable. The atmosphere of the room was stultifying, as though the concreteness of our discussion had weighed it down. In a short

116

time, it had become impossible to break through what could have been such an easily broken line.

Finally she raised her head and asked, 'Do you think they will approve it up there? With your current status, that is.'

'I expect they will. Didn't you say conditions are better now than before?'

She laughed, and it was a laugh with no vigour, no content, and no direction. It was a laugh of incomprehension. 'We pick ourselves up from wherever we're kicked,' she said.

I suddenly felt moved. This fact had been the cause of our meeting in the first place. She had, in that moment, become powerfully attractive. I wanted to take hold of the hand that she rested on the crate, to pull her softly to my chest.

At that instant, the yelling voice of Hei-tz came loudly through the window, as he ranted about not being paid for the leave that he had taken in Beijing. Cao Xueyi's voice came back in answer, telling him not to be crazy, that things could be worked out. And with that comic interlude, the scene was over.

Was this really love? Had that really been a marriage proposal? I tossed and turned under the covers that night, unable to sleep. It had all happened much too fast, as though it were missing most of the links in the middle. Even though the end result was firmly in hand, I felt cheated, as though it were not heavy enough.

The cool moonlight washed into the room through the window and, without sleeping, I entered the realm of dreams. Dreams had miraculously become reality, while reality had become an unreal dream. Everything seemed to be mysterious and unpredictable. With no control over the future, everything seemed pre-ordained. Fate was a worldly magician, making jokes that people could not handle: he had created imagination and ideas, and in the end made

117

none of it come true; he created disappointment, chimera and falsehood, and then put idealism and hope into the minds of men.

One by one, I remembered past loves. Perversely, those I had loved most were those I had no chance of marrying. Now, what I was going to marry was a hope, a body living inside a dream. Idealism had never coincided with reality, and yet I would now marry my ideal. How was this thought to be explained? There are those who say that love is giving—but what did I have to give her? I had nothing, not even love, not even tenderness. In the beginning, marriage was not the result of love, but the child of chance. One of the poets had it right when he asked, 'My wife, do either you or I know what love really is?'

'Lao Zhou! Lao Zhou!' I suddenly called out. I needed badly to talk to someone, anyone.

Zhou Ruicheng woke up in a fright. 'What's happened? What's happened?'

'Oh, nothing.' My mood suddenly disappeared. 'Do you have a match? I want to smoke.'

'Go to sleep.' He turned over in his bed unhappily. 'You know I don't smoke—what made you think I had a match?'

PART 3

1

I could not help glancing up occasionally at the newspapers plastered up and down the walls. One had a photograph with the caption: 'The invading American army has perpetrated a great massacre in the place called My Lai.' The picture was small and indistinct, but you could make out the corpses lying across each other in a pile.

To have our new room plastered with these newspapers, and to have that particular photograph placed front and centre made me extremely uncomfortable. Still, I had not yet peeled it off and exchanged it for another.

Then there was the matter of the bedspread. On it were embroidered two heavy tractors, pulling ploughs. Were she and I actually supposed to be able to sleep under such enormous machines?

The walls had been done by Hei-tz, who had originally intended to help me plaster them with lime. He had come in bubbling with excitement from the office of the State Farm Headquarters with a large pile of newspapers in his arms.

Throwing them down at my feet, he announced, 'Brother, you just watch me! It's obvious these walls can't be plastered with lime—best thing to do is cover them with newspapers. Haven't you seen pictures of the walls covered with paper in America?'

From out of the middle of the stack, he extracted a few sheets and slapped them down on the bed I was in the process of making. 'I know you like to read the *Daily Supplement,* so I stole a few just so you could take a look. You'll see what a joke it is. But there's one thing—it seems the foreigners have started learning from us! One of the Marxist Leninist parties has started praising our "7 May Policy".* Easy for them—once their bellies are full, they grab onto the idea. Just let them come down to the fields and work, they'll see what it's really like.'

As a result, I read the papers while he worked, and in the end the pile of corpses appeared on the wall.

The bedcover was a gift to us from the people in the Troop who like us had either been in the 'labour reform camps', or through 'labour education', or 'mass criticism' or had been in jail. The only one who didn't belong to those categories was the Big-footed Philosopher. Each family had donated fifty cents, and from this one small village they had been able to collect twenty dollars. What a huge number, and at the same time, what a pitiful number.

'I arranged it all,' said Old Lady Ma proudly. She had walked more than ten miles to collect the material from another town. 'None of the other colours was as good—just this bright red. That means you two will be bursting with happiness, and next year we'll see a fat little baby!'

The tractors pulling ploughs thus drove on top of our bed.

This was not the end of it, however. The dream continued. Now it had to be carried out to the end. The path that the world allows each person to follow is narrow: after the first step, you have to follow it on down. Once started,

*This is the 7 May Directive of 1966, when Chairman Mao created 'cadre schools' in the countryside.

122

you are not allowed to walk freely—the two walls on either side press you forward.

I paid a call on Hei-tz the same day I spoke with Xiangjiu. As soon as I walked in, he was shouting 'Congratulations! Great! I heard it from He Lifang. You two match perfectly—a brand new couple made out of two old spare parts.'

He Lifang scolded him, 'Don't joke. Our Lao Zhang isn't a spare part—he's never even been used before! In fact, he's a fresh, unopened bud.' With that, she winked at me behind Hei-tz's back.

'That goes to show what you know.' Hei-tz slapped his wife on the rump. 'You don't say "opening the bud" for men, you say "virgin boy". That's all right, Lao Zhang, you're a good fellow. Even that plaything you're going to marry is good material. Just let me know if you need anything.

I came straight to the point, and told him what I planned and what I needed.

'Say no more!' He patted himself on the chest. 'I'll go speak with Cao Xueyi myself. If he has any objections, I'll let him sample the full fury of our brothers in the Beijing Youth League. That bastard still doesn't know that even all the old war criminals have been released.' He quickly covered his mouth with his hand. 'Damn, and I forgot to bring him back a small present this time. All I've got left are two bottles of that sorghum liquor, I think . . .'

'And a tin of candy, to fatten up his old lady,' He Lifang put in.

'Say, that's right. Quick, find a piece of paper, let's start writing . . . Right, this is perfect. This damn letterpaper I bought at Xidan in Beijing. All right, here's a brush, now Lao Zhang, you sit here and write . . . You have enough ink? OK, like this: "The counter-revolutionary Zhang Yonglin and the released prisoner Huang Xiangjiu both willingly agree to become a counter-revolutionary team . . .'

We all broke up laughing.

Then I sat down in earnest and began to write something I had never written before—an application for marriage. It was written in an atmosphere of bantering, as though the whole thing were some kind of joke. Taking a sheet of paper—it wasn't letterpaper at all but a sheet off the 'Customer Suggestion' pad at the Xidan store—and turning it over to the blank side, I deliberated for a moment.

'Uh, Hei-tz, don't you think I had better write a Quotation of Mao's at the top?'

'Yes, I do. But what Quotation?' Hei-tz suddenly slapped the table. 'Just write something like "Dictatorship of the Bourgeoisie" and you'll be sure to be a bachelor for life! You'd be "reformed" in earnest then, damn you—they'd have you tying a different kind of knot. You damn "Stinking Nines"* will always be taking somebody else's whip to thrash yourselves.'

'Don't say that—we can take "to each according to his needs" as well as anybody else. In fact, I've got it now—don't bother me.'

Taking up the pen, I wrote the following lines:

QUOTATION OF CHAIRMAN MAO

'Stir up positive elements, unite all those who can be united, do your utmost to turn negative factors into positive factors, in order to serve the great task of building up a socialist society.'

*The author explains: 'From 1966 to 1976, the extreme leftists within the Communist Party divided "class enemies" into nine kinds of people: landlords, rich farmers, counter-revolutionaries, bad elements, rightist elements, capitalist roaders, spies, traitors and intellectuals. In general, "Stinking Nines" referred to intellectuals.'

APPLICATION

Whereby in Troop No. 3 the farm-worker Zhang Yonglin, male, age thirty-nine, marital status: never before married, and the farm-worker Huang Xiangjiu, female, age thirty-one, marital status: divorced, hereby apply to get married. Both parties come forward willingly. They guarantee that after marriage they will continue to remake themselves, will receive supervision and re-education under the leadership of the Party Branch and the Lower Middle Farming Class, and will do their best to aid in the construction of a socialist society. The attention and approval of the Troop's Party Branch will be appreciated.

Respectfully,

Zhang Yonglin
Huang Xiangjiu
APRIL 1975

'Hey!' Hei-tz looked it up and down as though he were a connoisseur of calligraphy. 'Damn! Will you look at that. "Will be appreciated"—ooh la la! And that Quotation, it's just like you were rolling out ripe melons. Damn you, you should be a Party Secretary. Based on this document alone, that bastard has got to agree. You just wait here, I'll go and find him.'

'Not so fast—what about a place to live?' He Lifang reached out a hand and dragged him back. 'You'd better clear up that minor detail with Cao Xueyi too.'

Hei-tz thought for a minute. 'Yes, about a place to live. It seems to me it would be best not to run either Old Lady Ma or Zhou Ruicheng out of their rooms—they're pathetic enough as it is . . .'

'Let those two move in together, that's what I say,' He Lifang cut in.

125

'Get out of here, will you! No, we have to think of another way . . . Ah! I know. Let's ask him for those two store-rooms they used to pile the old tools in. OK? OK, I'm off.'

After Hei-tz had gone, He Lifang looked at me and with some gentleness said, 'Eh, Lao Zhang, if she doesn't have children, don't blame her, eh!'

'How do you know she can't have children?'

'Is there anything about women that I don't know?' She snapped her fingers in front of my nose. 'All that book learning of yours doesn't amount to half of what I know.'

'I couldn't care less if she doesn't have children. Having children is precisely what I don't want.'

She stared at me, astonished.

Finally, all was, as Hei-tz said, 'Neatly done.' Suddenly, I had a home. It was, moreover, twice as big as the homes of most farm-workers. Instead of only one room, it had two. Granted, they were two broken-down storage rooms, but there was still an inner and an outer to them. I could only imagine what Hei-tz had done to Cao Xueyi to get them out of him.

Xiangjiu exhibited an extraordinary ability to manage the decor of our living quarters. I was instructed where to nail in the bamboo holder for the chopsticks, where to place a little shelf to put the soap, where to build the platform for the bed, how to pile up crates so they made a handy cupboard, how to make the frame for the stove and the cutting board into one extended surface, where to put the cooking pans, bowls and spoons so that they would be both convenient and hygienic—and at the same time would not take up too much space. I was taught where the face-basin and foot-basin should go when one was not using them, how to stretch a line for drying clothes. Each detail had its reasons

126

behind it and, as I was to discover, each was exactly right. The hat hook, for instance, had to be over the clothes hook, and under the clothes hook she pasted white paper onto the wall so that the clothes wouldn't get dirty. Over the clothes also came a sort of cover, so that the arrangement was almost the same as having a wardrobe.

In between the two rooms was a door, covered with slogans, but still in good condition. We borrowed a saw, and secretly cut a perfectly good door right down the middle to become two long halves. One half was put under the window, and on it went her bottle of skin-lotion. On it also went the one possession I could display—a full set of hardbound 'Works of Marx and Engels'. These were the only books that could be openly shown to the world. After eighteen long hard years, I finally had a bookshelf: in 9.6 million square kilometres of land, I could finally say that I had my own square metre.

The bottle of skin-lotion on the shelf did not give it a vulgar, cosmetic look, but actually heightened its feeling of elegance. In those days, the trademarks of all products were austere.

She used the other half of the door in this way: taking four sticks of about the same thickness and length, she sharpened their ends and stuck them in the dirt floor. On their other ends she placed the half door, and on the door she placed a cloth. The sudden appearance of this dining-table gave the room an air of domesticity. Our table was the one and only dining-table in the entire village.

She then proceeded to teach me a new trick about beds. Instead of the usual method of putting the kang and stove together, she insisted that they be separated, each in a different room. Dubious about this, I soon discovered there was no real problem in doing it that way—it only meant that the flue connecting the two had to be a little longer. The benefit, and it was substantial, was that ashes didn't get into our bedroom space. Since it was so simple, why had no one else thought of it?

We did not miss the door between the two rooms because she soon devised a clean white curtain, made from a length of sheeting. The sheet was much better than the mess of slogans.

As a gift, He Lifang brought over the plastic flowers together with their vase that she had been holding onto for over two years. In her home they had always looked miserable but, washed up with soap, they shone in ours. When they had been put in the middle of our new table, He Lifang could scarcely believe they had once been hers.

'You're pretty damn good!' she said with admiration. 'They look as though they've come alive in your hands.'

'A wife like you is sure to be able to pickle a good batch of salted vegetables.' Old Lady Ma was there, enjoying the house-warming too. 'I'll be over this winter, to see just how you've done.'

Zhou Ruicheng was sucking candy, and quietly sitting on a wooden stool. Everybody begged him to play a tune on his erhu but he declined, saying, 'It wouldn't be appropriate, not at all . . .'

'What's so inappropriate about a song?' everybody wanted to know. Only I understood.

At the most boisterous point in the party, Party Secretary Cao Xueyi made an entry. 'Hey, Huang Xiangjiu, you have really done something.' He looked around, then smiled at her. 'These old store-rooms really do look pretty.'

Hei-tz took a cigarette off the clean, new tablecloth and passed it to him. 'Secretary, this is for you. You see, under your intelligent leadership people are willing to put down roots on the frontier, make this farm their home!'

'How is it you're so eloquent today? But on the occasion of Huang Xiangjiu's happiness, I'll be glad to smoke that cigarette. After all, it was I who brought her over to this farm . . .'

He was formally correct in addressing his congratulations only to her. Huang Xiangjiu had done labour reform as I had, but she had never been 'hatted'. I was 'hatted', and therefore carried a dual identity. On occasions like these, the Secretary was very careful to distinguish grades and ranks.

She stood beside the curtain made of white cloth and smiled.

Her smile was beautiful.

The party was over. I sat on the edge of the newly made bed, smoking. She was still in the outer room, putting away the left-over melon seeds and candy. Every so often, the tiny tinkling of a sound would reach me. The sound was distant, as though it were issuing from a dream. This sound was the sound of a wife—it could not come from the hands of any other person.

'Woman', I mused: the word meant far more than I had imagined. It had a voice to it, a spirit, a magnetic field, it had its own breath and its own flavour. She was able to leave all those things on anything she touched. Even if she herself was somewhere else, those things carried on her charm, possessed a magic power that surrounded a man. She was ubiquitous, in every object of our room. All that was here, except for the annoying photos, was the life that she had created.

Life is made up of just things such as these: a bed, a bedcover, a bookshelf made from a door, a hook for clothes with its white paper underneath, 'Snowflower' skin-lotion. The world she had created was engulfing me, so that I had the feeling of losing my identity. She had cut into me, just as we had sawn through the wooden door. Slicing straight down the middle, she had cut away my past.

129

2

She put out the light in the outer room, brushed aside the curtain, and came in.

'Sleepy?' she smiled at me. It was as though she had already been living with me for several years.

'No, not particularly,' I said. 'Are you sleepy? I'll make the bed.'

'You needn't do that! Whoever heard of a grown man making a bed?' She climbed onto the kang, and deftly turned down the covers. 'You go out and bathe—I've got the water all ready for you outside.'

I learned two things from that: first, that from now on I would never have to make the bed, and second, that what she called 'bathing' was a prerequisite to what would come next.

When I returned from my bath, I found her already dozing in bed. How fast! It was difficult to know quite what to do. The kang had only one bedcover, but two pillows had been placed at the head of it. How very extraordinary to have a woman's head on one of them. Lying next to me would not be a man, but a woman. She was going to sleep right beside me. Nobody was going to come and interfere, in fact nobody but I thought it at all strange. Surely, there must be some proper sequence to this, some order of events . . . I lit a cigarette to think it over.

'Still smoking?' She wasn't scolding, just asking.

'I don't feel like sleeping yet.' I laughed a little apologetically. 'I'm too excited.'

She probably laughed too, but I didn't hear the sound.

'Xiangjiu, why did you want to marry me?' Sitting on the edge of the kang, I looked at her as I asked. Her eyes were looking straight up at the rafters, and she was quiet for a moment. Then she asked, 'Why did you want to marry me?'

'You still remember eight years ago? In the midst of the reeds . . .'

She laughed then, and I could feel the covers shake. 'Ah, you still remember that?'

'Of course I remember! It's always been in my mind.'

'I forgot about it long ago.' Her words cut me short, and she said it sharply. She forgot! My heart sank, even though I knew that she could not have forgotten.

'No, you didn't forget. Otherwise, how could you have known who I was as soon as you saw me?'

'Come, come to bed,' she said gently, impatient now. 'What's the point in saying these things? Since we're together now, let's think about how we're going to live from now on.'

'How to live?' I began taking off my clothes, somewhat embarrassed. I should have had a million things to say, I could have said a million emotional things, but all I could do was follow her lead.

'Yes, how to pass the days.' She was lying on her back, her body straight. 'With our two wages together we should be able to get by pretty well. At least we'll do better than those old bags out there. Those women, they've got mouths and not much else—what can they do! There's not one of them I respect.'

The tone of her voice suddenly became contemptuous. It sounded as though the entire point of her life from now on

131

was to compete in 'passing the days' with them. It was clear that in this competition she meant to win.

Women, oh women! Slowly I will come to understand you. I had taken off my shirt and trousers, and sat beside her, leaning against the wall. I wanted to finish a cigarette and prolong this time. It seemed a moment in one's life worth lingering over. She was here beside me. A pile of long black hair curled across a soft white pillow. Two shiny eyes looked upwards into the confines of a narrow space. Was that space moving with beautiful images in her mind? Her black eyes gazed ahead—they held hope, held prospects and also calculations. As her eyes gazed, she was also waiting, and seemed to be preparing herself for the coming encounter. Her body was clearly outlined by the bedcover. The harshness of the iron ploughs made a ludicrous contrast with the full curves of her breasts and little stomach. She was a woman with unlimited resilience, able to bear any weight. Image had become reality. Gone were the colours of my dreams, dreams that she had never controlled. I found reality had a greater power to move me.

'Come,' she said.

I pulled down the cover, and there before me, exactly as I had seen it in the reeds, was her beautiful body . . .

'Maybe I'm just too excited.'

I said it only to cover my shame, and my dismay.

This was a boiling swamp, which I was struggling to get out of; this was the hot magma of a volcano, magnificent and terrifying; this was a beautiful nautilus, suddenly stretching out sticky tentacles from the walls, wrapping around me and trying to draw me down; this was a shimmering sponge, attached to white coral, trying to soak out the fluids of my body; this was a giant's garden in a children's story; this was the most ancient of folktales and also the most fresh, the

132

most desirable . . . The first struggle of mankind was not between man and man, or man and beast. The earliest struggle was that between man and woman. It was a struggle that was unceasing and that still continued. It demanded not only strength, but a vital spirit, using emotions and some innate artistic sense in its struggle to find balance, to reach unity and harmony, to achieve wholeness while maintaining its own separate self.

In this struggle, I had failed. I had also lost my individuality and my independence.

My body was covered with sweat, as though I had just stepped out of a bath. Oddly, the soles of my feet were cold. Panting awhile, I finally sputtered out, 'I need to drink some water.'

'You're hopeless! There's still plenty left to do!'

None the less, she stepped off the bed and went to pour me a cup of water. The water struck the cup loudly as she poured it, making a sort of metallic clang of conflict.

'Here!' She passed it over to me. In the dark, I groped for the handle, and at the same time grabbed her arm with the other hand.

'I'm sorry,' I said. I wanted to pull her down to sit beside me, but she twisted free. Climbing onto the bed again, she burrowed under the covers.

'What is there to be sorry about? We'll just try again next time.' I could not see her face, but her voice was cold.

We passed the next few days quietly. I tried to find a measure of happiness in them. There was someone to cook for me, as I made my farewell to the collective dining-halls of the past eighteen years. After I had herded the horses into their corral each evening, and made my way back to the two old store-rooms, there was always a meal waiting for me on our pretty table. Although the ingredients were exactly the

133

same as before, she gave them new flavours and new colours. 'If you keep eating like this,' she said, 'our rations aren't going to be enough.' I took that as encouragement to eat more.

In front of our home, I cleared and levelled a small square of land. Long grasses bordered its three sides, which in the evening reflected the sunset, and then gradually the moonlight, like a wall of amber. When I had eaten, I went there to sit and to sink into a reverie.

The day that we were married, an Anhui man bicycled into town, an itinerant pedlar selling ducklings. She selected four of them, and with the downy yellow bits of life in her hands, said happily, 'Let's hope they're all female.' That same day we acquired a cat: the Big-footed Philosopher had commented that our store-rooms were probably over-run with rats, so she brought us a little kitten that had just been weaned from its mother. Grey with white stripes, it was a fierce little creature. Playing on that patch of land, it meowed as the ducklings quacked, getting used to their new terrain. We had suddenly become a whole family; I too was getting used to this new life.

Her condescension towards me cut into my peace of mind. A sort of pity hid under her solicitude, and her smile was unnatural. I felt inferior to her. This ruined my sense of well-being, and I asked myself if happiness really were only a matter of eating well and sleeping in a better place. I had even lost the contentment that I had found in solitude. The old sights were still there—the setting sun at dusk, the clouds on distant peaks, the wise old ram with his curls ruffled in the breeze, the dust that took so long to settle on the road, stirred up by patient animals whose hides were scarred by the shafts of carts and the whips of drivers. They composed a slow andante now, as their measured pace brought me a new and aching hurt.

134

Every night she tossed and turned in the bed beside me. Like a wild animal who has been loosed into the arena, she was waiting for me to make a move. Proud and contentious, she waited for me to try and conquer her. On that first night, however, I realized that I no longer had the power.

Perhaps it was some kind of psychological block? I tried many ways to relax the oppressive atmosphere. Taking advantage of her absence one day, I plastered a new sheet of newspaper over the tangled pile of corpses. I changed the tractor for a new cover, with the excuse that the tractor was too hot. Besides moving out the corpses and the tractor, what else could I do? Paralysed by anxiety, I waited for the 'next time'.

Several nights later, her hand took hold of mine as we lay in bed, and slowly began to guide it through strange waters. She took charge of it like a small boat on stormy seas, navigating by the shores of her own territory. Warm waves rose and fell, as I felt a quivering from the depths of the ocean. Trembling, I made discoveries: here was a mound covered with warm mist, here was a waterfall plunging into a soft, moist continent. Here no words existed to make into rational concepts: here was the most primeval state of chaos. We were two formless pieces of protoplasm; we were two paramecium vibrating our bodies' tiny hairs. Everything that existed issued from small bundles of nerves, and those nerves were sending waves of electricity through my body . . .

My head began to throb with pain.

'Are you sick?' She let out a long breath as she asked me, pushing me away.

'I don't know . . .' I massaged my temples, which were throbbing violently. 'In the past, I never . . .'

'You've really never done it before?'

'Never.' Panting, I said, 'Really, never.'

Sitting up, she abruptly threw off the covers. It had become as hot as a steambath under them, and I immediately felt more comfortable.

'Is it because in the past you couldn't do it either, or just because . . .'

'No, that wasn't it.' I felt like a suspect in the box, starting to defend myself. 'It's because there was never the opportunity, never the right situation.'

'Then,' she hesitated a moment, 'I didn't want to bring this up, but what about eight years ago?'

'Eight years ago . . .' I could hardly concentrate my thoughts, but if I had, there would still have been no way to explain. Even I did not understand.

I rolled off the kang and stood up, and reached for a cigarette on the top of the chest. 'Let me have one too,' she said suddenly.

Two flames lit up the darkness and soon went out. Two live stars were left glowing in the dark. I smoked half a cigarette before saying, 'I think it's probably because I've been inhibited for so long.'

'Inhibited! What does that mean, inhibited?' She was dragging hard on the cigarette, and seemed to spit the word at me.

'Inhibited, it means . . . suppressed, held back.'

She let out a mocking laugh. 'You have quite a vocabulary!'

Undeterred, I kept on. 'You know as well as I do that in the labour gangs that's all people talked about. But when they talked in the evenings, I would suppress it and think of other things. Then in the bachelors' dormitory, it was the same—when the others told dirty jokes, I would read a book, think about political problems. Holding back like that, I gradually lost the ability.' Unconvinced by the next sentence myself, I added, 'Perhaps it will slowly get better.'

136

'And where did all that thinking get you? Where did reading books get you? Thinking, reading, ha! What use are they?'

'People have brains, and so they have to think. Do you believe our lives can really go on like this to the end? Can our country keep going like this?'

'Be quiet. You're just a fast talker, you can't do anything.' She flung her cigarette against the base of the earthen wall, and in the darkness it made a red arc in the air. 'Others think too, they read too, but they're not impotent like you. I've heard that there are old monks who've spent half their lives chanting sutras—they never had a woman before either, but as soon as they climb on top they can do it. There's that saying, "a wolf when you're thirty, a tiger when you're forty". You should be a tiger right now. You can't fool me—I think you've had the problem since you were born.'

Hostility towards her suddenly swept over me. 'Of course you've had more experience in this than I have.' I had not won—both she and my own body had become my enemies. 'Even eight years ago, in the labour camp, you were already thinking of doing it!'

'Why do you bring up the past? You cripple! You're half a man!' My words had struck home—her fury doubled. 'Eight years ago . . . ha! If you had tried anything that day, I would have immediately turned you over to Gang-Leader Wang—let you taste a little more punishment! I was thinking of earning merit points! And you actually thought I was thinking of you, loving you. You ought to piss a puddle of water and look at yourself in it.'

Image and reality had totally parted ways.

3

Without warning, my horse and I suddenly found ourselves
stuck in a mudhole. He was 'Number 101', an old piebald
that I had taken to riding. His front hoofs plunged into the
hidden bog. His back hoofs instinctively tried to get a pur-
chase to haul out the front, but the harder they pushed, the
deeper they went.

I urged him on, lashing with the whip and beating his
sides with my feet in the stirrups. His head was up and his
ears pointed, and even from on top of his back I could see
the rolling of his wide eyes. All four limbs thrashed and
lunged as he found himself sinking deeper and deeper.

There was no point in beating him further. I rolled off his
back onto the grassy bank nearby and surveyed the situation. We had unwittingly walked into a grass-covered soft
pit made by a breach in the canal. Although it was mended,
the breach still leaked a small stream of water, which carried
with it accumulating sand and mud. As time passed, a layer
of reeds and cat-tails had covered the surface, making the
unstable mud appear to be solid ground. I had always been
careful to avoid these natural traps, but today, distracted, I
had finally been caught.

It happened as we were driving the horses back in the
evening. The strong final rays of the setting sun were flash-

ing a golden light off the trees and ground. In the distance they caught the ripples of water on the marsh. Frogs and toads had just begun to feel the cool breath of evening and were starting to croak. Brought to an unwilling stop by Dumbo, the other animals turned their heads around to look at us, as if to say, 'What on earth are you doing? Time to hurry back to the corral—the mosquitoes will be on us in a minute!'

'Hey!' I yelled over to him. 'You drive the rest on back. I'll get him out of here and follow later. Don't wait for me—it looks like we'll be a while getting out of this one.' I thought of asking him to go see Xiangjiu and tell her I was going to be late, then remembered that he could not talk.

He could not talk, but he could understand. He cracked his whip and started the horses on their way home again.

When they had gone, the land around became quiet. The old piebald gave a lonely, whinnying call, and mournfully blinked his large eyes at me. Then lowering his head until it rested just above the cat-tails, he settled down to wait for my command. Mosquitoes began an ominous hum around my head, and I lit a cigarette against them as I sat on the edge of the canal.

A group of crows passed overhead, returning from the mountains. I saw a wild grey rabbit hop by in a distant field. The shadows of the grass, the trees, the wild rabbit, the old piebald and my body lengthened, as everything in its tiredness seemed to stretch out on the ground. The world seemed to be playing in a stately minor key. Even my cigarette smoke did not loll around, but ascended straight into the air, until it faded into nothingness.

It occurred to me that I should take off the piebald's saddle, to let him gather energy for the next attempt. With the cigarette hanging from my lips, I used my herdsman's knife to cut the girth off from where I stood on solid

139

ground. Then, carefully, I pulled the saddle off without falling into the pit myself. A strong and familiar smell of horse sweat came from his back. I put down his saddle, sat on top of it, and let him rest.

Five cigarettes later, darkness had begun to fall on us. I combed out his mane with my fingers, picking out the burdocks that had stuck to it, and then worked on the tail that swished over to me. A small gust of air, like a silvery spirit, swirled around the tips of willow leaves dangling over the bank. Coming to the old breach in the canal, it reached out long arms to tease me and the horse.

The old piebald lifted and then lowered his head, as if courteously greeting the spirit. Time to move, I thought, and cut some cat-tails to give me better footing.

'OK, mate, let's put some muscle into it now,' I said. 'I'll hang onto your tail, and push with my shoulder against your rump. Just like that time you got stuck in the frost boils on that plain—remember? Right, now!'

His thick tail felt like a hard stick of wood. It was difficult to believe it had grown out of flesh and blood. One, two, three! I heaved with my shoulder, at the same time using the iron-studded sole of my mountain boot to slap him on the rump. He seemed to understand what he should do, and matching my efforts, tried to lurch ahead. The sucking mud under his feet sounded like some buried ghost that had suddenly been woken by our violent efforts. Up and down we went, back and forth, a push and a pause, trying almost twenty times. The mud seemed to melt into a running goo with the pounding, as the grass was trampled down beneath the surface. In the end, we had to admit defeat. The old horse simply stopped trying, indicating that he knew best his own sorry plight.

Wheezing from the effort, he again rested his head on the top of the cat-tails. I wiped the sweat off my face, as I squatted by the bank, fanning myself with my shirt. What could be done? Hey, mate, are we going to have to spend the night here?

The darkness had already melded the scenery together, the fields, the mountains, the trees had all become one. Looking out into it, I could not see a single light. The mysterious feel of night came over the land.

Suddenly, I heard a voice beside me that was both strange and at the same time strangely familiar. 'Man, don't pretend you're so worried. Humans really can fake it.' The old piebald raised his head, and one eye gazed steadily at me as he said, 'You don't really want to go home any more than I do. You've been married exactly one month, but you and your old lady are already sleeping apart. Am I right? You're afraid—afraid of the nights, just like I'm afraid of being hitched to the traces.'

Astonished, I fell over backwards and my rear-end hit the cold wet grass. 'You can talk?'

'Ha, ha!' With a strong accent, he laughed at me. 'Look at you, scared out of your wits. Don't forget, there's a loudspeaker set up just across from our corral. And I've been eating big-character posters ever since I arrived on this earth—it's true they taste a bit of ink, but they're still made out of vegetable fibres. Much better than the weeds those irresponsible horse-feeders try to foist off on us. With all that, I've discovered that we're living in an age of unprecedented linguistic development. You humans may have retrogressed in other ways, but you're definitely expert at playing with rhetoric. As they say, "he who sticks around vermilion gets stained red, and he who stays near ink gets stained black." After such a long period of edification it's natural that I can speak!'

Incredulous, I spluttered, 'I don't believe this!'

'That's the problem with you humans, it's a real shortcoming that you should try to change. You should learn a little silence from us, learn how to observe events with an objective, critical eye. That is the true way of "conducting oneself properly in the world with equanimity".'

'So why,' I asked him, 'have you opened your mouth to speak today?'

'I know you don't really want to go home.' He snorted a stream of breath out of his nostrils. 'As for me, it so happens I don't want to go back either. Sometimes you and I are alike—we feel the need to distance ourselves. We need to be quiet, and to think things over. Philosophy covers everything, you know, the way of horses and the way of humans are much the same.'

I couldn't deny he was right about that. Out loud, I said, 'It's true that secretly I don't want to go back. I need to be alone here in the openness, to try to get things into focus.'

'Perhaps I may be of help to you?' he humbly asked, in the tone of a scholar. 'I have not lived thirty-nine years, as you have, but among horses I am considered quite elderly. When they say "an old horse knows the road", that's me. Perhaps we could take a stab at it together.'

'Well then, since you know so much,' I said, 'just what advice do you have for me?'

'Dear, dear,' and he made clicking noises with his mouth. 'First off, I empathize with you completely. You and I have the same problems. I think you probably know that I was cruelly castrated by human beings when I was younger.'

'Yes,' I said, 'but I have not been castrated. I still have all the apparatus, I just don't have the ability to use it. So what does that have to do with me?'

'Before I was castrated, it only took the slightest whinny from a mare to set me off, the merest whiff of her perfume. It didn't matter if miles of mountains came between us, no distance and no fences could hold me back. My organ never

142

had any problem—it unerringly hit the mark, and transported me into uncontrollable pleasure. After I was castrated, though, I lost the stimulus of sex, and nothing interested me. As it is said, "There is no greater sorrow than the death of the soul." Humans, your insidious cruelty lies in this: you have eliminated the hope I once held in my heart. My beloved shepherd, you should take a good look at the state of your own heart, put yourself through a very strict self-appraisal.'

'No,' I said, 'you and I are different. I still carry the hope that you have lost. I still had it the first time, the second time, and even these last few times she has wanted to enjoy the pleasures of the bed with me. But recently I've begun to feel extremely upset—I feel a kind of terror because of my impotence.'

The old horse let out a strangely frosty series of laughs. 'You're worrying too much about that particular angle. Don't you think it's a trifle vulgar? What I'm trying to get at is your whole psychological frame of mind. That kind of "impotence" necessarily affects other aspects of your activity. You're an educated man—you should know that a unified approach is the only way to analyse different systems. Man and the world are in a unified continuum: if one particular system runs into problems, it's bound to affect others. Do you still feel you hold onto the same beliefs, ideals, ambitions?'

'I don't think my beliefs are very much affected,' I said, even as I was aware of my own uncertainty. 'Take Si Maqian, for example. After being castrated as a punishment he was still able to produce that masterpiece, the *Annals of History*.'

'Harrumph!' His snorting laughter rang out loudly, and ended with a great final blow through his nose. 'My dear shepherd, fortunately you are a man of letters. In this, you

143

have made a mistake in formal logic. Si Maqian is someone I know all about: during that "Movement to Criticize Legalists and Confucianists" I heard about him from the loudspeaker every single day. That so-called "castration punishment" was a crippling measure carried out on the corporeal body. Its effect was to spur him on to greater mental resentment, to forge a powerful motivation for completing what are now known as the *Annals of History.* I believe he never would have written it if he hadn't been castrated. The world lost one reproductive organ, but gained a great piece of literature. It's a perfect example of that constant exhortation of the loudspeaker: "Turn bad things into good things".

'You, however, are up against something different. You're like my fellow-brothers, who have to escort their own kind to the abattoir: the bullets of the firing squad have not touched a hair on your head, but your mind has been wounded by the experience. The sickness has settled into your brain, into your nerves, into the very centre of your being. You still think you should compare yourself with Si Maqian?'

'No, I think you're absolutely right,' I said, hanging my head. 'Please go on.'

'Therefore, in some ways you and I are surprisingly alike.' The kind glance the old piebald threw at me made his eyes flash in the darkness.

'On the one hand, due to my castration, my lustful desires have been extinguished. At the same time, however, it has made me refine myself. Unlike other animals, I have worked to educate myself, to the point of being able to speak the human language. You are very much the same. When you were doing hard labour in the camps and reciting Quotations, nobody could have said you weren't thoroughly familiar with the works of Marx, Engels, Lenin, Stalin and Mao. On the other hand, unlike Si Maqian, since

144

you hadn't actually had anything cut off (please forgive me if my language is inappropriate), you became mentally traumatized, ending up being just like me. The end result has been the same: like me, your life is not in your own hands. You are forced to allow others to order you about, to beat you, to control you, to ride you. Ha, ha! We really are a pair, we two! An emasculated man and a castrated horse! Please forgive me, my sense of humour sometimes carries me away. In that too, you and I are alike—a little satire and irony dropped in here and there.

'Yes, I even wonder if your entire intellectual community isn't emasculated. If even ten per cent among you were virile men, our country would never have come to this sorry state. I don't know how you feel, but I am just plain sick of hearing that loudspeaker every day. Can it be that even in that most advanced science language, we can't even create something new?'

'You think my life is finished?' I asked him sadly.

'What do you mean by "finished"?' He looked at me seriously. 'You arrive on this earth, you work, you see things, you eat, you hear all kinds of strange things, such as how in a moment a head of state can become an imprisoned criminal, how a small-time hoodlum can become Vice Chairman of the Party of tens of millions of people. And then, you die. The life of any person follows basically the same process. You are personally relatively fortunate, because you're living in times that are unprecedentedly ridiculous. Do you mean to say you ask for more? Ah, perhaps you want to breed descendants?'

'No, I don't want that at all. If, as you just said, the country is going to continue playing out this comedy, this farce, then any descendants I had would simply repeat my own wretched fate. Better that they not come into the world at all.' I rested my chin on my crossed arms. 'What I mean

145

is that through living, any person should add a little something to the world, make some kind of contribution to humanity . . .'

'Oh! Hear ye, hear ye! The old problem's cropped up again.' The old piebald cut short my words. 'Look at us horses, every day we have to plod along in the traces, hauling this and that—isn't that a contribution? You humans are always wanting to paint beautiful colours on the most trivial of things. You can even make scooping out a latrine the glorious result of studying the works of Chairman Mao.'

'You don't understand what I mean. I'm talking about creative labour, not just being ordered about by people, like you.'

'What do you want to create?' The big old piebald began to interrogate me. 'Humans, horses, all living things—their most fundamental creation is reproducing themselves. You can't even do that, and you're still thinking of creating something? Honestly, among you humans there are some very impressive people who work with a great spirit of self-sacrifice, and don't have children their whole lives. They don't forfeit the ability to have children, however, in order to be able to create or to invent new things. But you, you have actually forfeited that ability! Your mental state is unbalanced, your systems are not in harmony: I beg you, please don't assume that you can still create. Even if you did create something, it would be deformed, to the extent that it might well hurt mankind.

'My beloved shepherd, you are like a fellow horse I once knew. He was not properly castrated, and although he lost the ability he retained the desire. In the end, he was driven mad by his own body's contradictions. He was eaten by you all—his skin still hangs there over the rafters of our stalls.

146

Please, snuff out this desire to create. Be a peaceful, self-possessed man, just as I am a docile horse. Know your place, and abide by the rules they set.'

'If I understand you, you think that she's right? That I am a cripple, that I am half a man?' I discovered that tears were running down my cold cheeks.

From deep inside, the old piebald let out a long, long sigh. 'Yes,' he said, 'I'm afraid I do. You should admit it, because it is already fact. The power of fate is most obvious when people run into trouble, and fate is what you're up against. All your beliefs, ideals and ambitions are held in vain: worse, they've turned into this devilish blockage that is tormenting you.

'You know as well as I do why people have castrated us: it's to remove our creative force, make us tractable. If they didn't we would have our own free-will, and our superior intelligence could never be kept in the traces. Even Si Maqian himself said that "people who have been punished cease to be courageous in their speech". What "creation" do you still think you can talk about?'

I had no words to counter what he had said. I felt humiliated, and my stomach churned with bile.

'Oh!' The piebald suddenly lifted his head, as he faced the wind and alertly inhaled several large breaths. 'I have smelled the scent of carnal desire. It isn't coming from your body, but it seems to be coiled about you. Strange! My shepherd, you should be very careful.

'We'd best go now, I don't want you to get into any trouble. All in all, you're relatively considerate to us horses.'

With that, he vigorously lifted his front hoofs, and extricated the front half of his body from the mud. Nimbly putting his front hoofs on solid ground at the edge of the

147

pit, he tensed his buttocks and heaved the rest of himself onto the grassy bank. It only took him a few seconds to get himself out of his predicament.

'We're off.' Turning his head around, he called back to me. 'It's quite dark and you can't see the road ahead. I'll lead the way, and you follow on behind. My instincts are much keener than a human being's. In fact you humans have retrogressed the most in the animal kingdom. One indication of that is your tendency to think of yourselves as the most clever . . .'

With his hoofs clip-clopping, he strode on ahead. I trundled behind, saddle over my shoulder and whip useless in my hand.

The darkness was vast, and seemed to have no end . . .

Everyone had already gone to sleep by the time we reached the village. The only light came from our two old broken storerooms, showing that she was waiting up for me. It was still better to have a home than to have no home at all.

At the entrance to the corral, the old piebald turned once more to look at me. He curled up his upper lip, and gave a warning noise from between his teeth, indicating that I should not speak. 'Beloved shepherd, from now on I will remain mute and stupid, as I was before. Whatever you do, please don't let on that I can speak. If my comrades here were to know that I have this ability, they would take out their jealousy by biting and kicking me to death. At the same time, I beg you, for your own sake, don't stick out too much when you are with other people. Hide away your knowledge, and conceal your inner thoughts. That's the only way that you will preserve your life.'

148

She had not yet gone to bed when I walked in; she was sitting in the outer room cracking sunflower seeds between her teeth. A newspaper had been spread out on the table, and spat-out husks were scattered all over it. The grey cat lay curled on top of the stool.

'Why are you home so late?' She held a seed between forefinger and thumb, and with a theatrical gesture popped it into her mouth. The question was casual, almost careless in tone.

'The old piebald fell into a mudhole,' I said, hanging up the horsewhip on the prescribed hook.

'The food's in the pot.' She made no move to get it ready for me.

I washed my face and then chased away the cat before setting down my dinner on the table to eat. I noticed that the empty can on the table that we used as an ashtray held several cigarette butts.

'Who visited?' I asked.

Following my glance to the butts in the can, she hesitated a moment, then said, 'Secretary Cao.'

'What did he come for?'

'And what's so strange about his coming? He thinks highly of us and he came to pay a call.'

'That the Secretary thinks highly of us is already strange enough.' I started eating.

She cracked another sunflower seed and glanced sideways at me. After a brief silence she said, 'You're really odd, you know. It's as if you're not comfortable unless people are looking down on you. If somebody pays the courtesy of coming to call, you somehow think it's wrong. It's not as though we don't have noses or eyes like everybody else—why can't we live like others, openly, as everyone does?'

What she said made sense. There was nothing I could say, so I quietly finished eating.

When I was through, I put the bowl and chopsticks on the cutting board and suddenly felt an extreme weariness. I had expected her to say, 'Put those down, I'll do the washing up,' as she usually did, but tonight she didn't make a move to stop me.

Still at the table, she cracked one last sunflower seed. She stretched like a cat, and then began to roll up the newspaper. The can of cigarette butts was emptied in the middle, and the neatly rolled paper was tucked into the wastebasket. She took out a small brush and swept the tablecloth—even in the worst of moods, she maintained her habit of cleanliness.

'Take off all those clothes in the outside room—don't bring them inside the bedroom. It looks like you've been rolling around in the mud.' After this order she lifted the curtain between the rooms and went inside without so much as looking at me. I did as I was told, removing clothes that were indeed covered with mud and throwing them in the wash-basin. After a brief hesitation, I resolutely poured out some cold water and washed myself.

When I went into the inner room, she still hadn't gone to sleep. Her eyes were wide open, looking at the newspa-

150

pers plastered on the ceiling, as if she were reading some article written on them.

'Still not asleep?' I asked.

She turned over and faced the wall without answering. I spread out my covers with my head in the opposite direction. By now, I was back to using my own old bedcover and she used hers: the newly embroidered tractors we had been given at our wedding were placed between us, like a signpost at a border. Their bright red colour was a warning of danger.

After lying down, I reached for a book and, without understanding a word, read a few pages. She didn't urge me to turn out the light and go to sleep, as she had in the past. I couldn't even hear the sound of her breathing. The room seemed draped in a silence that was waiting for me to tear it.

'Xiangjiu,' I put down the book and said with determination. 'If you think it's appropriate, I can petition for a divorce.'

'You're crazy!' Her words followed immediately, in a wide-awake voice—it was obvious she had been waiting for me to begin. 'I've already been divorced twice. Now here I am just married and I'm going to get divorced again? If people heard about it they'd laugh till their teeth fell out. Forget it. I've just got rotten luck. I've realized I wasn't meant to be happy in this life.'

'How can you say that! You're still young . . .' A wave of pity squeezed my insides as I said it. 'You wouldn't have to apply, I could go do it for us.'

'You apply . . . you apply!' Her voice came back at me from against the wall. 'On what basis would you apply? What's wrong with me that you could use as a reason?'

'Don't get me wrong. It's not you, it's me who's at fault. The marriage law has a line that says, "A man and a woman

151

who are not able to live the life of a couple are not permitted to get married." It's just that I only found out when I was already married . . .'

'Oh lord, people will laugh even more if you use that as a reason. They'll say that I, Huang Xiangjiu, planned it all along . . .'

'What kind of thinking is that? It's an obvious and perfectly good reason.'

'Damn it all! Bedroom matters are obvious and good reasons are they? Only a bookworm like you would think such a thing.'

She laughed the cold laugh that I had begun to know well. 'No, I've figured it out already. Our marriage is like two single-member households getting together to make a co-operative. It's not a home, it's a non-married dormitory! We'll just continue as if I were still living together with Old Lady Ma and you were with Zhou Ruicheng. You live in one room and I'll take the other. As for the work, we'll just split it up and help each other. You do the heavier jobs like getting water and coal and cutting the firewood. I'll do the cooking, washing and all the cleaning up. What else can we do? That's the way it's got to be . . .'

Suddenly she could control herself no longer, and miserable sobs interrupted her words. 'I was hoping, oh hoping . . . hoping for a good man. I could do everything, even wait for him. I wanted to live the second half of my life peacefully together with him . . . not worry about politics, not think of what they were doing up there. They still have to let people live, don't they? Without people, what kind of country would it be? We could just close the door and live simple lives, not making trouble, not giving them any excuse to come get us again . . . Oh, I hoped so much, and look what has happened! What kind of man are you? Old Lady Ma told me you were at least honest and kind. But you

152

have no manliness to you at all . . . If you were a real man, I wouldn't mind if you beat me all day! . . .'

A great aching hurt seized me as I lay on the bed, and although the light was still on, everything went black, except for flashes of light behind my eyes. Tears wells up uncontrollably and I could no longer think. 'God, oh god!' I felt myself calling. I had no belief in any heaven or any hell, and yet I was calling out to someone. 'Why do you trample on me? You've thrown me down on the ground enough—why give me this final kick?'

She saw that I was silenced, and with red teary eyes sat up to look at me. Perhaps she saw my own tears, but she made no response. With a flick of her hand, she reached across and turned out the light.

I should move to comfort her, should stroke her and caress her, take her to my chest and hold her tightly. I should do everything I could to make her happy. But I was no longer able to do any of those things. Twice before when she was crying I had tried to hold her. Each time, she forcefully pushed me away and told me to leave her alone. 'You're only making things worse,' she said, with red face and large wet eyes. I understood then that I was not to touch her again. I was to stay to one side, to hide in the corners if possible. It would be best if I could become a mouse. She had slowly expanded, in our so-called 'home', until she filled all the empty space. She had taken over the store-rooms until there was no room for me. Before, when I lived in the bachelor dormitory, I had still felt that my space was my own. It was small, but mentally it had no bounds. Now, our space was larger, but my mental space had shrunk. I knew now what people meant when they said their minds were being suffocated.

I finally realized that there is a more terrible oppression than that of society. I remembered, one by one, the men

153

who had committed suicide during various Movements, and as I thought of them I realized that the critical element causing their action had been their wives or their children. Goading from their families had been so intense that it drove them to the final decision. And those who had been able to withstand the grinding of the Movements were those who had stable and warm backing from their homes. Even if they were denied a pair of chopsticks in the 'cow pen', they still felt the spiritual support of their family.

Again, I too thought of suicide. Since I was already a 'cripple', already 'half a man', since I could only be ordered around like the old piebald, what purpose was there in carrying on? Why spend the rest of a wounded life tied up in the stable?

During this period, my dead mother appeared to me several times in dreams. She still looked as kind and gentle as in her old picture, with an eternal smile touching the corners of her mouth. She would float in and out of sight, as though she were in a dense fog. When I hurried to reach her she would disappear. I would try to figure out the dream when I woke up: was she calling me to join her, or was she telling me to keep on living?

The morning after that encounter, I watched the room slowly lighten as day broke. It was a dilapidated room, but Xiangjiu had made it clean and bright. Spiders' webs were something I hated more than anything—they reminded me of jail—and in this room I had never found a trace of one. Slowly, our belongings became visible: the bookshelf with her skin-lotion, her round mirror, the white tablecloth, some roadside cowslips in a glass by the window. The ground had been covered with a layer of bricks to make a level floor, and even the newspapers on the earthen walls looked like wallpaper in the new light. It all seemed alive, as if it could start to move, as if it were ready and happy to

154

serve its master. Her nimble hands had created all of this, composing a song of the ideal home.

I watched her as she slept in bed, face up, her profile cut cleanly, beautifully from forehead to chin. All that I saw around me had a compelling attraction: instead of repelling me, it was trying to draw me in to a normal life. Yet between it and me, I had built a cold, unbreakable glass wall.

My physical body, down to the nerve endings, made me unable to enjoy the life of a normal man. In addition, it denied me the creativity of a normal man.

'To be or not to be?' I ceaselessly asked myself Hamlet's question.

5

'Hey, Lao Zhang! What about lending me a horse for the day, en?' Dumbo and I had shooed the horses out of the corral that morning and were already at the edge of town when we ran into Hei-tz. He was carrying an old flintlock rifle over his shoulder, and had obviously been waiting for me so he could borrow a horse to go hunting. Today was a day off for the Production Brigade, but naturally the animals still needed somebody to tend them. I could have asked someone else to take my place, and given him the overtime wage, but I was glad to have an excuse to get out of the house.

Down the street, I saw a number of idle men lounging around the door of the Troop office. 'Walk on a little further,' I said, 'I'll meet you where the woods start.'

From the back of the old piebald, I used my whip to herd the horses out to a stretch of fallow land. Wild grasses that should have grown there had long since been trampled flat; the yellow earth showed through, dry and split with little gullies. Fields close in to town had already been well patronized by pigs, sheep and horses—we herders had to go a long way out to feed our animals properly.

I rode the piebald to the belt of trees by the side of the bare land, and dismounted to tie him to a tree. Hei-tz

156

immediately came running out. He took a cigarette from his bag, lit it and then handed me another. 'Which one is most docile?' he demanded. 'Give me a good one!'

'Better take this piebald,' I answered. 'But make sure you get back early in the evening, and don't let anyone know. There's some grain in a small sack behind the saddle. Don't ride him too hard, take a break from time to time and let him graze.'

'I know, I know!' Hei-tz sized up his mount. 'Not bad, just like one in a damn movie.'

'The best horses have been ruined by this place,' I said, 'just like the best men have been buried.'

'Yes, well.' He suddenly turned around to look at me. 'Lao Zhang, there's something I want to tell you. I'm only talking about it because we're like brothers, in fact Lifang told me not to mention it. But I don't think we brothers should take things lying down. Last night Cao Xueyi came by our place to sit for a while—you know that damn bastard is always stopping by to get a drink. By midnight, he was getting pretty drunk. He started by saying that of all the women in this Troop your Xiangjiu is the prettiest. Then he began talking about how tiny her waist is, and how soft her cheeks feel. He said there's something in the way your old lady talks to him.

'Then he came right out and said he'd like to go to bed with her. That bastard always says what's on his mind. He has a pretty good idea of what makes the world go round— he hates being a petty official, would rather piss away each day as it comes. That's why he hasn't really joined in with that gang of "rectifiers". But I tell you, Lao Zhang, when it comes to women's bodies, what that man says he'll do, he'll do. Honestly, your woman is not what we call "standard goods". Flies don't get into a duck egg that hasn't been cracked. Lifang is in the same production team with her, and when they're working, Cao Xueyi is always circling around.

'Lao Zhang, since you've already got her, it's hard to say anything. But women, hell, you just have to keep an eye on them. I say give her a good beating, so she'll know she's got to behave. Use that damn whip, and just lay into her!'

I didn't feel anger. I didn't even feel surprise. Grass that has been trampled underfoot hasn't the strength to stand up even in a breeze. Rubbing my wrinkled forehead, I said, 'Let her do as she pleases, Hei-tz. I appreciate your concern, but she makes my meals and washes my clothes every day, and I figure that's enough.'

'That damn idiot, that lousy good-for-nothing bastard!' Hei-tz's bushy eyebrows came together in a scowl. 'It's a good thing you've already been in the camps twice, and been in jail three times. You're a tough man. But what has she got on you that makes her think she can get away with it? After all, she's done hard labour herself, she's even been married twice . . .'

'Get going.' I handed him my whip and clapped him on the shoulder. 'Remember, come home early this afternoon.'

Standing patiently by the tree, the old piebald nodded his head at me, as if in approval of what I had said.

Hei-tz mounted up and rode off muttering and cursing, and I walked on through the belt of trees to sit down by the side of a wheat field.

The wheat was already golden, and soon it would be harvest time. Heavy heads waved slowly in the breeze, like a chorus of women singing under the light shadows of clouds passing overhead. They were recalling the spring days of their youth: as snow-white shoots, as tender seedlings that were a soft green. They remembered the juicy vigour of life that had once filled their buds, and the grace-

158

ful charm of strong green stems that met the sky. All that had gone, and they knew it had gone forever. Their grains were golden now, stiff and hard, burnt dry by the sun. Their blond stalks were brittle, and they found it hard to withstand rain or wind. They were mature, yes, but they had lost a beautiful time, lost it for eternity.

The air was hot and dry. Leaves of white poplars rustled in the wind above me, and a small whirlwind suddenly started up from the wheat and took off straight into the air. I watched its patch of grey get smaller and smaller in the blueness. The clouds drifted along above, pure white tops capping their silvery foundations. They knew as little as I did where they were going. How fast it had all been! I had been married only two months before. This was the same wheat field I had passed on my way to Luo Zongqi's house, and yet just as the scene had totally changed, I also had changed.

A large castor-oil plant was growing by the edge of the field. Like a comforting hand, one of its large leaves rested on my shoulder. It seemed to pour out the sounds of nature to me in the wind, passionate and mournful, opening its heart to me. Hello, my castor-oil plant! Hello, white poplars, wandering white clouds! Hello, my golden wheat. I have received life from you, but this life has no value. My life has wasted you, and it has also wasted itself.

I stood up suddenly, and felt the earth spin for a moment beneath me. The pressure inside me burst out as I shouted, 'My god, my god, why hast thou forsaken me?'

'This man calls Elijah,' the people of Israel said beside me.

The tractor got as far as the front door of the primary school at Headquarters, and then stopped suddenly as the engine went dead. The cart it was pulling banged into it before stopping too.

'Move, you bloody tractor!' Xiao* Li-tz jumped off the driver's seat and vigorously began kicking one of the tyres. 'We're still using these rust buckets that they threw away years ago in other countries!'

The sun had already gone down and a full moon was rising in the sky. With no clouds, no sunset and no stars, I felt the fresh clarity of the evening even more than I had at dusk. Two vertical scrolls painted in red characters were pasted on either side of the school door. One read:

> The purpose of the school's work is to reverse the thinking of its students.

The other read:

> Workers' propaganda teams should spend a long time in the schools, participating in the schools' job of Struggle— Criticism—Transformation. They should forever be in command of the schools.

*Xiao' is a prefix attached to the name of a person younger than oneself.

Under the moon, the words of Chairman Mao glittered in the reflected light.

So schools were not places to study knowledge, but to reverse it. Did that mean to turn the innocent and guileless into the hypocritical? Or to turn capitalist thinking into proletariat thinking? Had 'capitalist class thinking' already taken hold of seven-year-old children so strongly that this school had to take responsibility for eradicating it? I felt the cold wind of evening brush across me.

It was very late. The cold wind seemed to have blown down from the moon.

Xiao Li-tz was pulling hard at the starting cord in the front of the tractor, trying to get the engine moving again. I was stretched out in the cart with a folded gunny-sack under my back, looking up at the moon. Were those continents I saw, or were they oceans? As I watched, I felt closer and closer to them, approaching the moon until I could almost touch it. Things on earth receded, as I began to look on them with an increasingly perplexed wonder.

'Damn it all! It won't catch.' Xiao Li-tz stepped up on the cart's axle, and craned his neck over the side to look at me. 'Lao Zhang, what are we going to do?'

'If it won't start, just keep trying a few more times,' I said, feeling very comfortable.

'To hell with that! You come try it for yourself.'

'All I can do is coolie labour—starting a tractor is way beyond me. If I could, I would have done it for you ages ago.'

Xiao Li-tz hesitated on the axle, muttering to himself, 'What to do? What to do?'

Earlier in the day Party Secretary Cao had called me over after the regular day's work, and asked me to put in a night shift. I was to haul phosphate fertilizer up from the railroad station together with Xiao Li-tz and his tractor. 'Work for

161

one night,' he had said, 'and you can take off tomorrow and the next day, to rest.

'The workers are all having a big meeting at the town hall tomorrow,' he explained. 'Everyone's supposed to attend. The leaders are calling on us to study the theory of the dictatorship of the proletariat again—something about criticizing somebody named Song Jiang . . .' If a man was sent out to work all night, he naturally would not be obliged to attend a meeting the next day, but more to the point, I would not have been allowed to participate anyway. The 'rich', 'landlords', 'antis', 'baddies' and 'rightists' were not included in meetings, so Cao was being doubly clever in selecting me for the night work. Dumbo could handle the herding for a day, and the great enthusiasm of the meeting wouldn't be dampened by any unexpected elements. The calls to 'assemble at the town hall', 'unite in raising the cry' etc., etc., would be unobstructed.

From my standpoint, I got two free days for one extra night. Moreover, she would be working in the fields those days, and I would be at home alone. Naturally I was willing to accept the deal.

'Hey.' Xiao Li-tz walked completely around the tractor before continuing. 'Tell you what I think—I think we should take a nap. Let's just go into the schoolhouse there, find a cosy spot, and take a snooze,' he snickered.

'Take a snooze! How could you think of such a thing? What about our responsibility?'

'Responsibility, responsibility! It can go screw itself.' But he wavered a moment in the moonlight. 'This old tractor's always losing its teeth—they shouldn't have sent me in the beginning, I don't know what to do. Whoever does, and has the patience, can come start the thing.'

I sat up, stepped over the side of the cart, and jumped down onto the ground. 'You have to have an explanation

162

ready for the bosses, you know. Even if it's broken, what if somebody came along and stole some spare parts while we were asleep? Worse yet, if somebody came looking for us, they'd find us sleeping and think we'd broken the tractor on purpose!'

Xiao Li-tz took off his hat and scratched his head, still muttering, 'What to do.' Despite a very secure backing as the precious son of the Vice Chairman of the Political Section, he never lorded it over me and he even tried to make my life easy.

'Well then,' he said, 'you go to sleep and I'll stay here and watch over the machine.'

'That's no good,' I said. 'This tractor's not going to move again until tomorrow. But Secretary Cao still thinks we're hard at work here hauling fertilizer. I think this is what we ought to do: you stay here in the cart, and I'll go back and report. We will have done our duty, and I can bring back a couple of horses to pull the tractor until it starts again. What do you think?'

'I think that's pretty hard on you. Our Troop's over nine miles from here!'

'Doesn't matter—I'm used to walking from my days of herding sheep. The moon's bright tonight, and at the latest I should be in town by midnight. Coming back with the horses will be even faster. You get some sleep—I'll be back before it's light.'

The open country looked like a lunar landscape under the rays of the full moon. Cold wastes stretched out to the black line marking the horizon, no human being was in sight. It was as though you would drop off into a clear, vast space when you reached that black line. I had returned to an environment I was familiar with, however, and my body felt weightless as I strode out in long fast strides. It is not very

163

difficult to walk from one world into another—it is just a matter of allowing the world to turn beneath you.

I reached our production team around eleven o'clock. My little village was tranquil, already deep in sleep under the moon. Row after row of earthen brick buildings slumbered next to each other, like farmers who had lain down tired after working all day. From the belt of trees just outside town, I saw that the first row of buildings still had two bright lights on. One was in the office of the production team, the other was in what had once been the team's store-rooms—and was now my home. A warm wave of tenderness came over me as I realized that at this late hour she still had not gone to bed.

I vacillated for a moment, trying to decide whether to go and see her first and tell her to go to sleep, or whether to make my report to Secretary Cao. Leaving the main road, I branched off into a small trail beaten out by human feet, that took a shortcut through the straight line of poplars. Dry branches crackled under me, left over from the year before. A cold night wind rustled through the leaves above, where small chirpings came from sparrows' nests. Oleaster trees had been planted along the border of the poplars. These trees were unique to north-western China, and in the midst of silver-grey leaves and thorny branches their little yellow flowers give out an extraordinary fragrance. Able to grow in dry and alkaline soil, the oleaster did not require very much of nature, but it was unstinting in giving off its own perfume.

The oleaster blossoms had already fallen at this late season, and the branches were heavy with hanging fruit. By autumn, the small green balls would turn and make the whole tree golden. I had almost reached the end of these trees when I saw the light in the office suddenly go out. A person appeared at the door, and in the light of the moon

164

I could see it was Cao Xueyi. He set out, walking purposefully, but rather than going towards his own house in the rear line of buildings, he turned in the direction of my own home. As I stood there astonished, he pushed open the door of my house, and quickly stepped inside. A flash of light pierced the darkness, as the door was opened to admit him. In less than a second, the beam that had illuminated the fields was turned off again.

Automatically, I continued walking forward a few steps when suddenly the light from the windows went out also. The village seemed to have blinked its two eyes shut right in front of me. The entire town slept: only I was left outside. Only I was wide awake.

'It has finally happened!'

My legs gave way under me as I sat down hard on the top of an oleaster root. I was conscious of the sound of the wind passing through the trees and beating against my canvas work clothes, but I had no sensation of feeling the wind itself.

Of all the insults and humiliation I had received in my lifetime, only this one remained for me to experience. It was surprising it hadn't happened before: fate seemed to have made an odd exception and taken care of me. It was as though it had been decided from my birth that I should pass through every kind of suffering. These past few days I had begun to have a vague premonition that the final mortification was approaching. I was a mangy dog backed into a corner, spine up and fur bristling waiting helplessly for the uplifted stick to fall. My only hope was that it would not pulverize my bones, that I would live and would recuperate some day.

Now the stick was coming down! Again all my instincts had been right.

Paralysed, I lay under the oleaster, one hand grabbing the rough bark of the tree, almost splitting the skin as I held onto firm reality. I needed it both to restore my senses and to test my own capacity for being hurt.

'Hey, what are you doing lying there?' A spirit wafted out of the air above and gave me a good swift kick. 'Grab your woodcutter's axe and get going! Isn't there a horse tied up behind your back door? You have the key—you could be through that door in a moment. A husband must stand tall between heaven and earth! How can you think of accepting this kind of insult?'

I raised my head and looked. It was fat and short and slightly swarthy and was wearing the costume of a Song Dynasty official. Its eyes were as red as the eyes of a phoenix, and its eyebrows were bushy like silkworm cocoons.

It stroked its moustache as it said, 'We brothers would never be as incompetent as you. Even Three-inch Peewee would have fought to the death with adulterers and seducers. Look at you—over six feet tall and broad of girth. A strapping fellow if I ever saw one. And yet you've allowed this to happen. How are you ever going to face your parents in the "nine springs down under"?'

I could act, of course. Perhaps those corpses that had appeared on the wall that day of our wedding had been an omen. And yet . . .

'Brother Song,' I called out, 'the times are not the same now. When you killed Yan Poxi* you could get off scot-free, keep your liberty. Nowadays, it wouldn't work that way. There is no more Shui Po Liang Mountain now!'

*Song Jiang is a famous character in the Chinese novel *The Water Margin* (also known as *All Men are Brothers*). He was used by Mao during the Cultural Revolution to make oblique criticisms of opposing political factions. Yan was the wife of Song Jiang's brother, and was killed by Song Jiang when she was unfaithful to his brother, who was impotent.

'That's your own fault. Shui Po Liang Mountain was made by heroes, don't forget. You're living in an age that's like the reign of Xuan He,'* Song Jiang said. 'Tigers and wolves fill the roads, honesty and decency have been knocked aside. The Emperor is ignorant and cruel. What are you waiting for? Raise the standard and rebel!'

'Brother, that's easier to say than do. In a different age, it might have been possible. But right now our leadership is more complex than in your ancient days. Some of our leaders really love their country—they're trying to help the people, and working hard to put things back on the right track. Rash acts by the populace are not really going to help matters.'

'Short-sighted, I tell you, short-sighted!' Song Jiang boomed at me. 'You need to unite the upper and the lower, unite the court and the frontier. Unite the inside and the outside—that's the only way you'll find what you call the "right track". If there were no lower, no frontier, no outside, your patriots in the court would be trying to clap with one hand. In the end it will be the tigers and wolves who clean things up more tidily than you would have wanted. Hurry up! Get together a band of fighters! Support the good men in the court. Liberate the court from evil ministers! Establish a correct dynasty!'

'Brother, this "band of fighters" that you want me to organize is what we would call a "revolutionary group" today. But I tell you, the policemen you had in your day are nothing to what we've got over us now. They've set up organs of dictatorship in the name of the proletariat: before we even had time to organize, they'd have us surrounded and arrested. These past ten years they've been willing to

---

*This means 'peaceful reign'. Xuan He was the period title of a famous Song Dynasty Emperor whose reign was not at peace.

arrest a thousand innocent people in the hopes of catching one real criminal, and yet they haven't let a single one of those innocent people go.

'When I came out of a labour camp in 1968, I thought there was something called the "Liu-Deng Headquarters". Like a fool, I set off in search of it. Not only did I find no "revolutionary group", I was "hatted" and thrown in jail again! You think it's all so easy?

'Song Jiang, take your own example. You shrugged off the living world hundreds of years ago. And yet they still drag out your name for "criticism and struggle". It's fortunate you don't come out in the daytime, or you would be arrested immediately!'

'Ah me,' Song Jiang said. 'Each age has its own problems. If there is really no possibility of you little crickets and ants rectifying the situation and saving the god of the grains* then the least you can do is get out and butcher those two dogs sleeping in your house. At least set an example for what happens to the wicked in this world.'

'That surely is one way to look at it, but there is one detail, Brother Song, that you may not know. Although she and I are man and wife in name, we are not man and wife in reality. I don't feel that it is necessary for me to abandon my own life for their sake, though it's true I don't really want to cling anymore to this dusty earth . . .'

As I said these words, a great gust of wind came bearing down out of the branches. The willow and oleaster leaves were sent scattering, throwing dancing shadows on the ground. Out of the wind came a thick circle of inky mist, and out of the blackness came a tragic voice.

'It's all because the moon is not on course! It's come closer to the earth, and hence everyone has gone mad!' A

*i.e. the country.

dark face appeared, and then an ancient Venetian war-costume. Othello's eyes glared as he hovered above the ground. 'I have lost my courage too! Any coward could easily wrest my sword away from me. Evil has triumphed over good—does glory remain anywhere? Let everything return to oblivion!'

He had been tormented in hell until he went insane, and his own conscience had played a part in his torture. His tragic voice was calling out a warning to every man who thought of killing his wife and then of killing himself.

The black mist slowly dissolved, and the two spirits disappeared without a trace.

Presently, the light of the moon brightened as the sky cleared up. My body felt as if it were riding along on my own line of vision, as I passed through the deep blue blue of the night sky, roaming through all the corners of space. From where I sat under the oleaster tree I could hold a conversation with any celestial body in the universe. Merely lifting my hand or my foot sent them out into the vastness of the world. I had thrown myself into the firmament.

I cried out to the heavens at large, 'Help me! Meng-tz claims that to be given responsibility one must suffer, must starve, must work oneself to the bone. I've suffered, I've starved and I've certainly worked. When will I see the end of all this chaos? If there's no point to all this, it would be better for me simply to end my life! That's as good a way as any other.'

A sonorous voice answered me from out of the sky. 'You can't discuss the wide oceans with a fish who lives inside a well, and you can't talk about the cold with an insect who only knows the summer. One is restricted by space, and the other is controlled by time. You can't discuss the Greater Truth with a student from the countryside, and this is because he is limited by the Confucian feudal code.

169

'However, starting from the source of a river, you have emerged to glimpse the sea. You have seen your own smallness. It is possible to speak of Truth with you.'

Although I couldn't see his form, I knew that the man speaking was Zhuang-tz. 'Master, I ask for your instruction,' I said. 'I will listen to your words.'

'Where Meng-ke* is wrong is that he thinks all of creation has a predetermined purpose. I have heard a man of great accomplishment in the past say: "The things one brags about have no merit; those with high and mighty reputations will come to no good." If a man can give to people without asking for recognition, follow the Great Path and yet not be self-satisfied, he will not in the end want from others, and will not have others want from him. Your labour, hunger, suffering and your chaos are simply a result of your participation in the creative process of the world. As for not seeking a purpose or a name for yourself, why do you love the concept and yet go on seeking?'

'The master's words are extremely profound,' I said, 'but I am not sure they meet the needs of my situation. I don't think that name and reputation are the reason for going through such suffering. I am well aware that an illustrious name can bring its own problems. All I want to know is what to do.'

Zhuang-tz laughed at me. 'First,' he said, 'you must realize that "only where there is that which is not is there the possibility of becoming," and "only by not Doing is everything able to be done."

'Prisoners don't care about their lives. They can climb to high places without fear. They can be menaced and oppressed without retaliating, and without worrying about being different from you and me. Rising above the differ-

---

*A familiar name for Meng-tz.

170

ences among men, they have reached the ideal state of the unity of man and nature.

'If you want to be at peace, then you must abandon yourself to the world. You must not fight it or try to control it. You must throw your entire self into the world as it is created day by day: in that creation is the Way. Only when you are in a state of unity with nature can you find that Way, can you do things in harmony with a state of not-Doing. You may express anger, but it comes from a mindless source: you resign yourself to not caring, to flowing with what happens in heaven and earth. That is the Way of the Sages.'

I was horrified, and my body had broken out in a cold sweat. 'Thank you, Master, for your teaching,' I said. 'In general, I believe I understand what you mean. I believe I have some of the qualifications you mention, and that I can "tolerate the small things in order not to destroy the big ones". But, Master, can you teach me more? I need to know the concrete way to do all this!'

From the middle of the universe, Zhuang-tz said, 'The sacred tortoise has the power to give Yuan Jun dreams and grant requests, but he cannot avoid Mr Yu Qie's fish net. Human resourcefulness can divine seventy-two ba gua symbols and foretell the future, and yet cannot escape an empty stomach in a calamitous famine. Even the most intelligent men have their difficult times—spirits too have their inadequacies. The fish doesn't know he should be afraid of the net, and yet knows enough to fear the pelican. People must discard their own small wisdoms in order to allow the Great Wisdom to stand out. A child does not need a teacher to teach it how to talk: its ability to speak comes simply from being with others who speak. I have studied the ways of Heaven, but I have been negligent about human affairs. If you want to know concrete things, you must ask for help from someone else.'

171

At that moment, Marx strode out of the middle of the round moon. 'My child,' he said kindly, 'I have heard the cry from your heart.' He tucked his hand inside the pocket of his waistcoat. 'In this specific matter, I cannot be of much help to you. As you know, I had a most beloved wife, and I in turn was her most beloved man. I'm afraid I have little experience in handling your sort of problem.'

'Master, I am not asking for help in that affair,' I said. 'I have already thought things through on that particular issue. I want to handle it with an even temper and good humour, and not damage my own morality. What I would like to ask you for is guidance about my country. What is the future of our society going to be?'

He gave a hearty laugh. 'My child, you think you've thought it through, but you haven't at all. The foundation of the Eastern philosophy is to cultivate the body and nurture the spirit: to seek wholeness in one's ethical being, and to commune with the essence of nature by "achieving unification of heaven and man".

'I believe you should first consider things from her point of view. You should start by treating her with an attitude of equality and respect. The main Western precepts are freedom and equality, while Eastern precepts are ethics and reputation. I don't mean to analyse which is superior or inferior, since they belong to different historical periods and are developing along the spiral helix of history. In the future, your Eastern philosophy will grow in importance in the world.

'I just want to point out that you and she are man and wife. But you, Zhang Yonglin, are not able to meet the obligations of a husband. So what right do you have to keep her from temporary happiness? You feel that pardoning her is a great act of generosity. In fact, you have no authority even to pardon her. I feel, moreover, that this "regarding

172

yourself as good" doesn't really tally with your own Eastern concepts of the "Way of the Sages".'

As he spoke, I felt the correctness of his words. 'Yes, Master, please continue.'

'All right.' Marx flipped up the tails of his coat, and sat down on a stump in front of me. 'First, I beg of you, please speak to me as an equal. Let the two of us, from different eras, talk together as friends. The reason I call you "child" is that I am considerably older than you. There is nothing of the Great Teacher or Master in this. I never advertised my own greatness before, but I also do not approve of stopping up the mouths of those who have come after me—this is a matter which gives me great grief up there in heaven. "The only reason a great man is great is that you yourself are kneeling to him." I remember passing on those words long ago, but now nobody listens to what I really said . . .'

Astonished, I said, 'It's true that there are those who distort your teachings. They carry your banner just to further their own devious schemes. There are even more people, however, who sincerely honour your teachings! Why do you say that nobody listens to what you really said?'

'Child,' Marx said, 'this is another thing that I worry about. The first group of people you mention are those who take sentences from my works and use them as theoretical weapons. They use passages for their own personal profit, either in struggling for power or in oppressing the people. Because of that, I have become terrifying to ordinary people. I have been made into something that opposes their welfare. Unfamiliar with my real ideas, they are frightened just to think about me.

'Why is it that those who misuse my words are able to achieve even temporary victories? Because they "Do as they see fit"!

'The second kind of person you mention tries naïvely to follow my exact words. These people often seem doomed to fail. Why is it that those who "honour my teaching" are often defeated? Because they on the contrary do not "Do as they see fit".'

'I'm a bit confused,' I said. 'You mean to tell me your teachings are not true? Why is it that those who don't follow them are successful, while those who do are bound to fail?'

'Don't be hasty—listen to what else I have to say.' Marx put his broad hand on top of my knee. 'The two most important points in my whole work were summarized by my good friend Engels when he spoke over my grave. One is the basic truth of historical materialism. The other relates to the particular rules governing modern capitalist methods of production and the society that they produce. As for the methodology of dialectical materialism and its world view, that runs through the entire process of my work.

'Both of the two kinds of people we mentioned, whether they have good intentions or whether their intentions are evil, are looking at my work only to find ready-made solutions. They are not adopting the methodology that was integrated into all I did. I admire very much your Eastern saying, "To take the meaning and forget the words". If one gets my "meaning", one can forget my "words". I'm afraid that after Engels and I left for heaven, many people on earth have taken my "words" and forgotten my "meaning".'

'I'm a little clearer now,' I said, 'but still not totally sure: why does one succeed only by "doing as one sees fit"? What exactly is the guiding significance of your teaching?'

'You still don't understand,' Marx smiled at me from under his great beard. 'If my discoveries are to be of use to people, it is because they use historical and dialectical materialism. If anybody wants to succeed in revolutionary work, that is the methodology that should be applied within the

174

framework of doing what one considers is needed at the time.'

'Anyway, we are going to carry on your great work . . .' I felt I should somehow comfort the illustrious ghost.

'Ha ha ha!' Marx bellowed out a laugh that was resonant and wise. 'My child, please don't underestimate my intelligence. I am not so stupid as to believe that what people who come after me are doing is to carry on my work. My work was already finished in 1883. The people of each generation can only do the work of their own period of history. The liberation of mankind is the work of continuing generations of effort. No single country, no single race of people, no single generation can solve everything—let alone one person.

'Only an old sex-crazed cretin would accept having other people tell him that he was the leader of World Revolution, and would ask them to complete his so-called work. Remember the words of Hegel, my child, "No race of people and no government has had very much to learn from history: each epoch has been too different and too special."

'What Hegel meant is that each period can be judged only from the standpoint of conditions prevailing at that time. The reason for the success of those who wave the Marxist banner while at the same time doing as they themselves see fit is that they have recognized this. If I were still living on earth, though, I would have to say to those people: "What about using your own words when you speak? You have unconsciously grasped my meaning but you still hang on grimly to my old words, often turning them into what they were not meant to say."

'At the risk of appearing presumptuous, I would say that all revolutionary work that is successful either consciously or unconsciously uses the laws of historical materialism and dialectical materialism. Using my words to describe it, however, is equivalent to asking me to die a second time. Ah, child, dying is not a happy thing. Especially when you are forced to watch people kill your own spirit, and you have no power to do anything about it.'

'Yes, I've thought much the same thing—although of course you and I can't compare. Looking at the future of our society, though,' I said, 'is there any guidance you can give me? This question concerns not only how I deal with life, but also my very life and death.'

'Economics!' Marx answered immediately. 'You must look at every problem from the standpoint of economics. I've described briefly the historical view of materialism. When the means of production of material goods have developed to a certain stage, contradictions form with the previously existing means of production. The previous means become shackles holding down production, and it is then that a period of social revolution has arrived. With changes in the economic basis, the whole monstrous super-structure will, somehow or other, go through a transforma-tion. This can all be seen from another side: when the means of production have declined to the point of not meeting the needs of society, then a social revolution tries to rescue productive power from the verge of death. It appears as if that kind of social revolution starts first in the superstructure. The transformation of the superstructure changes relationships in production.

'Right now, your productive power has essentially been neutralized. You're trying to scrape by with words and hot air rather than real action. It's ridiculous that at this time the mouth is developing rather than the hands or the body. Do you really think it can continue much longer?'

Marx had just spoken these words when the door of my house opened. Cao Xueyi emerged from the dark room, jacket slung over his shoulder. At the same time our grey

176

cat also sprang out of the door, and tripped him up as he hurriedly headed off to his own home. The grey cat gave a loud meow, and with a bound leaped up to the eaves of the house.

To think that this man, who was one of those offending the great soul of the deceased, was a Communist Party Member!

PART 4

1

'What in the world are you up to out here?'

'I'm looking at the moon. It's been full, you see, and now it's waning again.'

'What a fool. Married to a man like you, really, what is a person to do?'

I did my best to stay out of the inner room except to sleep. Since I had chanced on that incident, the room seemed permeated with Cao Xueyi. His smell, his shadow were everywhere. Right there, they must have . . . was it on this side of the bed, or that side? Surely they wouldn't have used the side that I sleep on. I imagined their every move: this is how he came into the house, she greeted him thus, they embraced like so and then went into the inner room. Who actually reached out a hand to put out the light? How exactly did they roll on the bed? I knew that her every action was practised, including the moaning and the little sounds. Had she played the scene out well in the arms of Cao Xueyi?

I knew it was senseless, but I could not stop turning the whole thing back and forth in my mind. It had reached the point where I would suddenly wake in the middle of the night and sniff the air: what was that odd smell, mixed up together with the others?

181

After returning from the animals and eating my evening meal, I spent most of my time sitting on the levelled garden, looking at the moon and enjoying the breeze.

As for writing, what would I have dared to write? This woman was more dangerous than Zhou Ruicheng had been. Anyway, my interest in writing had greatly diminished. I was a 'cripple', 'half a man'—best simply to exist, and to watch and wait.

The intense heat of summer was coming on; the wheat had been harvested and a scorching wind blew over the newly ploughed fields, bringing with it the rich smell of earth. In the distance, an 'East is Red' tractor was putt-putting along, sounding like some kind of animal. Despite being made of iron and steel, its spirit seemed to merge with nature. From in front of the house, I could look out unobstructed, at the rows of poplars and oleasters. They stood straight and tall, honest witnesses in nature's witness box. They were not going to retreat, not going to hide, and from time to time the evening wind brought me the grumbling of their discontent.

I watched the sad gibbous moon, high in the south at the beginning of the evening, then watched it go down in the middle of the night.

I watched the worried eyebrow of a crescent moon, appearing in the western sky as the sun went down. She seemed to be pursuing the setting sun, and almost caught him as they went behind the ridge of mountains.

'Look at you, so filthy and thin these days.' One by one she removed clothes that had been set out to dry on the line. Her tone of voice could be interpreted as either considerate or resentful. 'If people catch sight of you, they'll think I've been bullying you. Have you been eating too little? Drinking too little?'

It was as if in the eyes of other people I was reduced to

nothing more than eating and drinking. 'If I'm thin, I'm thin,' I said, quietly. 'As for looking dirty, you know yourself how fierce the sun is now.'

'Don't you have enough sense to stay in the shade of the trees? A herdsman like you, you're carrying a big responsibility. Better not get sunstroke.'

The stars began to flicker feebly in the evening sky. A bolt of redness in the sunset had not completely disappeared, and still silently shone over darkening slopes in the west. 'You bring out that little stool and come sit awhile too,' I said. 'Come and see for yourself how beautiful the evening is.'

'I'm too busy. Besides, why would I want to count the stars all night?' Carrying a large load of laundry, she brushed aside the bamboo curtain in the doorway and went inside. I had bought the curtain as I passed through a distant town with my herd. She had carefully stitched a white border onto it, saying, 'This way it will last for years.'

She was still thinking in terms of 'years'!

She was sewing soles on some shoes when I finally went into the inner room. 'Who are those for?' I asked with some sarcasm.

'Who else? There's only the two of us here—who else would they be for?' She lifted her hand, and very lightly scratched her head with the thick end of the large needle. Her movements were dextrous and her skill was beautiful to watch—every stitch was like the swish of a sleeve in a Peking opera. The soles were quite large—of course they must be for me.

I took off my clothes and lay down on the earthen bed. In the summer-time, the bed stayed as cool as the rays of the moon. With my bare back against the thin, cotton-padded mattress, I felt like a small leaf floating in calm water, letting the gentle wind take me where it would. Three months

183

earlier I had thought I would come to understand her. But three months had passed and she was even harder to grasp, to predict. The Big-footed Philosopher had been right: it was impossible to understand another human being. Especially if that person were a woman.

The morning after the tractor had broken down, Xiao Li-tz drove it back into town as I stood behind in the empty cart. We had tied the two horses behind the cart, and as the tractor rolled along at its leisurely pace they had no trouble keeping up. They plodded lackadaisically, nodding their drowsy heads in time to their hoofbeats.

We came in just as the large troop was setting out to work, and the entire crowd stood at the crossroads to watch our strange little parade. Xiao Li-tz forestalled any comments before we reached them by immediately starting to yell, 'Damn it! We couldn't get the—thing started! It stopped on us before we even got to the station, left us stranded out there in the open. Fortunately Lao Zhang came back in the middle of the night and brought two horses to pull-start it—otherwise the two of us would have been eaten by the wolves! Hell! If they don't give us four points, I'll have something to say about it. Whoever wants can try and get the thing to work properly. I'm going home to get some sleep.'

Xiao Li-tz jumped off the tractor, and headed off on a bicycle to get some sleep where his Daddy 'officiated'. I suddenly saw her staring anxiously at me from the crowd.

'Did you come back last night to fetch those horses?' Her face wore a worried and insincere smile.

'Yes.' I bent down to untie the lead-ropes I had tied to the cart.

'Then . . . why didn't you come home?' She followed along behind me.

'Ha!' I laughed coldly, the first time I had laughed like

184

that since we had been married. 'It seemed you weren't alone!' I answered very quietly, then mounted the horse bareback and rode off to the corral.

From then onwards she began to use a seemingly concerned, yet at the same time resentful, tone to talk to me. You could take it either way: at least it was more comfortable to listen to than pure resentment. She had previously simply ridiculed me.

She also began to wash the clothes so diligently that at times I felt it was much overdone. 'I'm accustomed to living the life of a bachelor,' I would say. 'It doesn't matter if the clothes are a bit dirty—I'm already cleaner than a lot of others.'

'You may be used to dirt, but I'm not,' she would say, forcing me to take off the thick canvas work-clothes. 'You smell like a horse. When you walk in front of people they hold their noses. Anyway, don't depend on others to know what to do—if they decide to go out and die, does that mean you have to do the same?'

Yes, perhaps!

She also made me shoes now, reinforcing the soles stitch by stitch. And she never complained that our rations weren't enough when I ate too much. I could barely carry on, but why should I pull her down with me?

'Xiangjiu,' I lay on the bed, eyes facing the rafters overhead. 'You're afraid of getting a divorce just after you've got married again, you're afraid it will hurt your reputation—so let's just quietly wait for a year. Next year, it doesn't really matter if you apply or I do—we came together easily and we can split up easily. As for reasons, we'll just say that we don't get along. A southerner and a northerner—our habits don't mix. What do you think?'

She didn't answer. The sound of a needle and thread sewing on the sole of a shoe filled the room.

Then a large beetle banged against the window. Trying

185

to get to the lamp, it fell on its back on the window-sill instead. It whirred beetle noises as it faced the sky.

The loudspeaker blared out the tune for putting out the lights. Ten o'clock, and everyone had to go to bed. This was a result of the injunction that 'the entire country should learn from the People's Liberation Army'. Even in this remote village, timetables were dictated by the notes of an army bugle. The tunes were recorded on a record: those for getting up, going to work, stopping work, lights out. The young girls who handled the broadcasting often made mistakes, however, and the stop-work bugle would blare when it was time to go to work, the get-up bugle came when it was time to go back home. Tonight they had it right, though—it was the lights-out bugle.

She finished her sewing with quick, neat movements. Then she took a brush and quickly brushed the cotton-padded mattress. Without lying down, she pulled the string turning out the light.

Time flowed past in the darkness, and life went with it, melting away. The beetle still called from the window-sill, not quite able to right himself. He might never make it, but he had to keep on trying. For a moment his rhythmic calls and the heartbeat throbbing in my eardrums became synchronized. I could not distinguish which was him and which was the blood flowing inside me. I began to feel that I might actually be that beetle. My back became numb, I was exhausted and my four limbs became terribly heavy. Just as I was dozing off, she spoke:

'You could go to the hospital. I've heard that it's curable.'

I finally figured out that this voice was her talking, and I made an effort to pull myself out of slumber and at the same time to calm my nerves. I wanted to show that I was reasonable and willing to talk, but at the mention of hospital, I could not hold back a laugh.

186

'You think anybody would even look at a sickness like this in a hospital? Right now, all they do in hospitals are abortions!'

'But if you went to a big hospital,' her voice seemed very distant, 'or else maybe found a "River and Lake Doctor"* . . .'

'You must be joking.' As if talking to myself I said, 'If I went to a large hospital and showed my identity card—don't even ask if the authorities would give me permission to try—they would take one look at it and not even let me register. And as for a "River and Lake Doctor", where do you think I'm going to find one these days? They've all been cut off as the "tails of capitalism"!'

Clearheaded now, I realized that I had already decided I could no longer go on living with her. I had rejected any hope of recovering from my 'illness', and I even wanted to widen the rift between the two of us. If possible, I would make the very earth between us split open.

There was silence for a long time. Yes, words spoken in the darkness are the truest, I thought. Everything is born in darkness, and all in darkness is real. You could say what you really meant in darkness, do anything that you really wanted to do. Lies aren't afraid of the light—the truth is.

'It's nonsense!' she finally said. 'I've never felt I couldn't get along with you. What do you mean, southerner and northerner? After all those years in the camps and in hard labour, how much southerner do you think is left in you? You mean you can't eat noodles, or round flat bread?† Anyway, whatever southern ways you have don't matter—I can go along with anything, as long as you get better.'

---

*A herbal-medicine doctor, practising traditional Chinese medicine.
†Southerners traditionally eat rice, northerners bread and noodles.

'That's just it—I'm not going to get better!' I quickly stated my loss of hope.

'Don't blame that on me!' she said, and I understood what she meant.

'I'm not blaming you. I only hope that we can get by peacefully for this coming year.' I felt sure that she would understand what I referred to when I said 'peacefully'. 'If you feel that's not possible, or not appropriate, then we can move the time up—we can even apply tomorrow.'

'Forget it—just forget it!' She began to get angry. 'I can't match you with words. You people who read books, your stomachs are full of snaky ways!'

'You read too,' I said. 'You've been to middle school, haven't you? You should understand the advantages of common interests and listen to reason. Aren't you concerned about your reputation?'

'Don't be sarcastic with me, OK?' She was furious, but her anger was still not quite enough to change her mind. 'If you want to apply, just go ahead. I'm not going to do it, and anyway, you wrote the marriage application.'

This woman was truly immoral! I held back my anger as I thought how she was using me. She had taken my forbearance as weakness, and now she was using me as a screen for her adultery. She had me in a stranglehold and was unwilling to let me go.

The downpour continued throughout the day and all the next night. It was unlike past rainstorms, which announced themselves first with a few tentative drops; this rain fell abruptly out of the sky in a blinding sheet, catching people unprepared.

Fortunately the wheat had been harvested, since it would have been a complete loss lying in the fields. The earth seemed to spread out flat in all directions, as muddy water filled in the low spots and made everything smooth. Trees swelled up with the water, and their heavy branches hung like drooping shoulders from the beating of the rain. Looking out the window, we saw a foreign landscape—we seemed to have been moved to another world. Everybody in the village began to feel uneasy, as if the earth under their feet might soon collapse.

The houses of the village were built in a slight depression on the top of a rise, and had not yet begun to flood with water. The village area was like a small dish that had been filled to the brim, however, and around the bases of houses flowed mud that was mixed with garbage from other houses. The refuse of toilets, of the pigsty, of the corral, had all oozed out and now surged around our homes. We were not yet flooded, but the muddy water was rising steadily. Some of the walls began to show cracks and a few of the

uninhabited buildings collapsed. Pigs of all sizes ran squeal-
ing through the lanes, looking for a place to escape the rain.
One by one, they huddled under the wet eaves of houses,
looking forlornly up at the sky.

I herded the twenty-four horses for which I was responsible into a large warehouse that was used for meetings. Since
the wheat was still unthreshed and the new rice unhar-
vested, the place was empty except for slogans. As the
animals squeezed in, they looked as though they were ready
to listen respectfully to a long report on 'Criticizing Song
Jiang'.

When the rain started, I had pulled two long poles over
to the house from the corral, and propped up our living
quarters from the outside. She had hot water ready for me
when I went inside, and solicitously handed me soap and
towel as she took my wet clothes.

'Good to have a man around the house!' She smiled
happily.

'Men—you can find them anywhere,' I answered. 'Material possessions are hard to come by but men are abundant.'

'Not necessarily.' In a change from her usual attitude, she
slapped me on the back. 'There aren't many men around
like you.'

My back cringed as I shrugged her off. 'Go on, to you any
man would do.'

I felt her stand stupefied behind me for a moment. She
didn't say another word. She spent the afternoon quietly
sewing shoes and making dinner, and only as we went to
bed did I hear her give a long, deep sigh.

The electricity was out that night. We were told that the
authorities were afraid that the bottoms of the wooden
electricity poles might get waterlogged and topple over, so
it had been turned off at the main switch. Inside and outside
were both pitch-black. In the darkness I wondered why I

190

still said things to hurt her, and I too let out a long sigh.

Around noon on the second day, just as people were beginning to think it would go on for ever, the rain suddenly stopped. It stopped as cleanly as it had begun, as if heaven had turned a central tap to stop the flow. Not a single drop was in the air, but the humid wind blew saw-tooth waves of water around land that had turned to marshes. Masses of huge black clouds still rolled in the sky, but towards their edges they were lighter, and gradually they parted.

We were all beginning to breathe again in relief, when suddenly from all four corners of the village came an ear-splitting whistle. It was penetrating and long, and felt like an iron rod boring into our eardrums.

'Quick! Hurry! There's a breach in the canal! Everybody get down to the canal—"marshal your forces"—to the canal!'

'Take a shovel, bring shoulder-baskets!'

Platoon leaders and team leaders went charging by in the mud, barefoot. Men and women came crawling out of houses to hear the news. No one really needed to ask: it was the same every year after the biggest rain of the summer. This time seemed worse than usual, however, and the workers hesitated, wondering what would be the best thing to do.

'Hell, if we all go who'll stay here to watch the house?'

'It's ridiculous! They don't even know how to give orders!'

'Let's wait and see if the big bosses go. If they don't go, then we won't go.'

'Right. If there's really a breach in the canal and the water gets up to here, there won't be even a bowl left at home.'

'And what about the children?' the women cried.

The big bosses were all on the move, however, shouldering shovels and running out into the mud-filled roads. Wearing plastic raingear issued by the army, Cao Xueyi threw back his head as he went running by and yelled, 'All men, out! Women, stay home and watch the houses. Don't forget, water has no pity: don't waste time trying to save things if the flood comes or you won't survive.'

Then his voice broke and changed its tone, and finally everybody knew that the situation really was serious. Grabbing shoulder-baskets and shovels, the men of the village rushed towards the canal in the west while the women ran inside to grab their children. They put them on the tops of the beds, and then sat there, waiting.

The team leader in charge of the herdsmen led all of us horse herders, pig herders, and cow herders to a shed to get gunny-sacks. These were to be packed with sand and stuffed into the breach. We were still far away when we started hearing the commotion of yelling voices on the top of the canal bank. By the time we scrambled up the bank, it was already crawling with people. The townsfolk of the nearby commune had come as well, in fact there were more of them than there were of us State Farm workers. Each team was paying attention only to that part of the canal that directly faced its own village, as if the water would not touch its town if it broke through somewhere else. Men were climbing up and down the side of the great canal, like ants crawling out of a hole on a rainy day.

It turned out there was no breach in the canal. Instead, the land to the west of the canal, outside the canal itself, had become a great expanse of water. Not a single tree or dry piece of land could be seen from where I stood on the canal bank looking towards the foot of the mountains. Large clumps of yellowish froth floated like icebergs over the surface; various grasses, rotten wood and what we called 'old crow firewood' were mixed together with sheep shit, swirling against each other in the water. The circling eddies of water looked as though they were trying to find the most suitable place to break on through the outer canal bank. Small gusts of wind whipped up the surface of the water into pounding waves which struck against the side of the canal. To farmers who had never seen the sea it was a terrifying sight.

The waters had come down from the mountains in a flash flood—they had not actually risen inside the canal at all. The flood-waters were on the outside of the canal bank, which ran parallel to the mountains to the west. The western side of the canal bank was fortunately serving the function of flood-protection now, but the waters were already within a foot of its top. If the western bank were to give way anywhere, miles of flood-waters would hit the eastern canal bank broadside, taking it out as well, and pounding through to wipe out several villages to the east of the canal.

The canal had not been built with a flood discharge tunnel, and there was no way to ease the growing pressure by channelling the water elsewhere. The only thing to do was move earth to the top of the canal, in a frantic effort to make it higher. People worked at first in a blind panic, but gradually a form of organization developed—line after line was formed to transport earth. People at the foot of the bank shovelled it into baskets, those in the middle moved it up, those on top were responsible for strengthening the rampart.

'We'll be all right if the water stops rising now.'

'The hell we will. Water this high is going to kill us if it decides to come through.'

'Can you float?'

'Who can swim? We're all dry-land geese here.'

'Well, don't worry—when you die you float naturally,' somebody laughingly tried to comfort the rest.

'You know, men's bellies face downwards when they drown, but women's face upwards.'

'Even then there's a difference between men and women?'

'Sure is, exactly like on a bed.'

Suddenly, a man on the bank of the canal yelled out, 'Look, what's that? Isn't that a body?'

Everyone on the bank followed the direction of his pointing finger, and there in the water was a corpse. It floated vacantly in the expanse of water, with its green jacket still on.

'Stomach floating down—it must be one of the sheep herders.'

'Damn, will you look at that. But where's the sheep then?'

'No, no—that man's from the forestry department up in the mountains.'

Everybody was even more terrified after the dead man had appeared. 'Faster, faster! Get the dirt up here. If this bank goes under, we'll all be like that bastard.'

I was one of those on the top of the bank, responsible for building it up. As the baskets of earth came into my hands, I poured them out one by one onto the outer edge of the bank, at the same time tamping the earth down with my feet to make the bank solid. In the freezing wind my body was strangely covered with sweat, as an unknown source of energy was added to my normal strength. I yelled continually as I worked, 'Move it over here, move it over here . . .' Whoever worked hardest was given authority over others. Distinctions among Troop Leaders, Secretary and ordinary workers had disappeared—at this point people were listening to whoever was most capable. We were in a situation of life and death, and the customary hierarchy had broken down.

194

'OK,' I shouted to everyone, 'it's not going to rise any further.'

'How do you know that?'

'When I came up I made a mark—see? More than an hour has gone by and the water hasn't passed that mark.'

'Hey, our Lao Zhang's a smart one. We just go ahead blindly.' The farm workers began to laugh appreciatively.

'Right.' Cao Xueyi was in one of the middle lines passing on baskets of earth, and he too began to laugh. 'We can take a breather now—whoever has a cigarette feel free to have a smoke.'

'Where would we find a cigarette? Everything's got wet through.'

'Take one of the Secretary's, he has high-class tobacco.'

'No resting,' I yelled. From my commanding position I gave Cao Xueyi a hard look. 'The greatest danger right now is if the water seeps through the outer bank of the canal. If a hole the size of a finger appears in the bank, the whole thing will go.'

'Correct.' Cao Xueyi hurriedly put away his cigarette. 'Everybody spread out and look for any holes . . .'

He had hardly finished speaking when a villager further down screamed out, 'A hole! It's broken through, stop it, help, stop it!'

'Bring a basket.'

'Somebody sit on it.'

'Captain, should we sound the gong?'

Some villagers gathered together in a confused group, as they rushed towards the water seething through the hole. People from our Troop also hurried over. If this stretch of bank went, both their village and our Troop would be the first to be destroyed.

The hole was the size of a bucket, and muddy flood water spurted out of it into the canal, making a sickeningly frightening pounding noise. It was as if the water were not liquid but a round, hard beam of metal. It had already beaten down everything in its path, and now it was pointing at the bank and smashing its way through.

The baskets of earth that the villagers had thrown on top of it were now being spat out in the form of mud, and the baskets themselves, now scoured clean, were riding along on the top of the pounding water. A number of villagers who had been sitting near the hole had been catapulted several feet away and were trying to climb back up the bank.

'No use trying to plug the inside of the canal bank,' I yelled, 'plug the outside, plug the outside!'

Not only had the strict work hierarchy been broken, but the line dividing commune and State Farm had also been erased. Villagers and farm workers were standing together, united in their terror of this hole.

The earth above the hole continued to collapse. The size of the hole increased with each second that passed.

The water on the outside of the canal bank was so deep that it was impossible to see the small hole where it must be entering. Anybody who has ever been in charge of irrigating paddies knows that the entry to a breach is much smaller than the exit. At least, it will never be bigger than the exit. Several villagers were lying flat in the mud, using shovels and poles to test the water and try to find the breach. They reached out until their shoulders were well into the raging water, and still there was no indication of where it might be. The bank appeared to be on the verge of collapsing before our eyes.

Looking out over the land to the east from where I stood, I noticed stovepipes coming to life in four or five little villages. The heavy smoke of firewood began to pour out into the clear air of the day.

196

'I'm going down,' I said. 'Find a rope to tie around my waist.'

None of the villagers could swim, and in their mounting fear they could hardly persuade their fingers to do the work. They untied the ropes attached to bamboo baskets and strung them together, tying one end around my waist. I plunged into the waters of the flood.

The water was three men deep on the outside of the canal, and as I went down I felt the uneven bottom. I was already wet through from sweat and had no consciousness of the cold. Feeling with my hands, I tried to find the opening. After I had gone several metres a great sucking force swung my legs around towards it. One foot was sucked inside the hole.

I thrashed out against the current, and managed to fight my way back to the surface, emerging amidst the branches and debris.

'It's all right,' I yelled out, 'the hole's only a little bigger than a wash-basin right now. Quick, pack a gunny-sack and throw it down to me. And throw that straw over.'

A gunny-sack brimming full of mud and piles of straw immediately came flying over. Pressing the sack on top of the straw, I once again dived down into the murky depths. Before I had time to push them in, they were violently pulled out of my hands and clamped into the hole by the force of the water.

When I worked my way back to the surface, a triumphant shout came down from the top of the canal, 'It's plugged! It's plugged!' Other voices followed, 'Like hell it is. What's that slurping noise?'

'Quick, now's the time to add earth—throw the sacks in there, right there.'

'Who is this guy? Is he PLA?'

'Forget the PLA! He's the one who herds the horses on

the State Farm over there. I've often seen him out there on the sandy flats.'

'He used to tend sheep, didn't he?'

'He should get a letter of commendation.'

Somebody hauled me up onto the bank as I crawled out of the mud. Looking up, I saw that it was Cao Xueyi.

3

I was the last to go home.

Families of the villagers brought over food and drink for the men at the 'emergency', and insisted that I stay and have a meal with them. The State Farm would never have been so generous: our cooks produced three meals a day at the appointed times and that was that. If you had risked your life in an emergency, who gave a damn.

'At least have something to drink if you won't eat,' a man who looked like a cadre encouraged me. 'Helps to fight the cold. Of course, I know your life's better than ours over there in the State Farm, you've got a regular salary every month, not like the few pennies we make for a hard working day . . .'

'That's right; if you don't drink with us, we'll say it's because you feel superior,' a man by his side cut in.

'Workers and farmers unite,' said another, not knowing quite what else to say. 'You workers are our older brothers . . .'

So I had to stay and spend some time with them, taking a few mouthfuls of food and drinking a bit of their alcohol. Towards dusk, I set out on the road for home. A beautiful sunset lit the road ahead of me, and the mud seemed to have dried considerably already. Insects came buzzing out in

199

swarms, not diminished by the rain at all. The croaking of frogs surrounded me as I walked along. It looked as though tomorrow would be a fine day.

As I approached the village, I could see that the electricity had been turned on again. Every family seemed to want to make up for yesterday's darkness, and to celebrate the narrow escape from catastrophe.

The cold food and alcohol of the villagers lay heavily on my stomach. The liquor had not been distilled from grains but probably from grasses or even gourds. Bitter and rough, it not only did not 'fight the cold', but right now it was making my whole body shiver. It also did not help my thoughts as I walked along. I was just a 'cripple', just a castrated horse—all I did was in vain, without any meaning. And yet there remained a ridiculous shred of vanity in my soul. A man could still comfort himself with 'heroism', never mind that it was used to save himself rather than others. With the minuscule consolation that I was proving myself, perhaps there was hope, perhaps I could still be saved.

I pushed open the door, and stiff with cold almost fell as I came inside.

She was standing in front of the stove kneading dough for noodles. In the light she looked like a branding-iron that had been heated to a scorching glow. She dropped the work in her hands and sprang towards me, and I felt the strength in her body as she half carried me into the inner room. Setting me on the bed, she deftly removed my clothes, and then tucked me under the tractors.

'Proves what you can do, but what tough guys were you showing off for?' She scolded me as she worked. 'All those other men of "superior backgrounds",* with their lofty

*Someone with a 'superior background' is from the 'poor farmer class'. Someone with a bad background is wealthy and educated.

ideals—why didn't they go in the water? I heard about it from the others when they got back—and all the time I was scolding you inside. You fool. Only somebody like you would go out and do a thing like that. You should have crossed your arms and stood on the bank and watched. Let the ones who are always yelling "revolution" get in there and do something.'

She ran quickly to the outer room and returned with a steaming bowl of ginger soup. 'Try it while it's hot. I made it for you ages ago. I've been waiting for you to get home. I thought you had drowned after the others all left . . .'

As she babbled on, I detected genuine concern in her voice. Women were unfathomable—was this pity, sympathy, or respect? Was it 'love' or simply a sense of duty towards her roommate?

My stomach warmed considerably after drinking the bowl of hot, spicy soup, and the icy feeling that had frozen me inside started to melt. My skin was chilled, however, as if it were still immersed in the flood waters. My whole body was covered with large goosepimples, like a nettle-rash— even my cheeks were covered with them. Kneeling by the bed, she began to massage my arms and chest. She worked them as though they were noodle dough in her hands.

'Why did you do it, unless you intended to drown! If you had drowned they might have given you a big memorial service—maybe they would have made you a Party Member posthumously. But to struggle to win some kind of "meritorious service", that's absurd. Nobody is going to put a good word in for you. People will even say you went down to make the hole bigger. Haven't your past experiences been enough for you? You know, you're just like a pig—you remember the eating but not the beating.'

The skin on my arms and chest began to relax and warm up. As it turned pink, for a fleeting moment, I felt a delicious shiver run through me. Her face was floating before me, like a beautiful kite . . . it was still better to have a woman in the house, I thought. Hadn't she said the same about a man? Perhaps that was what she had meant long ago by her 'two single families moving together to make a co-operative'. Thinking about it with my eyes closed, I must have smiled.

'What are you laughing at? You think I'm wrong?' She patted my cheek. 'Oh, feel that! Your face is still freezing cold, come, put it between my breasts.'

Taking hold of either side of her blouse, she ripped it open, and the buttons went flying. What I heard was not just the sound of buttons coming off—what she opened was not her blouse but her body. Two large mounds of milky white bared themselves before me, two lotus-like breasts. In the middle of each was a peony-red pistil. Both breasts and their red centres were larger than I had remembered, more fresh, more exciting.

I felt something I had never felt in my life before. Was this love? My arm reached out to wrap around her body . . .

'You're well.' Her voice floated up from the depths of deep water.

'Yes, I am. I didn't know myself . . .' and I started to laugh. I laughed a convulsive laughter, filled with sadness and a wild joy. The sound became louder and louder, until my whole body was shaking with it and I was crying.

'Can you . . . again?' Again the indistinct voice floated up to me.

'I can! . . .' I said savagely.

202

PART 5

1

The heat of summer had passed, but cold frosts had not yet settled on the land. The loamy plateau was as ripe and beautiful as Xiangjiu's full breasts. Water standing in the marshes was tranquil and clear, as if it had been made of quartz. I loved to send the horses running through it, watching it rise up in a million silvery splinters. After the horses had passed, the sun picked up tiny fragments of blue sky broken up by their hoofs. Sometimes I would give my horse his head and let him run. It was hard to make him stop after a wild sprint over the wide land. At those times, Milton's *Paradise Lost* would ring out beside me:

> *He spake: and to confirm his words outflew*
> *Millions of flaming swords, drawn from the thighs*
> *Of mighty Cherubim; the sudden blaze*
> *Far round illumin'd hell: highly they rag'd*
> *Against the Highest, and fierce with grasped arms*
> *Clash'd on their sounding shields the din of war,*
> *Hurling defiance toward the vault of Heav'n.*

The sky was transparent. The clouds were transparent. The light of the sun was brilliant and warm: in it, I too was transparent.

'My dear shepherd, I have felt a change in you,' the piebald under me said. 'Your grip on the reins has strength now, and your thighs are strong. The juice of a primordial instinct has flowed into your blood. I feel you are closer to being an animal, you have evolved.'

'Yes,' I said, 'and that's why I want to leave. I'm aching for action, aching to throw off all that binds me. Feuerbach kept himself a hermit for too long, and ended his own development. I don't want that—I want to see the wide open world.'

'You mean this isn't wide enough?' The old horse collected himself to jump across a small gully. 'Look at this sky, these fields, these plains . . .'

'This may be something that you just can't understand. I want to go where there are people—many people. I want to hear the sound of human voices. I want to talk to people about all I'm thinking.'

'And what about your wife?' The piebald lifted his head.

'I've been thinking about getting a divorce. First, I can't involve her in what I'm going to do; and second, there will always be a shadow over our relationship. Don't say anything—let's gallop for a while. Let me listen to the sound of the wind. If I shut my eyes, I can imagine you're flying through the air—you are Pegasus!'

Since I ceased to be 'half a man', ceased to be a 'cripple', a fire had burned in my chest. All my previous behaviour, including making allowances for her—'understanding' her—was not, as I had thought, the result of education, but the cowardice of a castrated horse. I now realized that the comfort and orderliness of her small household were designed to swallow me up. Now I wanted to smash it and escape: I had obtained what I desired, and now I rejected it. I thirsted for a bigger world. I was often agitated, filled with resentments and undefined regrets. They would melt away every time she satisfied me. Yet after each time, I felt ever more strongly the friction of an unnamed desire.

She would writhe beneath me, and use her fingernails to tease my body. Had she done the same with other men? Had others received the same satisfaction on top of her? Thinking these things, I would suddenly feel a greater stimulation, as the behaviour of love turned into the brutality of retaliation.

'If you don't think it's fair, you can sleep with other women a few times too . . .' she said hesitantly, shyly, one evening.

'I'm not like you,' I retorted. 'Any man's all right for you, but not any woman will do for me.'

'Then tell me what I can do.' Timidly, she tried to burrow deeper into my arms.

'There's nothing to be done,' I said coldly. 'You and I are going to break up sooner or later.'

My love for her was a mixture of attraction and repulsion. I wanted to comfort her and torment her, to love and hate her. Contradictions were coiled together, as hard to separate as they were to understand. My love was like a two-headed snake, eating out my heart.

'Get away.' Sometimes I would push her outside the covers and wrap myself up in them, trying to be alone. 'I can smell those other men on you right now.'

She would whimper, and the sound came from deep inside. The darkness of the room was like a grave, and the coldness outside was that of the netherworld. We lay in limbo on the borderline of the human world, without past or future, without thought. We were two living people who had already died, or two dead people who were still alive, unconscious. We lay in the Now, and in feelings that wrapped around us. The feelings came directly from the minute sensing of our nerves, and the messages from them changed a million times a minute.

'Don't cry, now. Your crying is enough to drive a person crazy. Come in and sleep then.'

'What you just said—was it just because you are angry?' she asked cautiously.

'It's human nature to get angry now and then.'

The nerves were vibrating, like a spider's web shimmering in the wind. Summoning up the courage, she said gently, 'Didn't we say before that we wouldn't bring up the past?'

'We're not bringing up the past!' My fury surged and erupted into words. 'What about afterwards—after getting married? How I regret not charging in, and taking the two of you and . . .'

The spider's web was smashed. 'Don't be like that, please don't be like that.' Terrified, she rolled off the bed and knelt beside it on the ground. 'I should die, I'm bad. It was only that one time—I'm being honest with you. "Come out with it and we'll be lenient, resist and it'll be tough." What more can I say?'

'Ha! That's true—except for the words of a criminal or an interrogator, what other words do you have!'

Even as I said it, memories flashed in front of me. Her words had summoned the past, which passed frame by frame like a movie of all we had been. In the beginning, we two had come from the same place. The spider's web hung limply, floating in the breeze. With anguish in my soul, I patted the pillow beside me and called her back . . . 'Come and sleep,' I said. 'I was only angry that you could . . . with him . . . What kind of man do you think he is? He's not like us.'

'I should die.' She sobbed into the pillow. 'But you don't

208

know, no matter what I did with those men before . . . it's only been with you that I felt . . . the feelings aren't the same.'

'Your feelings have always been too sensitive.'

'That's right.' She was eager to tell me all she felt. 'Listen to what I say . . .'

'I don't want to listen to you. I don't want to know about all those things.' I turned my back to her. 'I've heard people say before, "Never get married to a woman who's been married already—she'll always be comparing you to the one before.' "

'It's because I have a basis for comparison that I know . . .' she lightly drew two circles on my back with her little finger, 'know that you're the one.'

'Not necessarily. You can keep on comparing, me to the next, on down the line.'

'Even nine years ago, I felt you weren't like other men. In the reeds, in the labour camp, that day so long ago.' The hot breath from her nostrils brushed my bare spine.

'It's just lucky I'm not like other men. Otherwise I would have added three years to my sentence.' I snorted at her, 'You seem to have forgotten your own words.'

'I was lying when I said that . . .'

'How do I know when you're telling the truth? Which ones are the lies, I ask you. Forget it. Let's not fight. Go to sleep.'

She kept sniffling behind me, wearing me away. The tears of a woman are like the constant trickle of water—their gentle persistence bores through the hardest stone.

'Come,' I said, turning at last towards her.

What conspiracies was the darkness hiding at that very moment? What cunning tricks were being plotted, and what quiet plans to thwart those tricks? Under the white light of

209

bare bulbs, how many dossiers of how many people were being scrutinized? How many prisoners were waiting behind iron bars to receive their sentences? Throughout China where were the big-character posters going up—on seeing them, whose hair was suddenly turning white?

The rains had come.

The clouds, carrying their water, advanced with peculiar speed over the great sweeps of land, with nothing to block their way. Autumn is the season of rain, and when the sky changes, it changes swiftly.

Without waiting to block the sun completely, the clouds shot great raindrops like bullets to the ground. Pockmarks began to appear on its sandy surface and in a moment the fine dust and water mixed in a hazy mist. Then came a beautiful sight in the wide open country: the rays of sun shone out from between the dark clouds, every drop of rain carried its magnificent colours to the ground, and every blade of grass turned vibrant and golden.

The pelting rain excited the horses. They began to mill around, stung by the cold lashing on backs that had been warmed by the sun. Dumbo and I pressured them from two sides to get them to stay together, and tried to work them into the shelter of the trees. They jostled each other in confusion, however, and began to panic. Rear hoofs spattered mud into the eyes of the horses behind, who then trampled blindly on the horses in front. Suddenly, in the pandemonium one of the young colts broke loose.

Leaving the herd, he began to plunge wildly in all directions. He was a headstrong colt, driven wild by the wooden piece for fettering him that was still looped with a rope around his neck. His front legs kept hitting the wood in his panic, and the painful sound of bone hitting wood rang

210

crisply in the air. He neighed violently as he galloped about. I let go of the old piebald to try to grab onto him, yelling as I did, but he was not listening to any orders. Throwing me off, he plunged in the direction of the home corral.

It would be disastrous if he reached to the area where the unthreshed grain was stacked—he would scatter it to the winds with his trampling.

'This is all because he's not been castrated,' the piebald snatched a moment to remind me. 'Otherwise, he would be as obedient as can be.'

'Don't waste time talking.' I gave him a good hard whip.

'You've forgotten our philosophical discussion?' he asked resentfully. 'You certainly have changed.'

The colt was still galloping on. It was true he hadn't been castrated, and it was true that he was young, and both of these made him very much faster than the old piebald. By now he was approaching the oleasters and poplars that marked the entrance to the grain-threshing area.

'Faster!' Again, I laid into the piebald.

Just as the colt reached the trees, a white shadow leapt out and suddenly raised two arms to block the way. 'Don't try to stop him that way,' I yelled. 'Grab him by the wooden piece as he goes past.'

The colt charged straight ahead for the small white figure, as if there were nothing at all standing in his way. The figure stood doggedly still, firm in the face of the charge. Twisting at the last moment, it dodged the horse but gripped the wooden piece.

Slowed for only a moment, the colt shook its neck and stubbornly ran on, but changed its direction to angle off towards open pasture. The slight figure kept a death-hold on the rope around its neck, rump bumping along as it was

211

dragged upon the ground. The sheet of white plastic used as a raincoat was ripped off, and only then did I see that it was Xiangjiu.

'Hurry!' I squeezed my legs tightly around the old piebald and we flew across the ground. Coming up to the colt, I grabbed the wooden piece and the rope, and finally got him to stop.

'What are you doing here?' I demanded as I jumped off the piebald. I stroked the heaving sides of the colt to try and calm him.

She stood up, her entire body covered with mud. First retrieving the piece of white plastic that had been torn away, she panted as she explained. 'They blew the whistle at the Troop, calling everybody to the threshing area to help cover the grain. As soon as I saw it was going to rain, though, I put together some raingear to bring you, and just ran over here. That bastard Cao Xueyi saw me but he didn't call after me. Right now everybody's at the square working . . .' Excited and proud, she looked straight at me and said, 'Did I do all right?'

'You were fine, just great. You're a hero.'

I got to work taking off the fetter piece still hanging in front of the colt's chest, and tied his halter to that of the old piebald. The hard rain was passing, as drops came straight down now, even and regular. Our clothes were wet through.

'Get on.' With one hand I took the bundle of clothes she still clutched, and with the other helped her swing onto the piebald's back.

'Where to? Still not coming home?' She put her arms around my waist from behind.

'The rain may be stopping soon. Dumbo's still with the horses in the woods and everybody's working at the threshing area. It wouldn't be appropriate for us to go home now.'

212

Turning the piebald's head around, I said, 'We'll stay in the woods a while to wait out the rain.'

The sudden shower had not wetted the middle of the belt of trees. Filtered light made a chiaroscuro inside the woods, through air that was saturated with the fragrance of fallen leaves. Branches of oleaster and poplar crisscrossed each other above in a dense canopy. Grasses were still flourishing below, as if by hiding there they could escape the wind and rain. Crows gathered on the ends of branches, calling to each other in alarm and excitement. As they flew from place to place they shook down large drops of water, which painted the forest an even more verdant green.

'Hurry up and change your clothes.' I threw her the clothes which she had brought me and I tied the two horses to a nearby white poplar. The clothes had been wrapped in a plastic bag used for stuffing chemical fertilizer.

'What about you?' She looked like a mad woman, her hair wild and her arms akimbo as she stood defiantly on the grass facing me.

'I'm not covered with mud like you. See—I'm still dry inside. Now hurry, before you catch a cold.'

'Is anybody around? Where's Dumbo?'

'Just the ghosts and me,' I said. 'Dumbo's way over there in that far stretch of woods.'

She took my shirt from the plastic bag and smiled as she turned to face me. Then, without making any attempt to conceal herself, she took off every stitch of clothing until she stood there naked. I sat on a patch of leaves, smoked a cigarette and enjoyed the sight.

'You're still very beautiful,' I said.

Slowly putting on the shirt, she came to stand in front of me. She opened her arms wide and, kneeling, gently folded them around me. 'And you still say you want to leave me?'

She was very aware of her own attractiveness. Without

213

children and with years of vigorous work in the labour camps her figure had kept the beauty of a young girl. The large shirt draped over her body accentuated its slenderness. She pulled her wet hair back and tied it with a small handkerchief. She looked as though she had just come out of a bath. Her shining face gleamed with health and a seductive smile came to her lips. I didn't answer her, but threw away the cigarette and caught hold of her. For a second, I felt I was holding a patch of cloud, a swirl of mist—a spot of warm but formless steam. The large shirt had created a beautiful sensation of melting. She yielded to me, and carefully lay down on the bed of grass. I buried my face between the lovely curve of her neck and shoulder. I felt her small stomach, warm and firm. Her hair, her skin, the leaves, the fragrance of the earth, all mixed together in an intoxicating perfume.

From some hidden place an insect started whirring. A few yellow leaves floated down from the trees. The horses lightly clicked their hoofs together and snuffled gently through their nostrils. All the delicate and distant pieces of sound seemed like waves of rhythm, gradually building and becoming turbulent. To the background of a definite beat, like Ravel's Bolero, two melodies began to play, weaving through each other, rising and falling . . . Forgive me! Oh, understand me. Can you forgive me? Can you ever understand? My spirit is restless, and I hear voices calling me. This place is suffocating me—the village stifles and demoralizes, just as the nape of your neck seduces men. You've given me vitality, made spring glow within me again. But that vitality is now making me leave you. This spring can't belong to you . . .

After a while, exhausted and quiet, we lay on the grass.

'What are you thinking?'

214

'Nothing much.'

'Not thinking about anything?'

'That's right.'

'Do you ever think about having children?' She turned over, and propped herself up on her elbow.

I thought of what He Lifang had said, and answered, 'Yes.'

'Then let's adopt one!'

'Why adopt one? Better to have one ourselves, don't you think?'

'At our age? If we adopted a little child it would save us that many years of work. There are people in the villages over there so poor that they can't raise their children themselves. At most, we'd have to pay a little money to get one.'

'Where would we get the money?'

'I have it!' She laughed, happily.

'Forget it.' I did not want to keep it up and make things hard for her. 'Best not to have any child at all.'

'Why?' She pulled my shoulder around to look at me, and asked, 'You're still thinking of not staying with me—you think if you don't have a child, you'll be free. That's it, isn't it!'

I was silent. Her black eyes searched mine in alarm, but I could not very well close my eyes to them. The dim light of the woods seemed to have weakened, like tea leaves that have had the flavour washed out of them. I heard birds flapping their wings overhead, and heard their calls with a clarity that only open country could produce.

'Xiangjiu, we're living in a terrible time,' I said. 'I can't begin to fulfill the responsibilities of a father, whether the child is my own or not. Even the best families wake up in the night to find themselves split apart—brothers and sisters this way, parents that way—even the marshals haven't been

215

able to escape. I've seen it happen too many times. I've seen too much!' I took her hands in mine. 'Now is not the time to build ourselves a little nest.'

Pulling away, she rolled onto her stomach, with her chin in her hands, knees bent, her feet twitching as they pointed up to the sky. 'Why?' she demanded. 'Why are you so different from everybody else? It may be terrible, but it's just as terrible for others. Don't we eat and dress like everybody else? Why can't we raise children like the others? Even Dumbo is bringing up a little baby.'

'It isn't a question of whether or not we're able to raise a child. It's a question of my own self not being safe. Who knows when another Movement will come along? When one does, I'll be arrested and thrown into jail again.'

'If they send you in, we'll wait for you.'

'Ha!' I couldn't help laughing. 'Have you forgotten that you came out of there too? All right, let's not argue. When it's possible to have a child, I'll tell you.'

Branches waved back and forth above us and for a moment I could see through a crack to the slate-grey sky. A few balls of orange-coloured fruit hung from the oleaster. Still slightly juicy, they made my mouth taste sweet just at the thought of them. Drops of water spattered down on top of the sheet of plastic that covered us, forming small drops of crystal that rolled around as if they were alive.

Our bodies are pressed tightly together; your life leans on mine and mine on yours. Your passion and mine have to ignite in order for us to feel transported: for a moment we forget ourselves and are only us. Us! We are a wholeness, we are one life together. This is the significance of love, its content, its happiness and its materialism. When that moment passes, though, a small crack begins to grow between us: there are secret thoughts, there are small evasions, there are thoughts of leaving. You want to engulf me;

216

I want to escape. The mind again begins to fight against the body. Love is a net which take patience to create. But my heart is like that sparrow—you see it there, flitting from one place to another. Black clouds are rolling fiercely by up in the sky while we on the ground are kissing and making love. Are we merely apparitions, escaped from hell?

'Hei-tz has come back to town,' she said, tonelessly.

'Oh?'

'He brought something I had him buy for you, but right now I won't tell you what it is.' Crawling on top of my chest, she became more cheerful.

'What is it?' I asked, although I was not particularly eager to know.

'Guess. You wanted it a long time ago.'

'I can't guess.' I didn't remember ever having wanted anything.

A white-breasted magpie perched overhead and started to call, its handsome head turning this way and that to examine us, as if it were a zoologist researching the two animals lying below.

'It looks like we're lucky,' she said without enthusiasm. We were silent for a while. Then she asked, 'What do you write every night?'

'Nothing.'

'Is it a diary?'

'That's right.'

'What is there to remember these days? Each day is the same. Yet every day I see you writing page after page.'

I pushed her away and sat up. 'Listen, Xiangjiu, don't you ever tell anybody that I am writing things—don't even hint at it, understand?'

She sat up on the grass, leaned to one side and with a coquettish move brushed back her hair. 'I understand. I've never said anything to anybody. But would it be so bad if

217

you scribbled less of that depressing stuff? What do you care whether there are "rights of the capitalist class" or not? What do "rights of the capitalist class" have to do with us?'

'You've been reading what I write!'

'No,' she said, 'and even if I have I couldn't understand. I just saw a line that said something like the "rights of the capitalist class being above feudalism", something like that.'

'Don't read it if you can't understand.' I stood up. 'All right, let's put on our clothes—it's not raining anymore.'

We emerged from the trees leading the horses behind us. The sudden rain had left fresh air and clear skies behind it. To the west, rays of light still shone out from between the dark green ridge of mountains and a distant layer of grey clouds. Dumbo was both wise and stupid, and had moved the animals off to a distant patch of grass to graze.

'Damn it.' I mounted the piebald. 'If the animals eat that wet grass their stomachs will swell up. Come on, let's go.'

'I want to sit in front of you,' she teased.

'What would people think of that. You get on behind.'

'Who cares what anyone thinks? Besides, I want them to look!' I pulled her up to her usual place behind me.

'As soon as Hei-tz came back home, he and He Lifang kissed each other right on the lips in front of everybody. She said, "What are you all laughing at? On the streets in Beijing the foreigners are just like that.' " Then, scolding me, Xiangjiu said, 'It's only you who are afraid of everything.'

'Foreigners are foreigners,' I said.

As we went past the wheat fields, without objecting to what I had said, she let out a long sigh. 'Hei-tz said he'd come back after National Day, but he went twenty days over his allotted vacation-time and nobody dared to fine him a single cent. Nobody even dared to say anything. If we had done something like that . . .'

218

'That's right,' I said. 'You just remember what we are. We're not only people who can't do what foreigners do, we're people who can't even do what other Chinese do. That's our fate. Get on there!' I kicked the piebald, and we cantered on.

2

As I came back through the gate, I ran into Cao Xueyi inside
the corral with a stranger who looked like a commune cadre.
He had a jacket slung over his shoulder that was dripping
wet. Both were leaning against the rails, waiting.

'You're back—got wet, eh?' Cao Xueyi laughed as he
greeted me.

Without answering, I led the horses into the mucky corral
and together with Dumbo tied them one by one to the
feeding troughs.

Cao Xueyi and the commune cadre walked over.
'They're all here—altogether twenty-four head,' Cao Xueyi
told him. The man began examining them like an expert,
sizing them up and down, opening their mouths to look at
their teeth. As he looked, he shook his head and muttered,
'Not much to speak of, any of them.'

'What are you doing here?' I asked. 'Buying horses?'

'Yeah.' The cadre lifted his eyes momentarily to mine.

'Forget it,' I said. 'You think your farm has livestock like
this? The horses in the villages are all nags, they'd rather lie
down than stand up, rather shit than work, and their back-
bones are sharper than their brains. You see this one here?'
I patted the old piebald on the neck. 'Even if you paid good
money, he's not for sale.'

'Yes, he is,' said Cao Xueyi. 'He can have whichever horse he likes. If he likes them all, they're his.'

Astounded, I asked, 'The farm doesn't need horses any more?'

'It's like this: the bosses have said the whole country is to be mechanized by 1980. The people below them are even more enthusiastic, and they've moved the deadline up three years. Before the ink's even dry, everyone has begun to get rid of livestock. Seems to me this "mechanization" won't be happening for at least five lousy years—so if we need to, we'll just buy the animals back again. Who gives a damn about moving the money back and forth—it's the government's money, anyway.'

He shortened the distance between us with those words. I agreed.

As soon as I got home, Hei-tz, his wife and the Big-footed Philosopher came piling through the door one after another. 'Damn it all, Lao Zhang—the minute I came back they asked me to write a "criticism"—no way to get out of it. You write it for me, will you?'

'Me too!' the Big-footed Philosopher chimed in. 'What in the world is all this about? They even want Dumbo to criticize Song Jiang—who is this Song Jiang, anyway? And what did he do that was so wrong?'

'Song Jiang is Vice-Chairman of the Central Committee of the Party.' Hei-tz patted her on the shoulder as he told her. 'His crime is exactly the same as your Dumbo's: he won't talk.'

'Not talking is a crime?' She held a wad of paper in her hand, allocated to her by the head of the 'Livestock Team': paper for 'criticisms' had to be a uniform size, and there was also a time-limit on handing it back—just like paying the public grain tax.

'So it should be!' Hei-tz said righteously. 'Both talking

221

too much and talking too little should be crimes. Luckily, Dumbo is a stinking herdsman—if he were an official, we'd have to criticize him too.'

Unsure whether to believe what he said or not, the Big-footed Philosopher began to mumble, 'This world simply won't let people live in peace . . .'

He Lifang had combed her hair and cleaned up for a change. Today she looked glowingly healthy as she laughed, 'Hei-tz, quit fooling an honest old woman. Big sister, donate your paper to the cause—one sheet for each of us.' She neatly slipped the paper out of the Big-footed Philosopher's hands.

'Do I still have enough? Is this enough?' She was not quite willing to let it go.

'What, are you thinking of writing a whole dissertation like Yao Wenyuan?' Hei-tz asked. 'One sheet per person is plenty to dupe them with up there.'

'Leave a sheet for me too.' Xiangjiu was busy making dinner, but now spoke up. 'Our team asked me to write a "criticism" too. I forgot to mention it earlier to our Lao Zhang. Old Lady Ma and Lao Zhang are the lucky ones after all—those who have been "hatted" don't have to criticize Song Jiang.'

I washed my face and walked over to the table. 'Song Jiang should be criticized, because he butchered his old woman when she'd been playing around with other men.' Xiangjiu gave me a pinch as she walked by, and He Lifang shot a glance sideways at Hie-tz.

The amiable Hei-tz was plumper than before he had gone to Beijing. Squatting down beside me at the table, he began to speak in a low voice. 'Every blasted little alley in Beijing is filled with rumours. All talking about "criticizing Lord Zhou", "criticizing Song Jiang", all aimed at Premier Zhou and Deng Xiaoping.'

222

'Oh?' I lifted my eyes.

'Are they ever! You just watch—this Great Cultural Revolution is not over yet. If they don't carry it through and wreak total havoc, I'll be surprised.'

Picking out a sheet of white paper, I set it carefully in front of me on the table. 'Let's write,' I said quietly. 'Since it's not over yet, we'd better do as they say and criticize.'

'That's right.' Hei-tz pulled a newspaper from his pocket. 'I brought this for you to use as a reference. You can write down what it says here on the first page—just don't copy it word by word. Change the sentences around, that sort of thing. You know how to do it, anyway. Damn, just look at this quotation: "Song Jiang capitulates and becomes a Revisionist." I ask you, what kind of stupidity is that? Even I know that when Song Jiang lived there wasn't any Marxism, let alone Revisionism. That's really what you call pointing at the chicken and scolding the dog!'

I laughed at him, and said, 'You're so good at seeing through things, I'll just write down what you say—I guarantee you a superb piece of "criticism".'

'Oh, don't do that, don't do that.' Hei-tz put on a show of being frightened before breaking up laughing. 'People in Beijing all say that the leaders are carrying out a "policy for duping the people", and so we down below are also carrying out a "policy for duping people". It's the bosses fooling us and us fooling the bosses—no one speaking the truth.'

I picked up the pen, and said as I began to write, 'The first thing this Great Cultural Revolution has destroyed is not the country but the integrity of us Chinese. The legacy of that is going to cripple us for a long, long time.'

Hei-tz put one foot up on the stool and, quite taken with himself, declared, 'It's easy to live without integrity, harder to live with it.'

223

That was true.

I quickly wrote out five sheets of paper criticizing Song Jiang. Beaming with pleasure, Hei-tz took up the two for himself and He Lifang. 'Fine, fine. Listen to this, everybody: "Firmly and Resolutely Study from the Lower and Middle Poor Farmers!" Damn it all, that's just superb, Lao Zhang. Here, old sister, this is for you and your old man. Starting tomorrow, I'd better do my best to study from your Dumbo: he's the real thing, is Dumbo, a real Lower and Middle Poor Farmer!'

The guests all left in high spirits. She carried my dinner to the table, saying proudly, 'You write so fast! It would have taken them ages just to write a few characters.'

I shook my head and gave a bitter smile. 'Our lives may be hard, but they also have their small conveniences: everything has been arranged for us, we don't even have to use our brains.'

It turned out to be a transistor radio that she had commissioned Hei-tz to buy for me in Beijing.

She insisted on making me guess for half a day, but in the end I had to give up. I could not imagine why she would buy a radio—who knows what strange ideas lurk in a woman's mind. When I was getting tired of the game she pulled it out of a carton.

'Look, what's this?' She laughed as she held up the paper box. 'Hei-tz said it cost a hundred dollars—think it's worth it? Don't let him cheat us.'

'Worth it! Worth every bit of it.' This was the one thing she had ever done that exceeded all my hopes and expectations. I tore open the paper. 'Look, it's a three-frequency wave-band, and there's a line for an aerial, and it has earphones . . . wonderful. How did you think of it?'

'You mentioned it once.' She leaned against my shoul-

224

der, watching me. 'You may forget what you say, but I remember.'

'All right, all right,' I said, pushing her aside. 'Go close the windows.'

I don't know how or when it started, but radios had come to be associated with spies. They signified 'special agents' and 'counter-revolutionaries'. This had seeped into the awareness of every individual, so that anyone with a radio immediately was suspect. The small black boxes held unknown depths, concealed wicked worlds. The bright world of revolution was allowed to exist only in the broadcasts issued three times a day by the loudspeaker. Everything that one might hear, except for the loudspeaker, was to be considered a lie: the 'crying of false ghosts and demons'. But technology did not stop at the borders of our guarded country. It broke relentlessly through the steel bars of ideology. It held the world together in its net with invisible electronic waves, looping back inside pieces that had been sundered from the rest.

Greatly excited, I fitted the batteries, stretched out the aerial cord, and put on the earplugs. All the time, I felt I was committing a crime. I did not personally consider listening to broadcasts a crime—if one believed that the truth was already in hand, why worry about the people listening to lies?—and yet my hands were shaking uncontrollably as I tried to find a station on the dial. Waves were passing across the Pacific, over the Mediterranean and the Red Sea, over the highest peaks of the Himalayas, carrying the static of stormy winds all the way to my eardrums. That night I listened till all the Chinese-language broadcasts were finished.

The result was utter disappointment.

Foreigners in the West did not seem to have progressed in the past thirty years. With plenty to eat and plenty to

225

wear, they had not matured. We had been raised on adversity, experienced suffering. Compared with the great men these trials had produced, their Mechanized Men seemed immature. They had no conception of what politics could do—their awareness of its power was still at a kindergarten level.

They were blindly ignorant of the politics of mysticism currently being preached by our Eastern metaphysics. They were ignorant of the tortured ways in which it expressed itself, and the tortured minds that it produced. They were as uncomprehending, in fact, as the people of China had been when told that an American President had been hounded from office simply for listening in on conversations. Their analysis of China could only come from available reports: as these were issued by the existing regime, they were of the most superficial nature. Even Cao Xueyi and Hei-tz knew much more than what was in those reports.

That night, however, the Central Broadcasting Station of Beijing itself issued a very important piece of news. It was a famous 'Chi Heng'* article, entitled, 'Unite in Criticizing the Water Margin; Study Theory Deeply'. It included reference to 'the capitulating faction, and the road of capitulationism that has been known to us in the past, still exists today, and may still exist in the future'. This clause 'in the future' was not a shot in the dark: it was intentional, and it was aimed at a specific target.

'God damn it!' I pulled off the earphones. Exhausted, I threw the radio down on the bed.

She stirred beside me, and in her muddled sleepiness asked what the matter was.

'Not worth it after all,' I said.

*'Chi Heng' was the pseudonym for a group of professors and writers who composed the political announcements and writings of the 'Gang of Four'.

226

3

The piebald horse was finally bought and taken away, not by the commune cadre, but by another commune to the south. I heard it was a commune located in the mountains down there. Four farmers came up, bought all twenty-four head and drove them away.

That day was the first cloudy day since the start of winter, although it still did not look as though it would snow. A piercingly cold, dry wind was blowing. The sand, yellow leaves and dust of old horse-shit were picked up by it and blown about before ending at the bases of the walls to every house. A few black crows occasionally appeared out of the dark air, distracted, cawing. Fields which had been irrigated for the winter had begun to freeze, their surfaces contracting into the cracks of a chapped, pale skin. The trees had suddenly aged, their branches now bare. Only the oleasters still had a few tenacious dried fruits stuck to them, which shook in the wind. It was a day that seemed to freeze everything, even memories and hopes. It was as if this were the way the earth had been before man arrived, and as if this were the way it would be from now on.

On such a day the old piebald and his comrades were herded out of the corral. They took the familiar path after passing through the gate, and then took the branch connected to the main road. The piebald stopped for a moment and turned his head around to look at me, as if it were strange that I was not going along with them. One of the farmers gave him a sudden crack with the whip. Startled, he moved in the direction the farmer wanted, shaking his head but doing the bidding of his new master. The hazy greyness of the horizon waited as far as one could see down the main road. As the horses walked towards it, a heavy yellow dust slowly rose behind them.

Gone! My old piebald. How many secrets I have discussed with you, how many bad times you have seen me through. You have also seen my manhood restored. I am afraid I will soon be leaving, just as you leave. But unlike you, I won't wait for someone to come along and herd me into jail. There are indications now that the day my freedom will end is fast approaching. This too brief period of leniency is coming to a close.

After sending off the old piebald, I walked back towards the Troop, my path passing by the sheep pen. The sheep were being roused to head up into the mountains for their winter grazing. Zhou Ruicheng was there.

'The horses are sold—you'll be taking it easy.'

He laughed as he greeted me, but his laughter had a bitter ring. It had the tone of a beggar, the sound of somebody wanting something. It had been quite a while since I had paid any attention to Zhou Ruicheng, and I noticed that he had aged. An old sheepskin coat was slung over his shoulder, accentuating his curved back. His body seemed to have shrunk much closer to the ground. I walked over towards him, and we squatted down against the wall of the pen, sheltered from the wind.

'Isn't this the coat I wore last year?' I pulled the coat off his shoulder and had a good look at it. 'I see the sheep are

228

late going up to the mountains this year. This time last year we had already been up there a month.'

'They couldn't find anyone to do the job. No one was willing to go up in the mountains. You've shrugged it off this year—you have a family, so now I'm doing it together with Dumbo.'

'Don't worry,' I comforted him. 'It gets a little lonely up there, but the life isn't so bad—you can eat mutton any time you like . . .'

'Ha! So life is just a matter of eating mutton?' He spoke with that pointed little mouth that looked as though it were smiling and yet wasn't.

I was speechless for a moment—this was not the way Zhou Ruicheng usually talked. I intentionally put my hand on his knee and said, 'You just take along your er-hu. When there's nothing better to do you can amuse yourself with it. The winter will be over before you know it.'

'Yes, the winter will pass quickly, but spring-time won't be coming back.'

I was even more amazed, and shot him a sidelong look. I suddenly understood the significance of that begging, bitter laugh: what he wanted was for me to come talk to him. Pulling out a cigarette, I lit it and smoked awhile, then asked, 'What happened to your Appeal?'

'To hell with my Appeal.' With a complete change of manner, he spat out an obscenity. 'What should I appeal for? I tell you, I really regret things now. You haven't heard about it? Beijing's started a new Movement, called the "Counter the Rightists and Reverse Their Verdicts Movement".* They're starting with the education circles—you mean you haven't experienced it all before? All Movements

*This Movement was aimed at reversing the trend to 'rehabilitate' rightists.

229

start by twisting the knife in culture and education units first, and then go on to butcher everything completely.'

Butcher! Zhou Ruicheng could actually use that bloody and accurate verb. Unconsciously, I moved a little closer to him, afraid that he might start shouting his hatred out loud.

'You're the one who's better off after all,' he continued. 'You've been beaten down to the very bottom level, you've been sent to hard labour, you've been "hatted". Without anything to hope for, your mind has probably been more at ease than most. But me—I'm neither high nor low. I've been dangling in between, getting both the carrot and the stick. Only now do I realize it's all been for nothing. Don't you think that's hard to take? It's only now that I finally understand that political term they've invented—"to hang". It simply means to let a man hang himself.'

Amazing—however bad your situation, there would always be somebody around who envied you. It was a peculiar characteristic of the age we were living in. Since he still believed I never hoped for anything, I must have kept up a good show in front of him. There was no need to open up now and confide in him.

'Don't think like that,' I said with earnest stupidity. 'You've done "meritorious deeds", haven't you? They'll always remember you for that, and try to help you solve your problems.'

He spat violently on the ground. This man had changed extraordinarily—he completely betrayed the man he had been before. 'What "meritorious deeds"?' he said. 'Only an idiot like me would have done things like that. They pressed everything I knew out of me, pressed me dry. Then when I displeased somebody, they threw me out like an old, dry beancake, way out here, and forgot about me.'

Seeing that the herdsmen were not urging them to move on, the sheep lay drowsily on the ground or found corners

230

that were protected from the wind to stand in and think things over. They had been well fed in preparation for going to the mountains, and so they were not at all anxious to get out and find something to eat. One old sheep looked at me with fond eyes—perhaps he even remembered who I was.

Zhou Ruicheng's small mouth was working silently. His brows were knitted together, his eyes were dark and morose. He was sunk in memories.

'You think those days were easy ones for me?' he began again. 'From the time the "Loyalty and Honesty Movement" began in 1951, there was, as the saying goes, "nothing I knew that I didn't say and no end to what I said". All the way down to the Cultural Revolution it was always "Jianju!" "Jiefa!"* At first I turned them over to the leaders, later I turned them over to the "rebelling faction". I'm telling you, people being informed on have a lot easier time than the informers.'

'I don't agree with you there.' I couldn't play the fool on this subject.

'You listen to me.' He put his hand on my hand which still held its cigarette, and I felt him tremble. 'People being informed against have to endure only one excruciating moment, when the exposing material is actually placed in front of them. But informers are uncomfortable from the moment they begin to write that material. Time after time I've written reports—I can't even remember how many I've written. The leaders knew I was obedient, and that I understood things fairly well. I would probably write at least fifty cases in only one political Movement. All together, I must have written five hundred. My heart felt a kind of pressure as I

*'Jianju': To inform against others by reporting to the authorities. 'Jiefa': To expose or 'unmask' others in Criticism Meetings.

wrote each one. Lao Zhang, you can't imagine the lively young chap I used to be when I was young. I was full of life, full of fun. I played several instruments, I did sports—I could even do ballroom dancing. With each case that I wrote, I cut off a piece of my life. I did it to save myself, to make sure I could keep living safely—and for that I threw away the most precious thing in life. By now, I've become an inhuman man or a demon with human failings. I should have known that only sons of bitches write that kind of material. In the end, I've fallen into this god-forsaken hole . . .'

A little wrinkle had appeared at the corner of his mouth. Like a cruel line made by a knife, it pointed downwards towards his jaw. He was letting out all his suppressed anger, and he did not want sympathy. Nevertheless, I moved my hand from under his and held his thin, dry hand. 'Don't think like that—what's past is past,' I said. 'From what I've heard, some people falsely accused others and had them sent to jail. Some even had people sent to the execution ground. They themselves are still leading exciting, happy lives.'

'You're wrong.' He pulled his hand out from mine and made a violent movement to emphasize his denial. 'What kind of happy life could theirs be? I dare say that those men are the same as I am. There is no way they can feel that wonderful good fortune of a clean conscience. There's no way we can live now without a care in life. Maybe some people feel good about themselves—I don't know—but they still live just as I do, and it's a rat's life. Before a rat gets caught by a cat, it can feel pretty good about itself too.'

Dumbo appeared at the base of the hill, wearing another sheepskin coat and carrying a pack. He stumbled up the hill, coughing all the time into the wind. Dumbo had become thinner over the year, even though when he worked with me I always had him follow behind and didn't let him do any heavy work. If only he could let everything out, like Zhou Ruicheng was doing, he might get better. But then Dumbo had never had any education and only knew how to keep going blindly ahead.

Zhou Ruicheng stood up, and set his shoulders back. Seeing that military movement, I could visualize the man of twenty or thirty years ago: I knew what a handsome and talented young man he must have been. 'Going up to the mountains this time was something I asked to do,' he said. 'I'm willing and happy to go. Who knows, maybe when I come back out of the mountains, the world will have changed.'

'What kind of world do you think it might become?' I squinted up at him.

'Do you know who the target at the end of their spear is this time?' he asked me.

'No.' I thought it was better to let him say it first.

'Zhou and Deng!' His hand covered his mouth briefly as he muttered the three words, then fell away. His little eyes shone with a ghastly light. 'If those two go down, then the last little ray of hope for the Communist Party will be gone. Then it will be just like in the Dream of the Red Chamber—each will have to find his own escape route.'

'What would you do then?' I was curious.

'It won't matter much, because they won't bother with me for a while.' He looked straight at me frankly. 'I'm not like you: first, I've never done hard labour. Second, I'm not "hatted", and third, my family background is urban poor while you're from the capitalist class. Fourth, they still haven't wiped out my cadre standing, while you belong to the lowest class of farm labour. Also, I studied military affairs, and who knows in the future when they'll have to put weapons to use again. While you . . .' he returned to his sycophantish manner, using his finger to tap my chest. 'Lao

233

Zhang, do you remember when we spent time in jail together. The Captain would point at you and yell, "Zhang Yonglin! Don't think you can turn heaven upside down. All it will take is a small wind blowing across the grass from the Outside, and yours will be the first head they cut off to show the masses!" Naturally, he was only saying that to frighten you. He wanted you to obey orders, but what he said did have some truth in it. You had better be careful, Zhang Yonglin. Killing you would be like pinching a little insect in two. They wouldn't have the slightest obligation to report it, either—to any organization or to any person.'

Dumbo was still slowly making his way up the slope. The wind blew his too-long coat around his legs. Zhou Ruicheng watched him for a minute, then looked at me and said, 'You don't think so? Let me tell you, Hu Shimin and Li Yijun are good examples. Hu Shimin was Propaganda Chief at Division Headquarters. He started the work in 1949 when there wasn't a precedent, and later they killed him. When everyone was rehabilitated, there were no "apologies", no "memorial meetings". The Troop Leader even lost his position because of it—otherwise Cao Xueyi would never have been able to come here. I've heard that that particular lawsuit is still going on. Li Yijun was just a farm hand on the State Farm. He had done hard labour and been "hatted", like you, and he too was killed. Who is putting a word in for him, or for justice, now?'

This man who was usually taciturn and prudent had seen through everything. Remaining silent, he had remembered it all.

'Yes, you're right.' I shredded what was left of my cigarette butt into fragments. 'Actually, Li Yijun's death was a greater injustice than Hu Shimin's. You could rationalize Hu's death because he was already sick, but Li was full of life until they "rectified" him to death.'

'We actually saw those things with our own eyes when we were in jail.'

'Well then, what do you think I ought to do?' This man seemed to be very calculating, and I was in earnest when I asked him for advice.

'Lao Zhang,' although his mouth was ridiculously pointed, his words were honest. 'Chairman Mao got it right for once when he said, "Don't be afraid of having your pots and pans smashed." In the past, I was afraid of losing the security of my home—I wanted to protect my peaceful days, but it all turned around in the end . . .' His hands repeated his sentence. 'It's come to this mess—you're a smart man, you ought to know. As they say, "Of the thirty-six stratagems, the best is to run away." I'd get out of here if I were you.'

Dumbo approached, ending our conversation. Zhou Ruicheng went to meet him, and they began to rouse the sheep. Using short whips, they got them moving, one by one.

I helped them drive the herd towards the mountain path. As we shook hands in parting, I smiled at him and said, 'You and Dumbo together up there will be just right. In days like these, that kind of man is the safest.'

'Not necessarily.' He turned his head around, and gave me a meaningful look. 'The day when Dumbo opens his mouth is not far off.'

The piebald had set off for the east, and the sheep went to the west, headed for mountains layered with dark clouds. They spread sheep shit all over the trail as they went. The smell of it floated in the bitter cold, dry wind, until it slowly dissipated in the air. I never saw the men or the sheep again.

Returning home after work, I put the shovel behind the door and noticed my horse-whip still hanging in the corner. It had already collected a thin layer of dust. I ripped it off the wall, taking the nail with it, broke it in two and threw it out the front door.

'You're back?' She was sitting on a small stool, in front of a basket full of duck eggs. She smiled at me.

'I'm back.'

'The horses are sold—are you sorry to see them leave?' One by one, she was putting the duck eggs into an earthen jar. The jar had been filled with boiled and salted water.

'What do you mean, sorry to see them leave? I'm sick of humans, let alone of horses.'

The room was warm and bright and the lid on the iron stove glowed. I put my hands over it to warm them and closed my eyes, then placed my hot hands on my forehead and felt a wave of dizziness. This was home—this was the kind of warmth every man needed. What man had created soon wrapped around him and tied him down, however. This fire in the stove, these pots and pans, these two small rooms, were all given to me to enjoy, but I had paid the price of freedom for them.

'I'm pickling duck eggs for you. See!' She spoke from behind my back.

236

'What is there worth seeing?' I opened my eyes and turned my head to look at her.

She didn't seem to be insulted, just paused a moment before going on. 'Time goes by so quickly. Those little ducklings we bought when we were just married are already giving us all these eggs.'

It was true. The cat had also grown, and was now curled up without a care in the world on the warm top of the stove counter. Its eyes blinked sleepily as it yawned. This was the same grey cat that had darted out from between Cao Xueyi's legs that night. Like the old piebald, this cat had seen many things: what people fear most on this earth are other human beings—they don't fear animals, even if they are wild beasts.

She lowered her head, and continued to place the eggs in the jar. The duck eggs didn't sink to the bottom but stayed floating as a snowy white layer on the top of the salty water. In a happy voice, she asked me, 'I've heard that southerners love to eat duck eggs. Is it true?'

I snorted. 'There seem to be lots of things you've heard.'

She raised her head and looked at me, and the light in her eyes darkened as she cautiously rebuked me, 'You never let me forget what I've said in the past.'

'Words are easy to forget, things that happen are harder.'

With that, I flipped up the curtain and went into the inner room. I sat down in front of the desk made from half a door and took out a notebook with 'Red Guard Diary' printed on the cover.

The pleasure of writing does not lie in simply producing something. A good half of it is in the process of writing itself. Analysing, putting things together, reasoning and inferring, deciding: these mental activities are similar to physical exercise. You do not have to go after first place to be happy—simply by moving your muscles you can feel

237

yourself exercising your vitality. For almost twenty years I had not written anything properly, beyond the 'self-criticisms', 'self-analyses', the 'weekly thought-reports', a 'request for more grain rations' and that application to get married—plus a few 'great criticism articles' for others. Perhaps this was the purpose of my 'reform'—like skinning the pelt off an animal, I had to be scraped free of culture. Although the person being skinned undeniably suffered, for the hunter it was only a natural and necessary procedure.

Four months ago, after the danger of the flood had passed and I had become a 'normal man', I took up my pen again and tried to write. What appeared at the beginning was both contrived and obscure. I had to work on every character, like the ancients carving letters on bamboo strips. The drive-transmission between brain and fingers seemed to have rusted away. The words in my head could not easily be put down in writing. I would sit staring blankly, searching them out, one by one.

Gradually, as a result of exercise, the gears began to mesh again. Strange characters once more began to seem familiar. When there is no one at all with whom one can speak one's mind freely, solitary writing becomes the most effective way of continuing to think. Once a concept in the cerebrum forms itself into words on paper, becoming stroke by stroke a series of square Chinese characters, it takes on an independent and tangible existence. It leads you on to a new discovery, of its own accord, to the relationship between that concept and others that are to come. Slowly, the ideas are linked and matched together, random and chaotic thoughts are sifted through an ordering process of reason. Even the ravings of madmen and the mutterings of a dream can be set in order by the magic arrangement of a pen.

Besides the happiness of the senses, of tasting, seeing,

hearing, touching, there is another kind of happiness that the brain can set in motion. It is not a happiness that results from any consequence; in fact it issues from a deep place that hides from all the superficial vagaries of life. The only light this place has seen belongs to the flashes of man's intellect.

Being cast to the periphery of humanity is not necessarily all bad: one gains freedom of thought by it, and a certain purification of reason. This purified reason is like a phosphorescent light—it can't open up a new road, but it can at least illuminate the road ahead.

The road ahead was an increasingly perilous one.

Today I did not have the heart to write anything. It was more that my thoughts were confused than that my determination had finally crystallized. I closed and put away the notebook, and without undressing lay back on the bed. The soft collar of the jacket rubbed against my cheek. She had sewn it for me, stitch by stitch, and then proudly presented me with it. 'I'll bet you haven't worn such a warm coat for twenty years.' Ma Yinghua once gave me a pair of woolly pants stitched out of a carpet, but that seemed to have happened a hundred years ago. It was so long ago, I even wondered if it had happened at all. It had been very real at the time, though: women had a capacity for doing these things. They excelled in using a needle and thread to sew you to themselves. Wearing what they made, you would naturally think of them: their heads under the light as their thumbs and forefingers pinched the needle, as their little finger twisted the thread in that particular motion that only women have. Each stitch sewed in her warmth, her smell, her gentleness, her sexuality. In the end it was not cloth that wrapped around your body, it was her hot little hands, holding on to you.

'So life is just a matter of eating mutton?' Perhaps not, but

239

eating is a very important part, especially important to those of us who are poor. On the State Farm every person was given a monthly ration of one liang* of cooking oil. As soon as the first of the month came around, He Lifang would swear at the minuscule amount. 'Damn it all. The oil they give us is only enough to fill an eyedropper—one or two tiny drops is all I can use for cooking.' But Xiangjiu would save her one liang and use it all on me. She would heat a bit of oil with spring onions sautéed lightly in it, and then put that on top of my noodles at each meal. She herself would just lick the small spoon she had used to measure out the oil. This vulgar act was to express her great love and concern for me: she had to display her love, let me know unequivocally how much there was. In the same way, the pitiful ration of meat that the State Farm issued was all given to me. She would not eat the meat, but only gnaw at the bones. I often felt that this kind of love was a pressure and a burden, but she would comfort me saying, 'See how plump I am? I don't eat meat or oil, and yet I'm still strong and healthy.' Then she would ask me to feel her muscles, while she went on, 'I've heard it said that men need a lot more calories than women. You've been through the camps, and you still don't know?' This was something we both knew too well. Most of those who died in the labour camps in 1960 were men.

In short, the bachelor ways that I had once lived by had been completely replaced by family habits. To be more precise, they were her habits in which I was coached and trained. You could say that all my daily life relied on her; I had been spoiled. The warm padded coat, the freshly washed underclothes, the coverlet, the mattress, the sheets, the bed, everything in this room—not forgetting the Snow-

*A liang is 50 grams, or 1.7 ounces.

240

flower skin-lotion in its pure white bottle and the curtains at the window made from cheap cotton—all had come from her hands. Together, the objects hooked my life into themselves. She had created this little home according to her own concept of a household. She had placed me inside and I had accepted—I had become a part of it. Leaving it was not going to be easy, because I would first have to leave part of myself.

Without knowing what to do, I glanced up at the newspapers papered on the ceiling. They were densely covered with lines of words, yet not one line could explain life or guide a man in how to live. People had made a great show of being earnest during the last twenty years, and with great rectitude had spewed out nonsense and lies. The myriad words and lies created an unreal and yet terrifying world. It was as though I were living in two worlds, a world of my own, and a false world—and it was that second world that actually controlled my days, that decided my living and dying. I wanted to break through that false world, I wanted to break through my own current existence. But with the future so uncertain, at a time when great storms were raging, wasn't this world worth lingering in awhile? . . .

Suddenly, she ripped aside the curtain and stalked inside.

'I'm telling you,' she sat down with a thump on the bed, her face flushed with anger, 'don't keep hanging onto things in my past. You have things in your past too.'

Her apron was still tied around her middle, making her breasts unusually upright and large. She was rubbing lotion into her hands, turning them over and over as if painfully wringing them out.

'What?' I sat up, amazed. I had already forgotten whatever I had said that hurt her.

'It sounds like you want to use these things in my past as an excuse to leave me—well, I can use things about you in

241

your present, and neither of us will win.' Her eyes were filled with resentment and she looked as though she was about to burst into tears.

'What things about me in the present do you mean?' I should have realized long ago that she could erupt like this. Although she had always been placid and docile, she must have been slowly building up her strength. This fury had probably been simmering while she put the duck eggs into the brine. By the time they were finished, she was ready to explode.

'What do you write every night?' she asked. 'You're going to ruin this house.'

'When I don't have anything better to do at night then I write a bit. Does that matter to you?' I tried to stay composed.

'Yes, it matters to me. Yes, it does matter to me.' She began to yell. 'You know very well that you're not a bachelor any more. You have a home now, and in that home there are two people.'

I drew in a long breath: yes, there were two people. Why had I never thought about this point? I had kept her in the dark about what I did, and yet I was forcing her to take responsibility for it. Before I could answer, she began again, 'You must think I don't know. At night your body is beside me all right, but your mind has gone off to who knows where.'

This immediately washed the idea of explaining everything to her out of my mind. I smiled scornfully as I said, 'You must be joking. I told you long ago your perceptions of what goes on are totally different from other people's.'

'Don't act so dumb.' She looked grim now as she said, 'I told you long ago, the two of us can't make trouble. We can't fight things, and if you won't listen then you're looking for your own death. How many people do you think

242

have been sent into the labour camps just because they were keeping a diary? You still don't know those camps well enough? Haven't you had enough of the consequences of that particular crime?'

'No, I haven't had enough.' I had become brazen and obstinate.

'If that's the way you feel,' she said, 'then I'm willing to go along with you to the bitter end—just so you tell me you'll forget about things in my past.'

This stopped me, and for a moment I felt moved. This was a story that had been played out many times before in China. Should I tell her frankly what I was thinking of doing, what I was in fact already doing? Was she the kind of woman that could understand? I quickly glanced at her: pretty, sensual and also ignorant. She was a woman who could excite someone like Cao Xueyi, and she was the kind of woman who could be seduced by him. The image of a man came to my mind, a primary-school teacher who had written a poem in praise of love. The two of us had spent three years in hard labour together: he was in for 'counter-revolutionary opinions' and the person who had informed on him had been his wife.

My lips tightened as I said, 'Forget it. How could it ever get that far, anyway? Honestly, I was only afraid of forgetting everything I had studied in the past, so I began to write that nonsense in the diary.'

'Didn't you tell me before that you could never forget things in the past?' A whisper of a thin smile passed over her face, but swiftly disappeared, leaving a row of white, aggressive teeth. ' "Nonsense", you say. At least you know what you've written. Is there a single sentence in there that doesn't oppose the current policies? That doesn't oppose "criticizing the rights of the capitalist class" and "criticizing Song Jiang"? For better or worse, I've still been to middle school and I can still read. And that radio I bought for you: it was to let you listen to plays, to amuse yourself with. What do you think you're doing, when you put the earphones on every night, just like a secret agent?'

'All right, all right. I don't want to have a fight with you.' I wanted to stop her loud ranting, and I lay down on the bed to indicate a truce.

'Just what do you think you're doing? What do you think you're doing?' Her body was tight and she glared at me as the question came over and over, but she still held back the tears.

I want to leave you! Not just leave you, but leave this place. I remained quiet, however, as I stared outside the window. Something out there, in the far reaches of that grey sky, made me excited. A sparrow flew by, calling out in the cold wind. It was warm inside the room, but I would rather have been where he was.

'I thought you were like other men, that you were reasonable, not the "stomach of a dog and the guts of a chicken",' she went on. 'I tell you, I've watched you so many times when you were sleeping, caressing you, loving you . . . and now it turns out you're a man with no brains at all. At least you're better now, now that you're a man—and it was only that one time before for me, but you always grab onto it and use it to pressure me. I'm telling you, it isn't that simple. If I tell the bosses just one word about what you've been writing here, then you, Zhang Yonglin, will no longer be Zhang Yonglin. Do you think I'm a fool? You think I don't know what devilish ideas you've been hatching? You think I'm that easy to throw away? You just try!'

She began to sniffle, and the sound both moved me and made me angry. I did not want to look at her, but she insisted on staring straight into my face. When she was meek and gentle she was like a small cat, curled in my

244

embrace, letting me stroke and caress her. But when she was provoked, she was like a fighting cricket: she squared off face to face, ready to struggle until one or the other died. Her eyes were dark and determined, but tears now zig-zagged across her cheeks. Yes, this was Xiangjiu. 'Love,' that word repeated *ad nauseam* in tedious novels, had never once crossed her lips. Yet in front of me was her love: both wild and demanding. Love was something that made a person both want and despise it. One could not live without it, and could not live with too much of it.

'You say "just that one time",' I laughed coldly. 'If you want to kill somebody, all it takes is one thrust with the knife. That "one time" of yours hurt me too deeply, and can't be put right now. If you're thinking of reporting on me, I just wonder if you dare. If you say just one word about me to other people then you and I are no longer man and wife.'

'You just see if I dare or not.'

A momentary doubt and alarm appeared in her eyes, as she wondered how to retrieve the situation, but at the same time she didn't want to appear weak. She had read the coldness in my eyes, but not the reason. She didn't under-stand me: she still thought that I was a part of herself, and as a result she didn't understand even herself.

'If you just bring up my past one more time, you'll see if I dare or not,' she repeated.

'My past and your past are two completely different things,' I said. 'You can't compare them. So you're still thinking of using that to try and blackmail me?'

'Oh! So now you call it blackmail, do you?' She suddenly became righteous, as though there were nothing in her to blame. 'And what are you thinking of yourself? Do you think it's so easy to cast me off?'

'No, I hadn't been thinking of casting you off. But now

245

that you say these things, I don't see what else I can do. It's clear you've been thinking about reporting me for some time.' Sitting up cross-legged on the bed, I reached in my pocket for my cigarettes. I had to have an excuse, and there would never be a better one than this for leaving her.

She was so angry all of a sudden that her face went white. Her body seemed to coil itself as she finally made up her mind. I thought she was getting ready to jump on me but, like a cat, she leaped over towards the bookshelf. With one swoop she snatched up my notebook, and hugged it tightly to her chest.

'You don't have to grip it so tightly—nobody's going to try and take it away.' With that, I lay back on the bed and lit my cigarette. I threw the match towards the door and in the same motion pointed at it. 'If I see you go one step towards the door . . . just one step . . .'

I knew she could not do it, but at the same time I wished she would. I needed her perverse behaviour to salve my conscience. When you're thinking of leaving a person it's best to let that person do something to hurt you first. 'You just try it—if I see you go one step . . .'

'Well, are you going to bring up things in my past again or not?'

'Why not bring them up? I've already said that's something different.'

Her face changed so totally that it was almost unrecognizable. It went strange—it was the face of someone who has lost the power of reason. Hugging the notebook and crying now, she ran for the door. I sat bolt upright, threw away the cigarette and listened to what she was doing. She had run into the outer room, crouched down by the table, and begun to cry loudly. I heard the sound of the flower vase smashing onto the floor.

The rift was now made—should I close it over or make

246

it deeper? I stood dizzily at the edge of it, looking over into its depths. A great force seemed to be pulling me down. Only by throwing myself in would I ever break through both worlds. I would then find myself either in a new land or back in jail.

Pretending to be flustered, I jumped off the bed and in two steps strode into the outer room. I acted as though I were going to pull the notebook away from her. She had come this far and no further. I had not guessed wrong, for she jumped up when I came towards her. With the notebook held tightly, she headed for the front door, as if she would immediately take this 'evidence of a crime' to the bosses and report on me. I seized hold of her as she struggled violently. Her soft body, which in the past had aroused my passion, had become rigid and inflexible, full of enmity in my arms. I reached for the notebook; her hands gripped it in a death-hold. As in a play, the two of us pulled back and forth. But the script for the scene had suddenly ended: unsure of what to do next, the actors hesitated. They must now depend on their instincts to play their characters, as they made the fake play into a real one.

At that moment the door was pushed open, and dodging sideways past us, Hei-tz slipped into the room. Caught by surprise, we still held fast to the book. With one glance, he saw clearly what it was we were fighting over. He pulled her hands away and shouted, 'You let this go! Huang Xiangjiu if you have something to say, you'd better say it . . .'

She shoved the notebook at me and fled crying into the inner room.

Hei-tz winked at me. I stuffed the diary into the pocket of my padded coat, calmed my breathing for a moment, and then walked outside with him. The winter wind was exhibiting its authority, howling loudly as it blew the garbage of the town out onto the plains. Thick clouds of yellow dust

247

swept towards the bare trees from the dirt road leading out of town.

We found a corner out of the wind and squatted down together—each pulled a cigarette out of his pocket and quietly lit it. After smoking a few puffs, Hei-tz screwed up his eyes and said, 'I didn't see a thing, and I don't know a thing. I'm also not asking you what was written inside that notebook.'

He thought for a moment, and then spat out a large gob of spit. 'I've been through this kind of thing before. It was when I was a Red Guard, damn it all, on the streets of Beijing. This damn bitch took some notebook that her man had written, and she passed it over to me so I would "report". Hell, I was a fool then, I didn't think twice. I figured it would do me good to pass it on to the bosses. The man was found guilty and sentenced, and the bitch was awarded a divorce.

'Lao Zhang, it doesn't matter if a woman's lazy or if she's greedy. But god help you if she's KGB. Just think, every night you're hugging a time-bomb. I told you a long time ago, that woman of yours needs a good beating. And I also told you the bitch is on good terms with that bastard. I remember I was pretty annoyed with you then, but I figured she must be holding something over you. So this is what it was! Lao Zhang, how can you still want that woman? She'll send you into the camps again any time she wants. You have to think of a way to get rid of her . . .'

The lanes of the village were empty, as if the people had been blown away by the wind. After just a couple of puffs, my cigarette had already burned itself halfway down. Who could understand my feelings? Nerves could not be plugged into like electricity, to be transmitted to someone else. One's circumstances would always seem very simple to anyone looking in from the outside.

248

'Thank you, Hei-tz,' I said. 'You've helped me a lot. I'm still not sure what the result of all this is going to be . . . and as for her . . .'

What result could there be? I knew that she would not carry the issue any further after tonight's emotion. A woman's anger is like a river flowing out into the desert: at the beginning it is turbulent and surging, but after it has run on for awhile it begins to disappear. Angrily, I threw away the cigarette, which tasted of tar.

'Damn!' Hei-tz suddenly shivered in annoyance. 'All this almost made me forget. The thing I came running over to tell you was that this afternoon, when you were out working, the loudspeaker announced that Premier Zhou has died.'

'No.' Watching his face, at first I did not fully comprehend what he had said.

Too soon!

I pushed open the door, and with the same motion took the shovel from behind it and firmly propped it shut. Then I strode to the side of the stove and removed its lid. Inside the coal was crackling and alive, the flames were red. It was glowing like the eye of a one-eyed dragon. I pulled out the notebook from my coat pocket and ripped off the plastic cover. Sheaf by sheaf, I tore out the pages inside and threw them into the flames: Read that! Investigate that!

The paper spat out yellow tongues, then turned black, then white. Ashes fell onto the burning pieces of coal, which still glowed with light, like a spirit that could breathe. The burning words had a life of their own, they were my heart's blood, they were a chemical compound produced from my brain. Now relegated to the fire of the stove, they still moved restlessly back and forth. 'Paper, if you're going to burn, burn! Those marks written on you are permanently etched on my brain. It won't matter if I roam all over the world, or if I am put behind bars again—I will remember you, as a person can always recognize his own child. There will come a day, there must come a day, when I will take you out openly, in front of other people. "The winter will pass quickly, but spring-time won't be coming back." No, I don't believe that—I believe that spring will come.'

She was still in the inner room, and I couldn't hear what she was doing. After a while she probably smelled the burning paper and she quickly stepped outside.

'What are you doing?' Her whole body was shaking as she ran over and tried to pull the remaining pages out of my hands. I elbowed her aside, 'What do you think I'm doing? Do you still want to get some merit points?'

Her eyes opened wide, staring at me as if I were a stranger. Then suddenly limp, she dropped onto the stool.

'Zhang Yonglin, you are not going to die well. You've got a lot wrong in that head—did you really think I could go and do that? I am a human being too.'

She was painfully wringing her hands, her lips were pulled back in a grimace and her red eyes stared into the flames. Tears poured soundlessly from her eyes.

I know you couldn't have done it, but I must still do this. Because I love you, I can't stay on with you. I have to hurt you, hurt you so much that you put me out of your mind.

'Finished!' I stuffed the last wad of paper into the stove. 'And the two of us are finished too.'

5

The villagers walked in groups of two or three as they returned from spreading fertilizer on the fields. They were lively and stepped briskly, the energy they had kept back during the day emerging as the evening came on.

He Lifang came chugging up breathlessly behind me. 'Lao Zhang,' she said, 'I heard you and Huang Xiangjiu are getting a divorce?'

'What do you know about anything?'

'What don't I know?' She laughed, as though this were a lighthearted matter. 'Everybody knows. Huang Xiangjiu came running over to our place later that night, asking me and Hei-tz to plead with you.'

'What did Hei-tz say?'

'Hei-tz didn't pay any attention to her.'

'And you?'

'I feel so sorry for her.'

He Lifang had sent her only child off to Beijing, and now all day long she would ramble around the Troop, looking for gossip. Sometimes she would go out in the morning without even combing her hair or washing her face. Her greatest interests were eating and drinking and the relations between men and women.

'Why do you want to get divorced?' She followed the conventional order in asking her questions.

'Why should I tell you? After all, you're not a Leader.'

She laughed, 'I know anyway, even if you don't say anything.'

'If you know, you don't have to ask.'

'Ah, women.' She shot me a coquettish look. 'Lao Zhang, you don't really understand women. It doesn't matter how many men she's slept with before—in her heart Xiangjiu loves only one. Do you believe me?'

I did not answer, just kept walking and minding the road ahead.

'Take me, for example.' Full of energy, she turned the conversation around to herself. 'I'm telling you the truth— I've slept with lots of men before. But in my heart I only love one and that man is Hei-tz. Do you believe me?'

'I believe you,' I said.

'Well then, isn't that the answer?' She seemed to think the entire question was already resolved.

'What I don't understand is, if you only love Hei-tz, why do you sleep with so many other men?'

That didn't stop her at all, as she giggled, 'You just don't understand us women.'

'You're right, I don't understand,' I admitted.

The light was particularly clear today, like the weather at the beginning of spring. There wasn't a cloud in the sky, not even a haze over the mountains. In the distance you could see a small patch of exposed stones lying in a valley between the ridges. Last year at this time I was up there tending sheep, I thought, while this year here I am discussing divorce. After ten years of a mechanical life that had passed as though it were a day, these changes made me dizzy. I felt again that this year had been a dream. All that had passed seemed like a dream, and all that was yet to come also seemed like a dream . . .

'None the less, she's the kind of woman you couldn't

252

want.' He Lifang had a strange way of pleading with me. 'Why?'

'First of all, she can't have a child. Second, haven't you heard people say, "The more a woman divorces the brassier she becomes, the more a man divorces, the more cowed he becomes"? Women who have been divorced several times are not stable, not like me. Third . . .'

'Get out of here.' I stopped and frowned at her, shooing her away with my hand. 'You go your own way. Don't come bothering other people.'

'Look at you, all upset.' Her face was still full of smiles and laughter. 'I want to tell you something, this woman . . .'

'Are you going or not?' I took the shovel down from my shoulder and shook it at her. 'As for women, maybe my understanding is a lot better than yours.'

Not in the least offended, she grinned a toothy smile at me. Off she went, humming 'Sending You a Rose'.

I had thought I was bringing up the rear, but behind me came Old Lady Ma. As usual, she had her arm crooked around a bundle of firewood. From her pace, she seemed to be trying to catch up with me. I stood beside the road and waited for her.

'Suffer, oh how I suffer!'

Like the female character in a Beijing Opera, her voice came singing across to me in a melodious rise and fall. From the expression on her face, though, she did not feel any hardship at all. The wrinkles that had crawled all over her face bore smiles. She raised her head, stuck out her chest, and as she walked her feet had the kicking vigour of a female donkey. I thought of the saying she was always coming out with, 'A woman walks with her head down, a man walks with his up.' Whether I have troubles or not is all in the way I walk down the road.' This saying was meant to describe the general difference in character between a

253

woman and a man, and had nothing to do with Old Lady Ma, but if she wanted to understand it in her own way, that was up to her. She had analysed her own troubles, and felt that in the midst of them there was happiness.

'Lao Zhang, why do you want to divorce Xiao Huang?' she caught up with me and asked.

'Don't go back to that. Enough people have been asking,' I said. 'Funny how right now everybody seems to want to get involved in other people's troubles.'

'Everybody's concerned about you, that's all.' She looked levelly at me. 'Even though you're "hatted", nobody thinks of you that way.'

'You're right, everybody is very good to me,' I said in an undertone, 'but as soon as a Movement comes, faces change. It's hard to arm-wrestle with a leg—you know you're going to lose. Everybody has to protect himself. After all these years, you know it yourself—people's faces turn to the leader's tune.'

Making her lips very small, she furtively asked me. 'Is another Movement coming?'

'You're really out of it,' I laughed at her. 'It's already here. It's called the "Counter the Rightists and Reverse Their Verdicts Movement". Hey, what about that Appeal you were writing? Have you had an answer?'

'No, luckily I didn't write it.' She became happy, as though she had won the coloured ticket as a prize. 'Back then, Huang Xiangjiu couldn't phrase it very well. Then we asked you, but you wouldn't write it at all. I wanted to have Zhou Ruicheng do it, but the old guy just hemmed and hawed, putting it off today until tomorrow, and tomorrow until the next day. I got angry: forget it, I said, take what life's arranged for you.'

'You should count your lucky stars,' I congratulated her. 'If you'd been rehabilitated, you would now be one of the

254

"model examples" in our Troop for getting your "Verdict Reversed".'

'What about you?' She pointed at me with her chin as she asked.

'Is there any need to say it? Even without writing an Appeal, they'll still say I need my "Verdict Corrected". In this world, I've already been pre-registered for every Movement.'

She let out a sigh. 'And things had been pretty stable for a year.'

I laughed and warned her, 'That's something you don't want anybody else to hear you say. Recently the slogan has been aimed directly at what you just said: "Take the three Directives as the Programme, since stability and unity still require class conflict." You had better be careful.'

'Yuck.' She stuck out her tongue. 'How can you explain something like that? Wanting both stability and struggle?'

'You go work it out for yourself,' I said.

'Well, if it's like that, Lao Zhang, you'd better not leave Xiao Huang.' She lifted up a finger at me, plotting on my behalf. 'Just in case there's a "three longs and two shorts", if you were sent in, like in 1970, there would still be someone to send you clothes, and something to eat.'

'I should have a wife just so she can send me food in jail! These days are hard to believe.'

Luo Zongqi told me to get married so I could write a dissertation; Old Lady Ma begged me not to get a divorce so that I would have someone to send me food in jail. These were the current concepts of a family. I could not restrain a bitter laugh.

'Well, what to do?' Old Lady Ma also laughed. 'It's just life. I'm telling you that Xiao Huang—that woman has a bitter fate.'

'How do you know?'

255

'You haven't noticed?' Old Lady Ma said mysteriously. 'Right on her mouth, just between her nose and her lip, there's a tiny, thin line . . .'

'No, I hadn't noticed.' Amused, I said, 'Come on, let me see if you have one too.'

'You rogue, you.' She laughed and pushed me away. 'How could I have one? I've only been married once. It's only on people who have been married several times.' Her tone suggested she was envious of those who had this distinction.

She sighed again, 'You also haven't got any conscience. After all, you and Huang Xiangjiu are a "Catastrophe Couple".'

'How can we be considered a "Catastrophe Couple"? When we were married it was just as you said, a comparatively stable time. Don't you remember?'

'Anyway, you still don't have any conscience. Huang Xiangjiu did everything to feed you, to make things for you to wear, what could you fault her for? Have you forgotten how when you used to finish a little late, you would go to the door of the collective mess with that ricebowl under your arm, just like a beggar? And your clothes! All patches, just like an old camel whose hair was falling out. Now,' Old Lady Ma raked me up and down with her eyes, 'look how stylish you are.'

Perhaps she thought of her own fate then, as her eyes took on a far-off, sad look.

'Yes, how could I have forgotten?' Deeply saddened myself, I said, 'But I must say, it's not because I have no conscience, and it's not because I'm evil. It's because I have to think of myself. Things are beyond our control these days—to survive you have to think of yourself.'

She was sitting alone in the outer room.

She had not gone out to work for several days. If she was

not lying on the bed sleeping, she was sitting on the stool, looking blank. A thin layer of dust had settled on the various things in the two rooms. Even the snowy whiteness of the bottle of lotion had lost its sheen. Entering the room, one saw that its brilliance had been greatly diminished, even though outside the window the sun's rays were beginning to tease out the colours of spring.

She watched me come in, and gave me a cold, hard look. Her lips moved several times, but she did not say anything—she just sat there. She had become noticeably wan and frail. Like everything else in the room, she had lost her lustre. I surreptitiously glanced at her nose, but could not see any line between it and her lip. I did discover, though, that a row of creases had been added to her forehead, like the lines of a declaration, or a long string of dots of omission.

It required an effort not to go over and comfort her, to stroke her: since I was already preparing to devote myself to a cause, why add to her bitter memories? I took off the cotton-padded coat, washed my face, and rolled up my sleeves, showing that I intended to use the empty bowl that was sitting on the cutting board to get dinner for myself.

'You planning to make something to eat? I've already got it ready for you, it's keeping warm on the side of the stove there.' Quiet for a moment, she added, 'Don't worry, even if my heart were worse than it is, I still couldn't poison you.'

On top of the pure white rice was a fried duck egg. In the winter there was not much in the way of vegetables, but the chicken and duck eggs raised by the farm labourers were the best food they knew. Frying this egg must have used up at least half a liang of oil, I thought. Next to the fried egg were some braised salted vegetables, chopped very fine. On their deep green colour lay the bright red of a small pinch of hot pepper. The three primary colours of red, green and yellow combined to produce a depressing starkness, taking away my appetite. When we were getting married, Old Lady Ma had bragged about Xiangjiu, saying, 'A clever wife is one who can pickle up a good batch of salted vegetables.' But today she had said that Xiangjiu had a 'bitter fate'. Could it be that a 'clever wife' and an 'intellectual' put together were bound to have bitter fates?

It was hard to make the food go down. My chopsticks picked out the rice grain by grain. I suddenly understood: these days she was giving me all our tiny ration of rice, taking care of this 'southerner'. Although I had already been 'reformed' out of any southern habits, I couldn't help but raise appreciative eyes to look at her. She was still sitting by the side of the table, her back towards me, slightly hunched over, her two hands folded on her lap, like a work of art by Michelangelo. The rays of early summer came through the window, making a halo of softness around her. The scene cried out to me, 'You must remember this! You must remember. In the future, when you think over and over about this time, you will carry the sorrow and grief of this particular memory. You must remember this. Keep all of it locked inside your mind.'

In the evening, we went to bed without a word. After turning out the lamp, she suddenly drew a deep breath, and said, 'This home is finished, I know it for sure now. Today our ducks and the cat disappeared. They're smart, those little things, humans have nothing on them. When a family is breaking up or people run into problems, they know it before anyone else and they get out early.'

It seemed that her voice was coming through a very thick blackness before reaching my ears. It was a voice that had had all the colour of emotions filtered out of it by the darkness, so it seemed flat and bare and without any strength. If a dead person could speak, it would speak in a voice like this. My entire body went cold. Into these two rooms had bored a supernatural force, which quietly lifted the heavy curtain of time, and displayed for us a frightening glimpse of the future. I held my breath under the covers, waiting for her next words, but she did not speak again.

After a long time, I summoned up courage and asked, 'The cat and ducks have disappeared?'

She didn't answer.

'Just today?'

She still didn't answer.

'Strange!'

She didn't make a sound.

I was frightened, but I could still hear the thin, silky sound of her breathing, as it circled around this home that was soon to be 'finished'. After a while, the rhythmic breathing, one strong, one weak, began to float in the air like gossamer. It slowly coiled up like a snake, and became a faint blue ring of light. At first glance, it was like a completely full moon, but looking straight at it, it became the muzzle of an enormous gun. In the middle of the circle of light was an impenetrable blackness. At the very end of the blackness was one bullet, pointing straight at me. Terrified, I struggled to escape. As I struggled, I became that lost grey cat, on the stove, on the cutting board, on the table, leaping from place to place to get away. Wherever I jumped, the muzzle of the gun still pointed at me. Swiftly, I turned into the ducks that we had lost, shrinking into the inside of the ducks' nest. The gun blocked my way, pointing at the corner where I was hiding.

Turn into a mouse! No sooner had I thought it than I was a mouse. As I was scrambling for the hole, however, an army of little people ran out of it. The size of soybeans, they carried small flags and lifted high banners covered with slogans. They ran chaotically as they emerged from the hole, spraying like bullets in all directions. They were yelling as loudly as they could, opening wide their pitiful little mouths. I could not understand what they were shouting, so I told myself: they have just been changed into men from being mice, so what they are saying is still in the language of mice. They took no notice of this one big mouse, as group by group they charged, highly agitated, past my face. Soon they had all run off. Only one small person remained, who had fallen down on the ground before me. His face pointed upwards and all four limbs shook uncontrollably.

I moved my face closer to look at this small person, and discovered it wasn't really a small person but an abandoned child. It was a child that I had seen by the side of the road, as I walked towards Xinjiang in 1960. The child's face was full of wrinkles, like an old man without a beard. Crying loudly, he shouted out, 'I am a widow! I am a widow!'

The child was then corroded by its tears. The first to go were its eyes, then its face, and then gradually its entire head. What remained became hideous and frightful. In the end it melted completely into a pool of water. I felt wet and cold, as though my feet were sinking into some liquid. I lowered my head and looked: it was not water, but a boundless expanse of blood. Like a fetid marsh, it gave off a stinking smell. I wanted to run out of this bloody marsh, but raising my head, I again saw the metallic blue of the gun's barrel. It kept pointing straight at me, forever pointing at me . . .

The only thing to do was resolve to walk straight towards it. Closer and closer I approached, but it became smaller and smaller. The metallic blue of the steel barrel softened, fell apart, and slowly became a knot tied in the shape of a teardrop. It became a shiny and attractive noose, and I heard a voice loudly telling me,

'This is your end! This is your end!'

Violently, I woke up, but the sound of the voice seemed to go on and on without stopping: 'This is your end! This is your end! . . .' Before my eyes, the noose was still fixed, hanging in the middle of the darkness. A heap of covers was piled on my neck, giving me the feeling of having hanged myself. I threw them off violently, then lay back again quietly, not moving, letting the frightening dream slowly disappear.

I again heard her delicate gossamer breathing, pouring out into the dark night, as though it had nowhere else to wriggle into. Her breath was so intimate, so good to hear, and so heart-breaking. Xiangjiu! I want to take all the breath that you breathe out and absorb it into my own lungs. Let me take it to the edges of the earth, let it penetrate my soul. Let me carry it with me all the way until I throw myself into the predestined end, until I become ashes . . .

Luo Zongqi took several sheets of white paper out of a
drawer and put them in front of me.

'You've got pretty strange ideas,' he said, looking at me
as he sank heavily into a rattan chair. He was obviously
bone-tired. 'Here I am a Party Member—how can I stamp
an official seal of permission on a blank sheet of paper?'

Nevertheless, a regulation seal had been stamped on the
bottom right-hand side of every sheet. The letterhead of the
paper and the seals on the bottom were those of the farm
of which he was the Leader. With their bright red seals,
these white sheets of paper took on an uncommon importance. I picked them up from the writing table, carefully
folded them, and placed them inside the inner pocket of my
padded cotton jacket. I said to him knowingly, 'Who's
going to say you gave them to me, anyway? People are
being transferred all over the place these days. Blank letters
of introduction like these are everywhere—they might even
have been picked up on the road.'

His home looked as it had when I came a year ago. The
kitchen he had built was already beginning to look decrepit,
with wheat straw showing through earthen walls that had
been saturated by that big rain. Somehow the big room felt
more bleak and desolate than before. On its northern wall,

the photograph of the now deceased Zhou Enlai, taken by an Italian journalist, was draped like a coffin with a swath of black cotton. Its ends hung negligently over a ragged and lifeless fern. The sofa he had made with his own hands had long ago lost its bounce. Sitting on it now was like sinking into a pit. He was thinner than last year, and the hair at his temples had turned completely white. The rattan chair he sat on creaked, adding to the gloom.

Although it was spring, everything seemed to be cold. After settling our business, he said, 'The letter that you sent me took five days to get here. Only twelve and a half miles—why did it take so long? I examined the envelope for a long time, afraid someone might have opened it.' He made a face, then laughed ruefully, 'Doesn't matter if I'm head of this farm, it's the same as if I were still in jail—always on guard, always anxious . . .'

'We've never got out of jail.'

'That's true.' He heaved a deep sigh. 'These years, even my mouth has come to smell: all the bad things it foretold have invariably come true. The good things? I haven't seen one actually happen. Do you remember the things I told you last year at this time?'

'How could I forget? It just came too fast.'

'You think it fast? On the contrary, I feel it's been slow. These years, our country is like a stone that's rolling down a hill, the further it rolls into the future the faster it goes. It seems to me as though it's just about rolled to the end now.'

He lifted his head, his nostrils moving as if he were sniffing the odour of something that had wafted in. His eyes had the look in them of one who has suffered—who has been worn down by the despair that follows the end of hope. I understood his feelings.

'Almost to the end,' I said. 'I still keep thinking there will be one last Movement, a Movement that really belongs to the people . . .'

'Can there be a Movement that belongs to people?' He stirred, agitated, in his rattan chair. 'For years we've been "masses that were moved", for all they called them Mass Movements. A Movement that really belongs to the people? That would immediately be branded a "counter-revolutionary incident". If you don't believe me, just wait and see what happens.'

'Doesn't matter what kind of "incident" they call it, there is bound to be a real Movement by the people in the end.' I began to speak of what had been fermenting in my mind the past few days. 'Premier Zhou has passed away, Deng Xiaoping's been knocked off the dais. As the Movement to "Counter the Rightists and Reverse Their Verdicts" gets going, one by one "Democrats" like you will succumb. The screen in front of the people is being ripped away. If the Chinese people don't stand up and speak, if they don't move to the front line of struggle themselves, then one billion people will no longer have the right to live on this globe. We will have been the most stupid, good for nothing, weak, despicable race on earth.' I could barely hold back the tears starting in my eyes. 'We've been played with for almost twenty years, used like a guinea pig in an experiment—we've been cheated and tricked. Can it be that when the experiment has utterly failed and we are on the verge of death, we don't even have the guts to shout out, "It hurts"? People who are so numb they can't even yell "It hurts" are people who are really better off dead.'

My throat choked with emotion, as I sat in the hole of his self-made sofa. He also sat without moving or speaking as the room quieted for a moment, still reverberating with the waves of emotion.

264

Then he said softly, 'Well, what do you plan to do? Leave? Go where?'

'I haven't worked out an exact plan yet.' I calmed down, then said bitterly, 'In this age of chaos, even the country doesn't have a plan—how could an individual have one? I only know I can't keep living here. I have an intimate connection with both "Rightist" and "Reverse the Verdicts". As this Movement swings into full gear, I'll be the first to get thrown back in jail, just like in 1970. Letting the fire burn out slowly in jail is a lot worse than going quickly in a final explosion.

'There's another thing. You know that when I came out of the labour camp in 1968, I went like an idiot looking for some "Headquarters of Liu and Deng". Then it was bound to end in failure. Now, however, if you Democrats don't turn to the people, mobilize them, organize them or at least support them, it will be just like before, just waiting for the blows to fall. You'll be back in jail before you know it, begging for pardon for your crimes with your asses up and your heads down. What's more, it will be your own bloody fault.'

Raising a finger at me, he said wearily, 'Don't go writing things like that about us. At the very least, I've made things a lot easier for you.'

'That's right, and that's the reason I'm sure that all across China right now people are sitting together just as we are. We can't be alone, some special kind of phenomenon. One Communist Party Member, and one Rightist: each has walked his own road for eighteen years now. In the end they find they've actually had very similar experiences. Here we are talking together, feeling exactly the same way. If this hasn't been created by history, how else are you going to explain it? I'm sure that a Movement is gestating in China right now that really belongs to the people. I'm equally convinced that only that kind of Movement will allow the country and the Party to start anew.'

His deep eyes suddenly looked alarmed. 'Have you made preparations? Do you . . . have connections?'

'No connections.' My answer was straightforward. 'What connections could I possibly have? With whom? They've put great effort in these past two decades not into improving relations between men, but tearing apart the bonds that bring men together. I consider that to be the greatest crime they have perpetrated. They've destroyed a sense of trust among men. Instead of building good intentions and a readiness to help one another, they've made men into wild animals. Only a Movement by the people will be able to bring back decent relations between man and man.

'So don't worry that I have some kind of connections. You yourself were in the Revolution for over ten years—do you still have personal contacts with those old war buddies? Can you really tell each other what's at the bottom of your mind?'

'No,' he admitted. ' "Once the guest goes, the tea gets cold," as they say.' He drew a long breath, then said, 'That's not to say there hasn't been any communication at all. There has been. But it depends on getting oral news from people who are travelling. You might not hear of old friends for years, for instance, then suddenly someone will come through who knows their whereabouts and what problems they've run into.'

A sudden chill came over us. We lived in a stretch of land which we ourselves had turned to desert. The desert was in turn pressuring us. Yet in the midst of this hopeless place, at that moment we heard the lonely sound of a single voice singing from outside the wall of his small garden. 'The east wind blows, the drums of war are beating, who in this world

266

is afraid of whom? . . .' We listened, astonished, as if we could gain some enlightenment from the words of the song. But there was no revelation. These days any voice that could be lifted in loud song, or in loud yelling, was a voice without meaning, a hollow voice.

After a moment of silence, Luo continued talking. 'This thing you're thinking of won't end well. Because . . .' one finger was lifted upwards, 'he's still there. Nothing is going to change while the old man is still living.'

'I understand.' I leaned back on the sofa, then replied, 'Premier Zhou once asked, "How many chances come up in a man's life where you can really grapple with a problem?" At this moment, everything indicates that I have got to grapple. Others can wait—I too would be willing to wait, but right now I'm not even safe in my home at night. The clubs will soon be beating into homes too—how can I wait? If they want to take on Democrats like you, they first have to paste up big-character posters, incite the masses for awhile, cook up an "incident". Then they write up a lot of superficial newspaper articles. If they want to get me, none of those things are necessary. All they need is a pair of handcuffs and they'll come and get me. For all these years people like me have served as a foil for people like you. We fought your frontline battles.'

Luo Zongqi had to agree. 'That's called "first clearing away the outer defences".'

I laughed together with him. 'You could also say it was "first dismantling your so-called social foundation". These last ten years, I've been honoured to be the "social foundation" for all kinds of people. Starting off, I was the "social foundation" of Liu and Deng's Headquarters, then of the "16 May Incident", after that I was the "social foundation" of Lin Biao and Confucius. Now it's come around again, to this "Reversing of Rightists' Verdicts", which is simply to say that I am again the "social foundation" for Deng Xiaoping. Fortunately my back is as thick as a turtle's—otherwise I would long ago have been trampled flat.'

As soon as I said the word 'turtle'*, my heart jumped and I could not keep from blushing. Luckily, Zhu Shujun came in at that point, carrying a serving tray, calling us to come eat dinner. Her face had a shadow of worry on it, as if Luo Zongqi might soon be put in jail again. It had lost the good cheer of a year ago, and she seemed to be afraid now even of making a sound. Nothing had actually happened, nothing at all had happened yet, but already the newspapers, the broadcasts, every form of propaganda was spreading a poisonous atmosphere into every home. It made the men depressed and the women frightened. I ate my dumplings without really tasting them, silently thinking: I am right in my determination.

After eating, Zhu Shujun cleared off the table and asked me with concern, 'If you're going to go, then go, but why must you get a divorce? Is it her? . . .'

'No, she's good to me,' I said quickly. I could not say she was bad, and I didn't want other people to wonder what defects she had. Looking for the right words, I said, 'Some couples divorce because their feelings aren't enough, others because their feelings are too complex. Even if I don't go, we would probably divorce eventually. Couples who can grow old together must have just the right measure of feelings.'

Outside the door, the man who had been singing went by again, clearly singing another 'Revolutionary Song'. This is a happy man, I thought.

With her female intuition, Zhu Shujun seemed to under-

---

*The actual word used is a general term of abuse meaning 'turtle egg'; turtle is also slang for 'cuckold'.

stand, and did not ask further. Luo Zongqi did not understand, but he too did not ask. As our mood dampened, I felt it was time to take my leave.

'I'll be going,' I said.

Luo Zongqi struggled to pull himself out of the rattan chair and finally stood up. He did not seem to have shaken himself out of whatever he was thinking—his mind was not there, and his eyes looked absentminded. After a while, embarrassed, he extended his hand. As I shook it, I could feel that his palm was wet and hot—perhaps he really was suffering from some illness.

'Yes, it's time,' he said.

We walked to the front door, where I turned my head around and nodded back at Zhu Shujun: this was our parting. She stood in the middle of the room, using the warmth in her eyes to see me to the door. For a moment, I took a last look around this room, this home that had given me friendship, a place where I could speak without fear of investigation and arrest. I knew I might never have the chance to come back.

Luo Zongqi accompanied me through the small garden. On the edge of it, beyond a small levelled path, was a row of poplars standing like guards over us, their silver bark shining with an undercolour of green. On the far side of the poplars was the public road made up of pounded stones. I would be following that road on my way back into the wilderness.

'Lao Zhang, I would like to give this to you.' Looking in all directions to make sure there was no one around, he suddenly remembered and took the watch off his wrist. 'This watch still runs pretty well—when you're out there, you'll probably be needing it.'

I took it from him. The second hand was running quickly, as if something were pursuing it from behind. This watch really would be useful. The lives of fugitives were often decided by a matter of seconds. I did not refuse, and tucked it into my chest pocket, together with the blank letters of introduction.

'Thank you,' I said.

He waved his hands, and grumbled, 'Thanks for what? Looks as though everything is going to depend on time to get resolved. If anything goes wrong, you can write to us.'

'I will,' I said, 'if I'm still able to write.'

I walked along the road for about six miles without running into a single motorized vehicle. A few carts met me head-on and passed by in the other direction. Their drivers just gestured with their whips as they hunkered down, morose and sour. They were transporting bricks into the city, and the planks of the carts were covered with red brick-dust. As I walked, I could now see where the road ended, at a small black dot under the blue of the sky. That was the noisy city: a city that was even now violently declaring war against its own people. First it would use words and writing, then would come clubs and finally bullets. To the north, the other end of the road disappeared into the midst of desert wastes, like a river that has split into several channels, and then loses track of where it began. On either side of the main road were small trails beaten out by the feet of humans, extending out into the wilderness. I walked as far as a dried-up canal, then forked off on one of these small trails towards our own Troop.

The grassy plains had already been destroyed by those who 'Learned from Dazhai'. On the land before me abandoned fields stretched in all directions. Now covered with a thick layer of salt, they looked like dirty snow-fields, or like orphans dressed in mourning clothes. They had been through numerous storms since being abandoned, but you

270

could still see the scars of plough tracks running across their skin. Man and nature together had been flogged with whips here: the result of 'Learn from Dazhai' was to create barren land, on whose alkaline surface not a blade of grass would grow. A light spring breeze came blowing in from the banks of the Yellow River. When it reached this place, it suddenly dropped to a whimper, deploring the ruin of what once were grassy plains. This is what had become of my land.

Cutting across both salt fields and then a dried-up marsh was a stretch of sand. The roots of hardy grasses had been surrounded by small sand hills, which as the wind continued to blow grew thicker and higher, until every bit of green life was crowded out. When the soil was disturbed by farming, the sand took over. This landscape held no alternative, the greenness was retreating: weak and defeated, life itself was disappearing. Spring had returned to the earth, but there was no place here for it to get a foothold. On this stretch of yellow sand there would be no spring.

I walked on, beyond the fields and the open country that had turned to sand. My two well-trained feet were accustomed to walking in the shifting dunes. At birth these feet had been white and tender—shoes were too rough for them, they had been warmed in the palm of my mother's hand. Now they were used to walking barefoot through gravel and thistles, through salt lands that had started to hide away from people.

On the far side of the salt fields and the sandy stretches were fields of wheat. You could already see the beginning of alkalinization on the edges of those fields, where the stalks were sparse and weak. This was a borderline between life and death, a confrontation. Who would win and who would lose was still in the balance. Going on a little further, the wheat shoots began to look more flourishing. On the banks of the fields grew a thick, soft layer of grass. The land did not need irrigating in the spring—it was naturally moist and fertile. Last spring, I had returned to the Troop along this very road. The scenery at that time was identical to what I saw now: it seemed as though I had imagined everything that had happened this year.

Faced with sudden and incomprehensible calamity in the past, I would sometimes dream of reversing the passage of time. If it would only let me start again at a certain point, how much better things would be, now that I knew how to handle them. I would do things more intelligently to escape avoidable disasters, and make thorough preparation to meet disasters that were inevitable. Looking back, would I have wanted to escape the last year? No, I would have gone through with it just the same. Even if black magic were to allow me to start again, I would still come back to the Troop as I was doing now, and ask her to marry me. This past year had been the most beautiful of my brief life. My premonition told me that none of this could be played over again. I would never again be vulnerable to that humiliation and pain, but I would also never again know such happiness. Such powerful impressions come but once to a man's life.

I walked on, with long and heavy strides.

When I returned, I would get a divorce. Just as we were fated to be married, it was destiny that we should part.

My land, my salty land, my sandy Paradise, my vast plateau, I will soon be leaving you. Like her, you've been trampled on and ravaged by men. But you've also willingly lain beneath them, to give yourself. You've been unfaithful to me, cheated me and punished me—you are a dried-up marsh: how much of my sweat has gone into nourishing you and been soaked up without a trace. You are ugly, and you are evil, but you also have a beauty that approaches the mystical. I curse you and I love you, demonic land and

272

demonic woman. You have absorbed my sweat and my tears, you have also changed my soul: from now I have no more love to give to you.

I walked on. My final tear soaked into the spring earth at my feet.

QUOTATION OF CHAIRMAN MAO

'Conscientiously Struggle—Criticize—Transform.'

APPLICATION

Since their marriage last year, the farm-workers Zhang Yonglin and Huang Xiangjiu have not been able to achieve
harmony and unity in their daily lives or in their feelings for
each other. If this continues, it will be harmful to the production of the Troop, and will also be harmful to the transformation of the two individuals. Having consulted each
other, they have agreed to divorce. From now on, they
guarantee they will put greater effort into socialist construction and the transformation of the individual. The approval
of the leaders will be appreciated.

Respectfully,

Zhang Yonglin
Huang Xiangjiu
MARCH 1976

I put this application down in front of Party Secretary Cao
Xueyi.

He stared at it, avoiding my eyes, chewing his lips and

frowning. He looked it up and down, not immediately sure how to respond.

Without waiting for an invitation, I pulled over a stool and sat down across from his desk. Leaning back against the wall, I lit a cigarette. My eyes did not leave his for a second.

He took off his army-green hat and scratched hair that looked like a scrubbing brush, then put the hat back on again. His leg began to jiggle, making one whole side of his body shake. His hand touched the bottle of ink, then played for a moment with the paper in front of him. He picked up the pen, but just as I thought he was going to sign his name he put it down again.

'I'd heard about, I'd heard . . .' He finally mumbled.

'Who from,' I asked aggressively. 'From Huang Xiang-jiu?'

'No, of course not,' he said hurriedly. 'It's going around, that's all.'

I remained silent, waiting for him.

I had thought he might give me trouble for using that incongruous and irrelevant Quotation of Chairman Mao, but he did not pay attention to that angle. If he had brought it up, I was all prepared to ask him for advice: exactly which Quotation of Chairman Mao was appropriate for the heading of a Divorce Application? Before leaving the Troop, I wanted to have an opportunity at least to play with the current political hysteria. When they came to arrest me, I imagined, I could have already escaped. But he did not give me the opportunity to redeem myself as a man.

Outside the office, twilight came on. Somebody's shadow passed by the window, and Cao raised his head to look. He was obviously hoping for someone to come in and disturb us, but I had specifically chosen a time when even Huang Xiangjiu would be out in the fields working.

'Would it be possible . . . for someone to come and

mediate?' He held the paper in one hand, put his head sideways and asked me slowly.

'Who?' I asked. 'Someone from Headquarters?'

He heard the measured significance of that sentence, and quickly demurred, 'No need to have someone come from there—someone from our Troop would do fine, eh? What about Hei-tz?'

'I think it's best not to have an outsider get involved,' I said coldly.

'Oh, well that's fine, that's fine . . . As they say, "Even an upright official finds it hard to settle a family quarrel." '

I wanted to pick up the bottle of ink and splash it all over his square, dark face. It was a momentary impulse, however, and I found that I was ashamed of my cowardice. To make a statement, the statement of a real man, in front of a 'Leader' would still require of me a certain education. I would have to be 'reformed' in the opposite direction. Even though my words had been pointed, I found that at some time or other my posture had slipped into being bowed and bent. A self-demeaning attitude had become my second nature.

Patience, just hang on a little longer, I told myself. Just get him to sign that piece of paper, which was mainly for her peace of mind. I knew that he was only too anxious for us to be divorced, but he still had to put on this little show, this short scene in a long play.

'Does Huang Xiangjiu agree?' He muttered to himself, then asked again out loud.

'Of course she does,' I told him.

'This doesn't seem to be her signature.' He brought his face close to the paper, as if to say, 'See how responsible I'm being about this for you two?'

'Do you want me to call her here so you can ask her?'

276

'Uh, no, that's not necessary.' He laughed without humour, beginning to rub his hands together nervously. 'I remember last year when you were married, you also wrote the Marriage Application.'

'Secretary Cao's memory is excellent.'

He had established enough 'evidence' for his peace of mind, and now took up the pen. 'If you both agree, what does the Leaders' approval mean anyway? Marriage is a free matter, you know. Later, if you both feel you can come together again and want to get married all over again, that's fine too. Right now there are plenty of divorces, and there are also quite a few re-marriages.'

The 'Leaders' meant him, he was the 'Leader'. He signed his name with a few quick strokes.

I suddenly had the feeling that I had both lost something valuable and heaved off something of great weight. I instinctively stood up and took the sheet of paper. The stamp, the signature—these were the laughable notations that decided our lives.

'I'm thinking of moving back into Zhou Ruicheng's old room. Is that all right?' I said.

A look of surprise passed over his face, followed by a look of sympathy. He said, 'You needn't hurry for the time being. That room hasn't had anyone living in it for some time—the fire hasn't even been lit for a whole winter. As soon as it warms up you can move in. Anyway, you two have two rooms, don't you? Can't one of you take the inner and one the outer?'

'I think it would be best to move out.'

'Well, that's up to you.' He slapped his hands together.

I had finally caught his eyes with mine for a moment. In that second, I understood at last what she had said so long ago in the sheep pen. He had already signed his name on the application, however—what point was there in locking horns with him now?

'You can go to hell,' I said to him silently.

After dinner, a pitch-black night descended. It was a sinister night, a dark night that could drive a man crazy. The rays of remaining daylight retreated from the unpainted window-frame, like life slowly leaving a body. At the same time, the oblique coldness of spring came seeping in through its cracks, invading all the corners of the room, making the air clammy as a grave.

Out in the country, the belt of trees had not yet sprouted leaves, but the branches had filled with sap, already making them soft and limber. They made a hundred different sighing cries of mourning in the wind. It was a night that brought with it both despair and hope. With hands behind my head, I lay back on the kang. A small grey spider began crawling down one of the columns of the newspaper plastered above my head, as if it too were a person, looking for the most appropriate Quotation to fit its life and future. In the past, today would have been the 'Waking of Insects'* day, when all sorts of small insects were supposed to crawl out into the world.

She finished washing the dishes in the outer room, then brushed aside the curtain and pulled on the light as she came. The rafters of the room were suddenly bright light. I squinted my eyes and stayed where I was, not daring to look at her. She sat as she usually did on the edge of the bed, her body bent over, continually wringing her hands. She was rubbing in the skin lotion sold in clam-shells in town—she loved adornment and took good care of herself. This was not a characteristic of women who were born to farm-

---

*A folk festival which, like other traditional holidays, has been abolished in China.

ing families. If she hadn't lost her position in life and been sent to hard labour her fate would have been very different. She had done 'labour reform', however, and she had been driven to prostitution: this was also her fate.

She was wholly absorbed in rubbing her hands together. Meanwhile, I thought how I could begin. Women's patience is great, especially in the talent of being quiet. Finally I could stand it no longer. I cleared my throat lightly and said, 'Our application was approved today.' I placed special emphasis on the word 'our'.

She still didn't say anything, just carefully inspected her fingernails. It seemed she had to get lotion into the edges of each nail.

This was a mine-field, but I had to go through it to get to where I wanted to be. I sat up, took the paper from my pocket, and placed it in front of her on the bed.

She glanced at it without changing expression. After rubbing a while longer, she then reached out two fingers and picked it up, and with one motion tore it cleanly in two.

Amazed, I began to protest but stopped immediately. I did not dare say more. This layer of ice was extremely thin, one uncertain move and I would fall through, never to float to the surface again. Ready for anything, I watched her face.

She did not lift her eyes, which still scrutinized her nails. Calm and composed, she said, 'What kind of game is this? If you want to get married, nobody stops you; if you want to get divorced, nobody forces you to stay together. Since there aren't any feelings between us, what's wrong with splitting up even if it's not approved?'

'Of course, of course,' I quickly expressed my agreement. 'But don't we still have to take this toy to Headquarters to go through the proper procedures?'

Then in a flash I remembered: last year, when Hei-tz brought our application back to us with Cao Xueyi's approval, I had been afraid that it would meet obstacles as it went on up through the bureaucracy—so since the local Party Member had already approved it, we didn't continue to the main headquarters to complete the process. The 'mountains are high and the Emperor is far away' was the rationale. Even if soldiers came and broke in the front door, they weren't going to want to examine some 'Marriage Approval'. That was the way we had been married.

I gave a strangled laugh. Here was a person who had been 'under the discipline of the masses', illegally married to a woman for a whole year! And it had been the same masses who recognized the marriage, together with time and our own feelings. Even I had forgotten that we had not completed the legal process. So my anguish over these past weeks had been unnecessary. If I had wanted to go, I could have just got up and left.

I had forgotten, but she had remembered. She looked at me with loathing in her eyes, and spat at me viciously, 'You were insincere from the very beginning of our marriage!' The full luscious contour of her lips was now drawn into a thin line, exposing white teeth. 'Your belly is fully of demons,' she continued. 'Today I've finally seen through you.'

Her words fell like hail on my face. I was hurt and said, 'Don't be mistaken. I was not sincere and I was not playing around. I laugh only because the whole thing is so ludicrous. Hei-tz said that immoral days are easy to live through—well, it seems to me that illegal days are pretty easy too.' I drew a breath. 'It really is as if we were in a play, as if we were in a dream.'

'I have woken from that dream,' she said.

The one who had awoken should have been me. Yet here she was saying it was she who had woken. Cautiously, I stopped on the thin ice, not daring to go another step: I didn't know what she was really thinking or what she would say. Are a man and a woman always living in a dream? Once they wake, will they invariably part company?

Yes, the life of a couple really is a dream: if it is not a beautiful dream, it becomes a nightmare. Whatever you do, couples, do not wake up.

She looked as though she had remembered something, and, standing up, she lifted the cover off the chest. One by one, she began to take out my clothes. Every article carried something of herself in it. She was icy-cold, or at least she seemed to be on the surface. She was familiar with the process of divorce.

'It's not so bad to be poor—it's easy for poor people to divorce: you, me—one simple split and that's it.' At least she had that much humour left in her. Finally she took the transistor radio and put it on top of my clothes, saying, 'This I give you—spies should never be too far away from such contraptions.'

I could not believe it. 'Reality' had destroyed her life. Yet she still made anything that tried to counter 'fate', that tried to find a means to another way of living, into something 'counter-revolutionary'. When it was necessary, she too could ball up her little fists and scream out: 'Smash these counter-revolutionaries!' Dully, I said, 'This is something you bought. I can't take it.'

'So there's something you can't take?' She pretended to be astonished. Spreading out both hands, she said, 'These things, take them all. Just leave the room behind. I'm not a fool. You're leaving me behind, and I have to take care of myself.'

She drew one more thing out of the open chest, which like a magic box seemed to contain an endless number of objects. She drew out a wad of bank-notes from a small handkerchief and, with practised speed, peeled off twenty of them. 'Here's two hundred dollars, take it with you.'

This time I was really surprised. 'What do you mean by

giving me money? Anyway, we can't have saved that much over this past year.'

She could not keep up her pose any longer. Like the sticks that a small child has painstakingly built up, her icy, critical stance suddenly collapsed. Using her small hand to cover her mouth, she quietly began to cry.

'Zhang Yonglin, you were born with a wolf's heart and the lungs of a dog. If you want to leave this town, just leave, why go on playing around like this? There's absolutely no need to pretend you're not going. You should just say "I'm leaving" and go! Nobody's stopping you, nobody's going to pull you back . . .'

Her shoulders drooped and her head hung down tiredly. As she stood there, she was the very picture of the beaten and oppressed. Her attitude was clearly calling me to go comfort her, to clear up this one last particular debt. I hesitated. I knew there was no way I could explain. I couldn't make this divorce into something that was purely for her sake, or even something done purely because of feelings at all. The action also sprang from other complex motives. Her brain could only understand black and white, however. Grey or fuzzy things were too obscure for her. They were also beyond my power to explain.

Reason cannot substitute for emotions, or even analyse them properly. When two souls cannot respond to one another, any spoken words are insufficient. What had held us together was the excitement of physical need: it was simply the contact of flesh against flesh. The love that we had felt came only from that feeling of pleasure—without it, we lost both understanding and concern for one another.

All the same, I moved over to her and put my arm around her shoulders. 'How did you know that I was going to leave this place?'

'How could I not know? I know your stomach is full of

worms.' She snuggled into my chest and, snuffling, said, 'You think I can't see? If you didn't leave this place, could you separate from me? I know you too well—you've done twenty years of hard labour, yet in your heart you're still a little master. You need somebody to wait on you, serve your needs. And don't forget, it was me who made it possible for you to find your true calling. I've opened the way for you to search for what you must do. If I didn't accept this divorce, do you think you could still leave me? Even if you join those American Imperialists and Soviet Revisionists, or Liu Shaoqi and Deng Xiaoping, that's fine—don't worry. If your counter-revolution is successful, I won't come to stain your "glory, splendour, wealth and rank"! But why do you have to be this way with me?'

She was charmingly stupid, and laughably clever. She spoke as if she had waited on me for twenty years, bringing me meals as I did my 'labour reform'. She had her own understanding of the world. Everything that came into her basket was vegetables, everything that opposed 'Mao's Revolutionary Line' was 'counter-revolution'. And yet she loved a 'counter-revolutionary'!

I was unable to stifle a laugh, and shook my head in disbelief as I said, 'What "glory, splendour, wealth and rank"? It's more likely to be a lot of misfortune and very little luck. That's why I didn't want to let you know.'

'Ha!' She snorted abruptly through her nose. Her teary eyes looked tenderly at my face, but her voice was full of poison as she said, 'That's not true. I tell you, you are not going to die well, and it's because you have a guilty conscience.'

'Yes,' I laughed sadly, 'I do have a guilty conscience.'

She seemed to calm down then, leaning against me in the middle of the room with her head against my arm. After a while, she drew a long breath. 'At first I thought of making a big scene with you. I was going to report you to the authorities, expose you, and send you off to hard labour again. Afterwards, I thought, how pitiful. Here you are, so educated, and you've been cheated in your own home. You have your reasons for suffering. Best to divorce and split up quietly, leave a few good things for each of us to remember the other by. No matter how well off you are later, no matter how beautiful the women are who circle around you, you won't find anyone who can love you as dearly as I have. As for me, well I've thought it through pretty clearly. Old Lady Ma's lived her life alone and she's still happy. I figure I can be the same as she is.'

'You'd be fine alone, but you're still young, Xiangjiu. Find someone who's better than I am for you.' Against my better judgement, I began to comfort her.

'Forget it, don't make a fool of me.' She wiped the tears off her face, her little red nostrils quivering. Her eyelashes were wet with round drops, like the dew covering the grassy edge of a lake. She was still beautiful enough to bewitch a man. 'I won't look any more after this,' she said. 'I was not destined to have a good man in my life. If I found one, I couldn't keep him, he'd want to go too. You take that money, you'll need it on your way. The two times I was divorced before, I fought for money, for things. I even took it to court. This time I'm happy to give you some. Take it and don't worry, I still have three hundred left.'

Saying that, she twisted her body round to press against mine. Her full breasts were against my chest, as she said in a hot, commanding voice, 'On the bed! Tonight I want you to play till you're satisfied. Take me so you'll never forget me.'

The moon had risen until it hung high in the sky. As the light was put out, the moonlight poured into the small room like a waterfall. The tiny sound of her voice rippled in the

284

waves of moonlight. '. . . You've betrayed your heart, Zhang Yonglin, and you won't die well. But however many people there are weeping for you at your grave, the only one really mourning will be me. And afterwards, I'll burn money for you every year at Qingming,* wherever I am. You can come to where I am and take it to spend . . . come, take off your clothes—quick! Why are you looking so confused?'

I felt two burning hot arms wrap tightly around me, and pull me down, pull me down . . . deep into the bottom of the lake of moonlight. From the bottom of the water a voice came floating up:

'Don't forget, I'm the one who made you into a real man . . .'

A woman is the most lovable thing on earth,
But there is something that is more important.
Women will never possess the men they have created.

A small insect climbed slowly up the wall. So spring had come. In another month it will be Qingming.

Would I return to her side to accept her memory?

How large, how round the moon!

22 July 1985

---

*A spring festival during which Chinese traditionally offered gifts, paper money and prayers to the souls of the deceased.